WHAT WE MAY BE

LAYLA REYNE

What We May Be

Copyright © 2021 by Layla Reyne

All rights reserved. No part of this book may be reproduced or transmitted in any form or by any means, electronic or mechanical, including photocopying, recording, or by any information storage and retrieval system without the written permission of the copyright owner, and where permitted by law. Reviewers may quote brief passages in a review.

Cover Design: Cate Ashwood Designs

Cover Photography: Wander Aguiar Photography

Developmental Editing: Edits by Kristi

Line & Copy Editing: Susie Selva

Proofreading: Lori Parks

First Edition

August, 2021

E-Book ISBN: 978-1-7373524-0-2

Paperback ISBN: 978-1-7373524-1-9

This is a work of fiction. Names, characters, places, and incidents are either the product of the author's imagination or are used fictitiously. Any resemblance to actual persons living or dead, business establishments, events, or locales is entirely coincidental. All person(s) depicted on the cover are model(s) used for illustrative purposes only.

ABOUT THIS BOOK

What we were…

Sean found love once, with his college roommate, Trevor,
and Trevor's best friend, Charlotte.
The missing piece, Sean made it possible for Trevor and
Charlotte to find love too.
But then Sean left and took the love with him.

What we are…

Now an FBI agent, Sean is back in town, ten years later, to
investigate a murder.
A case that pits him against his ex-lovers—Charlotte, a
local detective, and Trevor, a literature professor sucked
into the Shakespearean mystery.
Everyone guards their hearts, but before long, desire sparks
anew the feelings that burned hot a decade ago. That still
burn true.

What we may be...

Love is within their grasp again, but as the killer escalates, it's more than just their hearts and futures on the line. Sean, Charlotte, and Trevor will need to work together to solve the case.
If they can't, lives will be lost and pieces of their love gone for good.

For my grandmothers,
one a Southern storyteller, the other an English professor...
the perfect storm.

CHAPTER ONE

Standing at the edge of the crowd in Hanover's centuries-old cemetery, his dress shoes dusted with sand and pollen, Sean watched as two flag-covered caskets received a three-volley salute. He didn't flinch at the gunfire—police and Bureau academy had trained that out of him—but when the Stars and Stripes were lifted and folded with snapped precision, when the long, polished caskets were lowered into the ground, his insides clenched, a flinch worse than muscles and bones could betray.

They were gone and Sean had missed his opportunity to say goodbye, to explain, to apologize.

To find out if the cruelest betrayal was worth the broken heart that had never healed.

"You a friend of the family?"

Law enforcement academies had also trained Sean to not betray his surprise at the voice immediately to his right. Never mind the training to always remain aware of his surroundings, a skill that had apparently deserted him in his grief. The uniformed officer who'd approached was white, late twenties or so with a summer sunburn that had caused the rosy skin of his too-thin nose to peel, an errant flake caught in the lashes of his light blue eyes.

Sean smiled politely. "I went to school with Charlie and Cal."

The officer—*Sylvan* according to his badge—swiped at his eye, flicking away the bothersome flake. "HU?"

Probably not a local, then. At a minimum, not an HU sports fan. If he'd spent much time at all in the memorabilia-filled halls of Hanover University's baseball complex, he would have seen the pictures of Sean. Sure, ten years had given him a few more wrinkles, shorter hair, and thicker facial scruff, but he was still #10.

"I did," Sean answered. "But I haven't visited in some time."

"You live out of town?"

The questions were annoying—nosy digging cloaked in polite conversation, a Southern specialty that had taken Sean half his time in Hanover to get used to. Never really had, which made the irony of his career detour even more ironic. That said, Sylvan's nosiness was warranted. To him, Sean was a stranger in the crowd. The officer was just doing his duty at the funeral of his fallen colleagues. As a fellow LEO, at least until the end of the summer, Sean respected Officer Sylvan's commitment. As a fellow LEO, Sean also knew how to keep his answers equally polite— and vague.

"Washington." Not technically—*yet*—but that's where

he'd be living once he retired from the FBI and moved back across the ocean.

"Nice of you to come down," the officer said.

"Least I could do."

Two days ago, his phone had rung and the voice on the other end of the line had delivered a punch to the gut so severe Sean had had to grab the closest chair to hold himself up. He'd been struggling to regain his balance ever since. He shoved his hands into his pockets and glanced back across the cemetery, through the crowd of mourners to the Henby family gravesites. "What happened?"

After the call, he'd scoured the web for information. He'd found a few articles, then culled more detailed reports from various law enforcement channels. But an account from someone local—someone in the department—was likely to be more colorful and possibly more accurate. That's what Sean had told himself, the rationalization he'd used to justify hopping on an eight-hour flight from Amsterdam to DC and driving six hours to Hanover, despite the razor-sharp claws of self-recrimination and regret tearing apart his insides.

"Bust on a local drug dealer," Sylvan said. "Charlie's been building the case against him for years. We finally got the go-ahead to move in as part of a joint takedown with the county sheriff's department." He swallowed hard and dug his toe into the sandy dirt. "Someone tipped off the bad guy, though. We still got him, but one of his soldiers also got Cal and the chief."

The reason they were gathered there today. "*Two fallen heroes, two decorated officers of the law, two native sons of Hanover,*" the minister had said at the beginning of the service. Detective Callum Henby—Sean's former friend and teammate and Charlie's twin brother—and Hanover Chief of Police, Mitch Henby—the man who a decade ago had affectionately called Sean "son" and carved out a place for him in his family.

"We're lucky we didn't lose Charlie too," Sylvan added.

Sean doubted Charlie saw it that way. He peered at Charlotte Henby through the crowd of mourners and the abundance of graveside flowers. She was seated in the front row of folding chairs, dressed in her own police blues, her dark hair pulled into a bun at the base of her neck beneath the lip of her cap, her gloved hands folded in her lap, resting atop two bouquets of red roses. She had remained stoic during the service, likewise not a flinch at the gun salute or when the uniformed officers had handed one of the folded flags to her.

The minister concluded the service, and the family rose. Sean tore his gaze from Charlie and shifted a couple steps behind a group of officers. "The tipster?" he asked Sylvan.

"A mole in the sheriff's office. Behind bars too." A faint glimmer of pride belied the officer's sad smile. "Don't think Charlie or Abel slept a wink until they nailed him. None of us did. We owed it to Cal and Mitch."

Sean chanced another glance at the gravesites. Abel Champion, Mitch's brother-in-law, now the acting chief, was as massive and imposing as Sean remembered. He had his big hand on the shoulder of Charlie's sister, Annie, who, folded flag clutched to her chest, sobbed in the arms of a uniformed Black man about Sylvan's age. Abel's worried gaze, though, was on Charlie, who knelt between the graves and tossed a bouquet of roses into each. He shot a concerned look over her head, toward the final member of the gathered family.

Trevor Caldwell, his dirty-blond locks in a knot, his broad shoulders straining the seams of his jacket, gave Abel a sharp shake of his head. Abel let whatever he wanted to say to Charlie go, knowing as well as Sean did that Trevor read her best. They'd been thick as thieves since childhood, the too-smart kid from the wrong side of the tracks and the police chief's daughter. Trevor had always understood what Charlie needed better than anyone.

"I didn't catch your name?" Sylvan said, snapping Sean's mind out of the past and back to the present.

"Shane," he replied, the alias easily rolling off his tongue. He held out a hand. "And yours, Officer Sylvan?"

"Wallace." The young man smiled wider as he returned the handshake. "There's a reception back at the station. You should swing by. I'm sure Charlie would love to see you." Sean doubted that too, but he smiled and nodded anyway. "You remember where it is?"

How could he forget? "I do. Thanks."

Sylvan wished him a good day, then snaked through the rows of graves to pay his respects. Sean tracked his every step, wishing he could do the same. He owed the Henby family so much more.

Caught in a web of grief and wishful thinking, Sean's training faltered once more, and he missed the shift of the parting crowd. Missed moving out of view of a pair of hazel eyes that stared across the distance at him. Sean held the piercing gaze, not bothering to hide the regret and guilt that threatened to gut him. Trevor had always been able to read him too, better than anyone.

Sean sat in his parked rental, staring out the windshield at the For Sale sign in the front yard of the place he used to call home. His chest ached, quite a feat after the beating his heart had taken on his drive through town after leaving the cemetery. Hanover, North Carolina, had changed over the past ten years. The red-brick station house and the cluster of matching government buildings remained intact, but they'd been expanded with multiple annexes. Crowds still lingered outside the downtown barbecue joint and the dive bar by the pier, but so many of the other local places he used to frequent were gone, their storefronts either empty or replaced by national retailers. None of those heartbreaks, however, compared to the parking deck on campus where his beloved baseball diamond used to stand. A shiny new ballpark had been built in the shiny new sports complex across campus. Maybe there weren't any vestiges of #10 left for Officer Sylvan to find. Once the gray-and-white clapboard house was sold, would there be *any* evidence left of the best five years of Sean's life?

Charlie and Cal had inherited the beach house when their mother, Alice, had died in a car accident their senior year of high school. Mitch, then deputy chief, had moved into town to be closer to the station and to Annie's middle school. But Charlie hadn't wanted to part with her childhood home. The summer after their sophomore year at HU, Charlie had moved back in, bringing Trevor and Sean with her and making the house their home. Three years later, Sean had abandoned that home—and their future.

He worried what it said now that Charlie was selling the house. Their history aside, she had cherished the house because it kept Alice close, even after her passing. Had Charlie learned the truth about the night her mother died? The truth Sean had stayed away to help keep buried? Knowing it, were the memories—the lies—too painful for Charlie to bear? Or was she simply moving on, leaving the last vestige of their lost future behind?

Sean wondered if Trevor had made a pitch to keep the house or if he was ready to move on too. Trevor had already tried to move on once and failed—a marriage to and recent divorce from a nurse in town. Maybe Trevor, like Charlie, needed to cut all the ties to their past in order to have any chance at a different future. Or maybe Trevor and Charlie were finally moving on together. That's what Sean had hoped. It had devastated him to learn his hope had been for naught. Or God help them all, were Charlie and Trevor, lifelong best friends, also going their separate ways? Sean didn't think that was possible, not for two people so in sync and not after what he'd seen at the cemetery that afternoon, but he hadn't thought Charlie would ever sell the beach house either.

He swallowed down the upset the swirling worst-case scenarios caused and focused instead on the vintage

Mustang parked next to an F-350 truck under the house between the stilts. The former was familiar, Charlie's cherry-red ride all through college. In a way, so was the latter, a mega-sized version of the beat-up truck Trevor used to drive. After a day like today, Charlie and Trevor were as helpless as he was to resist the call of this place.

Shoving open the car door, Sean angled his long legs out of the too-small rental and planted his feet on the sand and gravel driveway. He kicked the door shut behind him and leaned back against it, rolling up his shirtsleeves, closing his eyes, and inhaling the heavy, summer sea breeze. Working at The Hague, living in an apartment near the North Sea, he'd frequently catch whiffs of salt-tinged air, but it was never as strong as it was here on the North Carolina coast. He'd found it oppressive at first, but over time he'd come to appreciate the enveloping nature of it, the warmth and comfort it offered. In a way, it represented everything good about his life in Hanover before he'd deserted it.

"Mr. Anderson."

Sean smiled at the use of his rarely spoken first name. He shied away from it—the memories of his namesake painful—but Trevor teasing him with it in a faux-Matrix voice had always made him laugh, had eased the pain.

"Saw you at the cemetery," Trevor continued, speaking normally. "Thought you were a figment of my imagination."

Sean savored the richness of Trevor's accent. Another clue that Officer Sylvan from the cemetery wasn't local. He lacked the low country accent that was a unique blend of Southern drawl and Elizabethan-era English, totally unlike anything Sean had ever heard outside the coastal counties.

He opened his eyes and looked up at the house, drinking in the sight of the teammate and roommate he'd fallen for all those years ago. Trevor stood with a muscled shoulder propped against a porch pillar. In the hours since the funeral, he'd traded his dark suit for cargo shorts and a faded HU tee that hugged his broad chest and cut upper arms, and he'd untied his hair, the long strands tangling with each breeze that lifted it around his angular face, made more so by the sharp lines of his beard.

His hazel eyes were hard, though, as was his expression. "You shouldn't be here." He looked like one of the Smiths, ready to vault over the rail, miraculously land the jump, and beat the shit out of him. He'd only ever seen Trevor throw that look at opposing teams, never at him. Trevor had always been the romantic of their trio, the English lit nerd who spent his days studying sonnets, poems, and plays. Trevor had also been Charlie's fiercest ally. The protector was pummeling the romantic today.

Sean couldn't blame him one bit. "I just wanted to pay my respects."

"You should've sent flowers. Anonymously."

"Trev—"

"No!" The splintering crack of that one word was like a well-hit line drive off Trevor's bat. Sean didn't doubt that if he were in reach, Trevor's fist would have connected with his face, same as his ball often had the bat. "She's hurting enough."

"Damage is done," Charlie interjected. She appeared at Trevor's side and leaned a hip against the wraparound deck's railing. She was similarly dressed down in a pair of cut-off denim shorts and a black lacy tank top. Her hair was down too, the same shoulder length she'd always worn it, the same dark brown that was nearly as black as her eyes, as far as possible from Trevor's every-color hazel. They were a perfect complement, the two of them impossibly more beautiful at thirty-three than they had been at twenty-three.

"I already saw him at the cemetery." She laid a hand on Trevor's forearm, then slid it down, curling her fingers over Trevor's white-knuckled fist. The tension in his frame eased a measure under her touch, but his expression remained furious.

Sean regretted his decisions. So many of them. "I'm sorry. I'll go."

"You loved them too," Charlie said, her accent the same as Trevor's. "And you're not the one responsible for today's damage," she added, letting him off the hook for today's pain at least. "And fuck flowers. If you're here to pay your respects, you better have brought a bottle of scotch. The stronger the better. I don't want to feel anything."

She turned on her heel and strolled out of sight, disappearing around the corner of the house. Trevor held Sean's gaze as if he were trying to determine how much more pain Sean was likely to cause Charlie.

Sean raised his hands, palms out. "It's your call, Trev."

"Not really." He pushed off the pillar and turned to

follow Charlie. Then stopped and glared over his shoulder. "Though let me be clear. If you hurt her and are dumb enough to come back here again, I won't be so deferential." Meaning he'd beat the shit out of him, like he wanted to do now, just as Sean suspected. Trevor didn't wait for his response. He continued in the direction Charlie had left, his flip-flops smacking the deck, the tread achingly familiar.

Sean was as powerless to resist the pull now as he had been when they'd first been roommates on campus at HU. As he still was in his dreams. He circled to the back of the car, popped the trunk, and grabbed the bottle of Ardbeg from where he'd wrapped it in his discarded tie and suit coat. Bottle under his arm, he climbed the exterior stairs that ran up the side of the house, his fingers coasting along the wide, flat railing, over the dates and initials carved into the weathered wood. Memorials of important occasions in the lives of its inhabitants.

Alice and Mitch's wedding date.

Charlie and Cal's birth date, then five years later, Annie's.

High school graduation dates.

The date, their junior year at HU, when he, Cal, and Trevor had won the College World Series.

Two steps from the top, Sean's gait faltered at the last carving, one he'd never laid eyes on before.

The date he, Charlie, and Cal had graduated from the police academy.

The same day he'd proposed to Charlie and Trevor.

The Saturday that had started amazing then turned

awful with one phone call and one wrong decision that had altered the course of his life, that had put him on a path away from his heart.

He'd never seen the carved initials and date because he hadn't come home that night or any night since. He'd left Charlie and Trevor waiting in a house packed with friends and family for a celebration that was never to be. That had been the worst day of his life. Before today. Standing on the outskirts of the cemetery crowd, fighting everything in him that screamed to go to Charlie and Trevor, had been a special kind of hell. Not one he'd ever experienced.

He'd been a fool to throw them away. Honor and obligation, duty and loyalty, fear and worry had gotten all mixed up in his twentysomething head. He'd been lucky to be a part of their lives at all, lucky to somehow fit with them. That sort of luck—that sort of love—came along once in a lifetime, maybe twice if you were supremely lucky. For him, nothing had come close in the decade since.

The clink of glasses inside filtered through an open window and jolted Sean out of his memories and up the final steps. Turning the corner and walking along the back deck, he shifted his gaze away from the too-painful sight of moving boxes inside to the expanse of sand dunes and beach just beyond the house. The ocean was calm, its waves breaking gently against the shore, the setting sun giving way to the rising moon's reflection on the rippling water.

Roughly bumping his side, Trevor yanked the bottle from under his arm and hopped up on the wide deck rail.

He leaned back against the corner pillar and examined the label. "You always did like the peaty stuff."

"They were out of Blue," he replied, referring to Trevor's favorite.

"Well," Charlie drawled as she appeared at the door, "seeing as that's the only alcohol in the house, beggars can't be choosers."

She set three glasses on the round metal table between two rockers and snagged the bottle from Trevor. She filled the glasses, handed them their drinks, then claimed the chair closest to Trevor, rocking back and propping her feet on the railing near his thigh. Sensing she needed the reprieve and that Trevor would deck him if he interrupted it, Sean followed her lead, toeing off his socks and shoes, settling in the other rocker, and lifting his bare feet to the railing. He stared out at the ocean and sipped his drink, drowning under the weight of the silent, mounting tension among them. There were things that needed to be said, but more than anything, he just wanted to hear their voices again, to be part of a conversation with the two people who'd mattered most to him at one time. That still did.

So, when Charlie dropped her feet and angled to refill her glass, Sean moved, catching her wrist halfway to the bottle. Trevor shifted, and Sean lifted a hand, wordlessly pleading for the chance to say his piece. Trevor held his gaze a long, assessing moment, then resumed his position against the pillar. A single deep breath later, Sean removed the empty tumbler from Charlie's grasp and set it on the table next to his.

"I need to—"

His long overdue apology was cut short by the last thing he expected Charlie to say. "I caused today's damage. They're dead because of me."

Surprised, Sean tightened his fingers around her wrist. He brought to mind the details of the police report, plus the details Officer Sylvan had shared, and he couldn't recall a single scrap of evidence that suggested Charlie was involved with or at fault in Mitch's and Cal's deaths. "How can that be?"

Given his sigh and pinched expression, Trevor agreed with Sean. "Charlie, we've been through this."

She glanced away from both of them but not before Sean saw the tears gathering in the corners of her eyes. "Week before the raid, family dinner at Dad's house. I was giving him shit for becoming a desk jockey in his old age."

Trevor rotated toward them, both legs dangling off the rail. "Charlie, you can't—"

"He was in dispatch when the call came in—*from me*—requesting backup. Dad took it, Cal was covering him, neither came back alive." She shrugged, her voice barely above a whisper. "My fault."

"You"—Sean grasped her hands—"did not tip off Hector Salazar that the cops were on their way. You did not put automatic weapons into his drug dealers' hands. You did not fire Kevlar-piercing bullets into Cal's and Mitch's vests."

Her eyes widened. "You get all that from your FBI contacts?"

And so did his. "You knew?"

"Of course we knew," Trevor said as he hopped off the

railing. His next words were for Charlie, though. "And Sean is right. This isn't your fault."

The detective remained focused on Sean. "Were you keeping tabs on me?" Her gaze flicked to Trevor. "On us?" She withdrew her hands and scooted back, pulling her knees to her chest and wrapping her arms defensively around her shins. "Is that how you knew about Dad and Cal?"

"I check on both of you from time to time," he admitted. Moments of weakness overcame him occasionally, but being an ocean away had kept him from acting on them. "But in this case, Annie called me."

Charlie's tears instantly returned, and she angled her face away, angrily swiping at the wetness on her cheeks. "Annie was there that night. She heard what I said to Dad. She blames me. Aside from the funeral today, she won't let me near her. She's inconsolable, and all I want to do is help, to grieve with my sister, but I just make it worse. I had to leave her at Dad's house with Jaylen."

She buried her face in her knees, and Sean glanced at Trevor standing beside her chair. "Jaylen?"

"Jaylen Sims. Another officer with the department," he answered. "They've been dating a few months, under the radar until today."

Charlie lifted her tear-streaked face. "He's the—" Her voice cracked. "He's the only one who's been able to calm her while we…"

While she and Abel made sure everyone responsible for Mitch's and Cal's deaths was behind bars. Sean slipped out of his chair and knelt in front of Charlie. He clasped her flailing hand in his and gently squeezed. "Charlotte, you are not to blame for this."

Trevor steadied her chair. "That's what I've been trying to tell her." His smirk was small and sad. "She's not much better at listening than Annie."

Charlie swatted at him with her free hand, and Trevor caught it, holding tight. Sean continued to hold the other as she struggled to choke down a sob, but otherwise she made no reply, keeping her gaze focused on the ocean's inky black water. They sat like that for several long minutes, the three of them connected yet never further apart.

Trying to feel nothing and feeling everything.

"When do you leave?" Charlie asked after an eternity.

"Tomorrow." Sean peeked around Charlie and Trevor at the boxes inside the house. "When's the big move?"

"Later this summer," she answered. "Washington."

Sean's heart skipped a beat, a flame of hope igniting. "DC?"

"Georgetown, technically," Trevor said, his smile a little truer, a little wider. "I got a tenured professorship in the English department there."

"I thought you were tenure-track at HU?"

He opened his mouth to reply, but Charlie beat him to it. "We needed a change."

Sean's heart skipped another few beats, the flame burning brighter. "You're moving there together?"

"I only decided to go last week," she said. "After..."

Beside her, Trevor's smile dimmed, and Sean's hope darkened with it. They were moving to DC as friends, then, nothing more. The two of them fleeing Hanover.

Fleeing home. Did they have any idea they were running toward him? Sean didn't think so, and now didn't seem the time to tell them. "That the reason you're selling the house?" he asked instead.

Twin tears raced down her face, and Sean's heart more than skipped, fearing the worst. It only began to beat again when she mumbled, "Yes."

He reached out and brushed away her tears. "You sure you want to do that?"

She nuzzled his palm, her warm breath caressing his skin and igniting a flame of need instead. Her next words doused it, and ice replaced the warmth. "I need to move on."

"We both do," Trevor added.

A freezer-sharp burn seared Sean's soul and his own eyes filled with tears. When he was able to speak again, he asked the one question that would put his mind, if not his heart, at ease. "You'll be there for each other?"

Charlie opened her eyes and stared directly into his. "Always."

Trevor echoed the response, his unspoken *unlike you* loud enough for Sean to hear over the waves of sorrow crashing around inside him, louder even than the tide lapping at the shore. They didn't need him any longer, no matter how much he would always need them. He wouldn't bother them in DC.

"Good." He gave Charlie's cheek a final swipe, then grabbed his socks and shoes and stood. Charlie rose with him, and Trevor shifted to stand beside her. Stepping close, Sean gave in to the urge to trail his fingers down Trevor's arm, needing to touch him too, one last time. Goose bumps rose along the tan skin, and Trevor's shiver rolled through Sean too.

Fighting the lump in his throat, Sean said the words the two most important people to have ever entered his world needed to hear... to move on. "I'm sorry. More than you'll ever know, but if the two of you are happy or on your way to being happy, then I'm happy too. That's all I've ever wanted for both of you."

Trevor's body trembled, Charlie's breath hitched, and the salty smell of tears, from one or both of them, tickled Sean's nose. Enticed him to stay. But he didn't dare linger. If he did, he'd surely fall to his knees and confess all his sins for another shot at a future with them. A future that was the opposite of moving on. So instead, he swiftly turned and headed for the stairs.

He made it as far as the corner before his world imploded.

"Sean!" Charlie called at the same time Trevor shouted, "Wait!"

All they had to do was call his name, ask him to stay, and Sean was undone.

His socks and shoes hit the deck and he erased the distance between them. At Trevor's nudge, Charlie lunged forward first, and Sean wound an arm around her waist, plunged a hand into her hair, and hauled her body close, hungrily reclaiming her mouth. It was all better than he remembered—the smokiness of the scotch mixed with the taste that was uniquely Charlie, the weight of her thick, silky hair gliding through his fingers, the way her warm, soft body fit perfectly against his.

The way the other hot, hard body fit perfectly along his backside. Trevor's hands landed on his hips, the grip bruising in its intensity, all of that earlier anger channeled into his grip, but the flash of pain was nothing compared to the spike of pleasure as Trevor notched his erection against Sean's ass, yanked aside his collar, and licked a stripe up his neck. The lust that had always sizzled between them winning out and fueling the romantic.

Deprived hands roaming, Sean aimed one south, squeezing Charlie's firm, denim-clad ass and pressing her hips against his. The other he reached behind him, weaving his fingers into Trevor's hair, holding Trevor's mouth to the crook of his neck, and moaning as Trevor kissed and nipped the tendon there. Sean rocked his hips, and Charlie and Trevor countered, friction from both sides ratcheting his need higher. And higher still when Trevor kissed a path up his neck and over his jaw. He lured Sean's mouth from Charlie's and claimed a kiss with the same intense hunger that had always threatened to drown Sean.

He lost himself in rough kisses, in Charlie's featherlight touch as she unbuttoned his shirt and ran her hands over his chest, in the tangle of arms and legs as they wound around and thrust against each other. Fuck, he wanted them, had always wanted them, more than any others who'd ever shot him an interested look. He was back where he belonged, between the only two people he'd ever loved. But he was leaving tomorrow, and they were moving on, together but separate, each hoping to find a new path that would make them happy. He didn't want to cause them more pain. Didn't want to damage the fragile hope they were hanging on to. This wasn't moving on.

Tearing his mouth from Trevor's, Sean forestalled Charlie's advance with a hand to her shoulder and eased Trevor back with the fingers still in his hair. He gulped for air and struggled for control. "What are we doing?"

Charlie stared at him, a stormy mix of lust and despair churning in her bottomless black eyes. "Saying goodbye."

A single tear escaped her eye and raced down her cheek, only to be intercepted by Trevor's thumb as he gently held her face. There was a second of hesitation, two deer caught in the headlights of the unexpected, and then they lunged, mouths colliding, their bodies sighing and melting into each other.

Sean's stomach clenched with the undeniable confirmation that his hope for them had been lost until that moment. That it would be lost again—forever—after this night was over. They hadn't been together after he'd left, and they wouldn't be together again after tonight. But if Sean could give them this goodbye, this resolution they all needed, then at least maybe he would've done something right by them. Would've healed a little of the pain he'd inflicted.

He circled behind Trevor, used his nose to push aside his hair, and kissed his nape. He wrapped an arm around his front, a hand slicing between him and Charlie, and snuck his fingers under the hem of Trevor's tee. He splayed a hand against his tight abs, and Trevor shivered in his arms enough to draw back from the kiss with Charlie.

Sean met her gaze over Trevor's shoulder and nodded. She shifted her attention to Trevor, and hand in his, tugged him forward. With her hair tousled, her pale skin flushed, and her full lips swollen, she was as good as any siren from the sea. There was no denying her; there never had been. Trevor followed her into the house, Sean on his heels, unable to tear his hands from Trevor's body, stripping Trevor to nothing as they stumbled after the woman they loved.

In the bedroom, the tables were turned. Trevor claimed Sean's mouth once more and Charlie stripped him from behind. She dragged his dress shirt down and off his arms, unbuckled his belt, and shoved his pants and boxers to the floor. Sean kicked them aside and used the momentary distance to draw Charlie back around to his front. He grabbed the hem of her tank and yanked it up and off, exposing smooth skin and more black lace. Mouth to her neck, he groaned when he discovered her skin still smelled and tasted of cocoa butter and the salty air that coated everything here. Pure heaven, pure Charlie.

He kissed the swells of her breasts and traced the bralette's cups with his tongue, dipping inside each to swipe across her stiff nipples while Trevor worked the clasp behind her back. Once undone, she freed her arms from the straps and the delicate fabric fluttered to the floor. Trevor slipped his arms around her waist, holding her gently, as Sean lifted one perfect breast to his mouth. He sucked deep, causing her to moan, to rock her hips back into Trevor's and draw a deep, delicious rumble from him. Smiling, Sean took her other breast in his hand and gave it equal attention, his fingers rolling and tugging, just the way he remembered she liked it.

Her hands fisted in his hair, holding him to her. "More. Fuck, more."

He continued to worship her breasts as Trevor sank a hand inside her shorts. She thrust into the touch, arching her back and offering more to Sean as well. He drank of her, of them, of their moans and thrusts until he was drunk. Unable to hold himself up, he sank to his knees, taking her shorts and underwear with him. With her legs spread, Sean buried his nose in the patch of dark hair between her thighs. He flicked out his tongue, licking a path from her opening to where Trevor was torturing her clit. Then he took Trevor's fingers into his mouth and sucked hard, the taste of them both on his tongue almost enough to make Sean blow.

Trevor too, judging by the moan and the thud against the wall that could only be his head. Charlie's affectionate, sexy chuckle confirmed as much and was enough to break through Sean's lusty haze. Her nails scratching under his chin drew his gaze all the way up. The sight—Charlie's naked body flushed and arched against Trevor's, his erect dick in her grip against her hip, his hand clasping her breast—was second only to her sexy, in-charge smile.

"Get on the bed, Sean," she ordered softly. "I want you inside me, and Trevor needs to get his cock inside you." A cock that eagerly thrust into her fist, the darkening head glistening with precome.

Sean dropped a hand to his balls and clasped them tight, praying he didn't come from the sight and words alone. A picture, a fantasy that had haunted his memories and dreams, unexpectedly reality again.

"Now," Trevor rumbled from over Charlie's shoulder, the earlier anger in his hazel eyes replaced with fierce hunger. He thrust again. "Please. If you want this too."

Sean did, no question. He staggered to the bed and lay on his back, bared to them, his cock straining and leaking, his gaze and words pleading. Trevor knelt beside him on the bed and silenced him with a kiss, tongue invading his mouth as if he could lick up every drop of Charlie that Sean had devoured. Every drop of Sean too. And mixing a heady cocktail of Charlie and Trevor that Sean was getting all of.

Charlie's weight settled on his thighs, and she rolled a condom down his length, making him hiss into Trevor's mouth, which curved against his. Trevor drew back and dragged a thumb over Sean's smile. Sean nipped his fingertip, flicked it with his tongue, and Trevor growled. He shoved his thumb all the way into Sean's mouth, and Sean sucked hard. Trevor fell forward, hand braced on the mattress beside Sean's head. "Do you want me to put a condom on? My last test was negative."

Sean released Trevor's thumb with a pop and shook his head. "I want to taste all of you on my tongue."

Another growl, and then Trevor straightened, shifting on his knees, spreading his legs more, and bringing his cock right where Sean wanted it. Lower, Charlie took Sean's aching shaft in her hand, positioned him at her entrance, and sank down onto him. He pushed into her warm, wet heat, savoring every inch until he was buried to the hilt inside her. He bent his knees, bumping her forward, and her lithe body spread atop him, her hands splaying over his chest.

All while Trevor filled his mouth and his senses, the sharp taste of his precome, the musky smell of his groin, the tickle of hair on Sean's nose and on Sean's fingertips as he skated a hand around Trevor's thigh to his ass, fingers teasing his crack and speeding Trevor's thrusts. Sean traced his other hand up Charlie's side, into her hair, holding her close as their hips rocked, as her breaths quickened and the heat and wetness around his cock intensified.

Surrounded by them, this was contentment. This was home.

And in that instant, Sean realized he'd never have it again.

The agonizing revelation that he was doomed to spend the rest of his life as a nomad, banished from the only place, the only two people he'd ever loved, drove him to tears.

"Sean?" Charlie whispered, her voice trembling with worry as Trevor murmured a quiet "Baby." He wove his fingers into Sean's hair and eased him off his cock.

The soft words and familiar endearment made Sean's chest ache more. He hid his face in Trevor's thigh and mumbled, "Need a minute."

Charlie stilled atop him but for her hands, which soothingly coasted over his chest, whisper-soft against his skin. Trevor's fingers played a gentle melody in his hair, tapping lightly, threading through the longer top strands. Breathing deep, Sean focused on their scents—musk and salty sea breeze; on the sounds—the waves outside, their breaths, their kisses as they drifted back together above him; on the sight of that kiss—full of love and longing as he peeked out from his hiding place.

When he finally had his despair locked down, Sean nudged Trevor forward with the hand still on his ass. He slid his tongue along the underside of Trevor's cock and took the thick length back into his mouth. Trevor hummed his approval, Charlie hers, and Sean rocked his hips once more. Rhythm steady, he closed his eyes and listened as pleasure took hold of them again.

Slow and steady quickly escalated to wild and abandoned, the years of separation and longing getting the better of them. As teeth and lips clashed above him, Sean greedily sucked Trevor's cock while his own pounded inside Charlie. Her nails dug into his chest as she tripped over the edge with a shout, as Trevor's release filled Sean's mouth, and as his own climax filled the condom inside Charlie. Sean wished like hell her nails on his chest and Trevor's bruises on his hips would last, would permanently, impossibly, scar so he'd have physical memorials of this night. An entirely different kind than the ones on the banister outside but marking the date nonetheless.

The last time they'd come together. The first and last time they'd properly said goodbye.

Hours later, when dawn was beginning to break outside, Sean silently slipped out of the bed where he, Trevor, and

Charlie had said goodbye two more times during the night. One time leisurely and tender, the other, their last, as desperate as the first. Walking through the house, Sean gathered his things and dressed, soaking up the quiet peace of home, storing it in his heart and mind.

He was sitting on the edge of the living room couch, rolling on his socks, when Charlie appeared in the bedroom doorway across from him, Trevor's T-shirt hanging off one shoulder and skirting her thighs.

"What time's your flight?" she asked.

"Two hours." He slipped his feet into his dress shoes. "Out of Wilmington." It would take him forty-five minutes to get there, leaving just enough time to check in, board, then have the inevitable breakdown with an in-flight beverage in hand and his face aimed out the window. No witnesses but the clouds and the morning sun.

"So, this is it?" Charlie said.

"Yeah, this is it." He swallowed hard, stood, and crossed the room to her. Looping an arm around her waist, he rested a hand at the small of her back and with the other, wove a dark tendril of hair through his fingers.

Charlie fiddled with his unbuttoned collar as tears pooled in her eyes. She gave a watery chuckle. "I failed at not feeling."

His own sad laugh was equally damp. "I should have picked a stronger scotch."

She leaned forward and kissed his knuckles. "I'm devastated that more of my family is gone. I'm angry as hell at the way they were taken and at myself for playing a role in that."

"Charlie—"

She talked right over him. "And somewhere below all that grief and anger, I'm still pissed at how you left and that you came back. And I'm pissed that Trevor and I have to move on from all this, from our home, if we have any chance of being happy. But despite all that hurt and anger, despite the fact I know I'm supposed to say goodbye and let you go, the only thing I can think to do is tell you we still love you and beg you to stay. That's the only way I can think to make some of this pain and anger go away."

But it wouldn't truly go away, and the pain and anger would only be worse if Charlie ever learned the truth of why he left and stayed away in the first place. He couldn't cause her more pain, couldn't cause more damage. He'd made a promise.

Brushing aside her hair and curling his hand around her neck, Sean pressed his lips to her forehead. He breathed deep, a final inhale of all that was home, a final melody as Trevor snored in the background. When he was sure every aspect of home was committed to memory, he drew back and held Charlie's tear-streaked face in his hands. "I love you, Charlotte. I love Trevor too. Always have and always will," he vowed. "But I have to go."

"Are you going to keep tabs on us?" she asked, repeating her question from the previous night.

"No." After the night they'd just shared, after learning they'd be in DC too, there'd be no way Sean could resist seeking them out if he knew exactly where they were. And that would be the opposite of moving on. So no, he wouldn't be checking up on them any longer. He wouldn't be looking back. "I'm going to let you live your lives, Charlie. Let you and Trevor be happy."

"But what about you?" She rose on her toes, her lips soft against his jaw. "Is that enough, Sean?"

"Knowing you're both happy is all I need." He nuzzled her cheek and inhaled one last breath of cocoa butter and salt. Listened once more for the sleepy rumble from the other room. "Take care of him."

"Always."

That would have to be enough.

CHAPTER TWO

Jefferson Marshall was a legend.

A legend for his oft-cited treatises. For the gilded awards lining his office walls. For the well-placed students who had crossed the threshold of his lecture hall. Marshall's scholarship and his progeny were an institution of their own.

Standing slouched and unconscious, a gag in his mouth and a thick rope noose around his neck, the man known as the Kingmaker seemed anything but legendary.

He awoke slowly, attempting to open his eyes, but his eyelids dragged, and his legs ached as if he'd conducted a day full of lectures. And there was some sort of pressure around his neck, scratching his skin like the rough wool of a cheap overcoat.

Inhaling, the strong stench of hay and manure assaulted his senses, causing him to gag against the cotton between his teeth and depressing his tongue.

The dense fog clouding his mind dissipated instantly.

In the dim light emanating from below, Marshall's well-trained mind quickly surmised he was in a barn on a raised wooden platform above horse stables. He attempted to look at his feet and met resistance. His eyes flared with panic, and he lifted his hands. He clutched at the thick, braided rope around his throat with tingling fingers. The more he tugged, the tighter it became.

Shifting to the gag that strangled his cries for help, he fumbled for its knot behind his head, stilling when his fingers brushed the hang knot at the base of his neck. He turned his gaze skyward, following the rope to where it disappeared into the rafters above—the symbol of his imminent mortality.

Mortality that grew closer when a terrifying sound echoed out of the darkness, chilling him to the bone.

The first cackle was muted, far away, but then it became louder, more hysterical.

Panic made his palms wet and caused his fingers to slip on the knot.

If he could just get rid of the gag...

Working with renewed resolve, his focus was rewarded when the gag slipped from his mouth and fluttered silently into the abyss below.

Relief coursed through him as he took his first unencumbered breath, oxygen filling his lungs with air and his heart with hope.

Now for the knot at the base of his neck...

Abruptly, the manic laughter stopped, replaced by a far more dreadful sound.

The swoosh of the trap doors opening beneath him was the last thing the legendary Jefferson Kingmaker Marshall heard before swinging to his death.

CHAPTER THREE

The sun had barely been up an hour when Charlie parked in front of the HU Equestrian Center. The middle barn of the large complex was swarming with police officers and crime scene techs. Thankfully, the only van in the lot so far was the medical examiner's. No press on the scene yet, thank fuck. But in a town Hanover's size, it was only a matter of time, and once the reporters caught wind, city hall would too, and Charlie's day would be shot to hell.

She and her team needed to work fast. She stretched to the glove box, grabbed her weapon and badge, clipped them to her belt, and shoved open the car door with a booted foot.

"Deputy Henby," Officer Sylvan greeted as she entered through the open barn door.

"Morning, Wally." Wallace had been her brother's partner and was a friend of the family. Shortly after the funeral, he'd come to her and asked not to be immediately repartnered. He'd needed some recovery time, and HPD had needed a new local affairs liaison, which included dealing with HU and campus security. "Keep it locked down out here for us?"

"Yes, ma'am," he said with a nod. "Let me know if you need anything."

She joined Detective Diego Perez where he stood next to one of the barn stalls. "What've we got?" Dispatch had given her the basics, but she wanted to hear it from the officers on the scene.

"Professor Jefferson Marshall. Distinguished member of the faculty at HU."

Hanging by a noose from the barn rafters, his face so swollen it was hardly recognizable, Professor Marshall looked far from distinguished.

"He was found like that by one of the stable hands," Diego said as the crime scene techs loosened the noose and lowered Marshall into a body bag. "Last person here yesterday closed up around nine. Time of death looks to be between then and five this morning."

"We'll let your wife be the judge of that." Diego was married to the county ME, who was also one of Charlie's best friends.

"Maggie's dropping the hellions off at my mom's. She'll meet us at the morgue."

"I won't tell her you called your kids that," Charlie said as she snapped on a pair of gloves.

"Me?" Diego splayed a hand over his chest. "Those are her words. Direct quote."

Charlie didn't doubt it, that Maggie would say such a thing or that she and Diego, two fiery individuals, would have equally fiery children. They came by it honestly.

"Got something," said the tech peering into Marshall's mouth. Using a pair of forceps, he extricated a rolled strip of paper and held it up for Charlie.

She took the tiny piece of paper and carefully unfurled the scroll, revealing the strangest suicide note—hand-written in red, block letters—she'd ever read:

#1 – A PLAGUE UPON YOU, MURDERERS, TRAI-TORS ALL!

One word caught her attention, making her heart pound and transforming the scene from merely disturbing to potentially dangerous.

"Move away from the body," she ordered and took several steps back herself. She raised her voice so everyone working the scene could hear. "We've got a quarantine situation. Shut the doors and call the biohazard team."

A stunned moment of silence and a shouted "Now" later, Wallace kicked into action and swung the barn doors closed, plunging them into darkness.

By late afternoon, the only piece of good news Charlie had received all day was the all-clear earlier that morning from the biohazard team. No toxins or pathogens were found at the scene, but neither were any more clues. The body, the barn, and the surrounding areas were all clean.

She'd left the Equestrian Center at noon, then spent

the next two hours working the phones with Wallace to deal with city hall, HU, and the local press, who'd finally gotten wind of Professor Marshall's death. After escaping that hell, Charlie had made another pass at the crime scene, recentering herself in the process of picking apart the stable. Aside from evidence that the bale lift had been used to lever the professor to the upper level, something anyone would need to use to haul him up there, she'd found nothing more on her second look around.

She hoped Maggie would be more successful. Cause of death—hanging—appeared obvious, but underlying toxicity, pinpricks, or the like would be critical in ruling the death a suicide or murder. There was the note, but the professor's son, an FBI cyber agent who worked out of The Hague, insisted to Charlie on a call midday that it would be very unlike his father to commit suicide. Granted, father and son were estranged—perhaps Agent Marshall didn't know Professor Marshall that well anymore—but everything Charlie personally knew about Jefferson Marshall, everything she'd also heard from others she or her officers had talked to that day, confirmed as much. Still, until evidence to the contrary came to light, suicide remained on the table along with murder.

She was back at her desk, combing through interviews and reports, when a commotion at the front of the station distracted her. Through her office window, she spotted Trevor towering above the crowd, and then a moment later, Annie appeared, her face as dusty as her and Trevor's purple-and-white uniforms.

"Ten and oh!" she shouted to the cheers of some and the groans of others.

Hanover had an active municipal softball league, the teams fielded from the HU staff and various governmental departments. The HU team had two ringers—Trevor, a CWS champion, and Annie, a former softball pitcher for UNC. They were going to be hell on HPD when they faced off in the league playoffs next month.

Charlie met Annie just outside her office. "I expected nothing less with you on the mound and Trevor catching." She looped an arm around her sister's shoulders, ignoring the dirt and sweat and hugging Annie to her side. She was proud of them both, but more than that, she was so relieved her sister was smiling and talking to her again. It had been a rough six weeks since their brother's and father's deaths, a rough month since their funeral, but they seemed to be coming out the other side of it, and Annie seemed to be on the way to forgiving her, even if Charlie would never forgive herself. "I'm sorry I missed it."

"Jaylen's wishing he'd missed it too." Annie snickered at the officer who joined them, an umpire's mask dangling from his fingertips. Sweat dappled his short, cropped hair and an indented strip from the mask's band darkened his forehead above his brown eyes. The teams rotated officiating duties, a few players from a third team providing the line judges and umps for the two teams playing. Jaylen had filled in at the last second for Wallace, who'd remained trapped in the barn with Charlie.

"They're gonna wipe the floor with us, Deputy. I didn't need to see that." Except he'd been seeing it all month, dutifully attending Annie's games now that they'd gone public with their relationship. He sighed dramatically, but the corners of his lips turned up as he caught another of Annie's grins.

Another light in the dark of the past couple months.

"You got off easy, man." Trevor's amused voice carried over the din of the bullpen. He shuffled through the rows of desks, balancing a cardboard tray of food in one hand and holding two bottles of Cheerwine with the other. "You didn't have this one"—he pecked Charlie's cheek, then strode into her office to unload the ballpark bounty—"heckling you the entire time too."

"I would have behaved myself," she called after him.

Everyone laughed. Rightfully so. All of Hanover knew she was a grade A heckler. It was her favorite thing about sports, especially since she was otherwise shit at them. She'd grown up surrounded by athletes, but athletic talent had skipped her completely, so she'd made up for it with moral support.

"How many strikeouts?" she asked her sister.

"Twelve," Annie said. "The last one was a wicked rise ball."

Charlie opened her mouth, and Jaylen held up a hand. "Don't say it should've been fifteen. You weren't there."

"Just in case, I'll have Maggie check your eyesight."

"It's all good." Annie swaggered over to Jaylen and slapped his shoulder with her glove. "Lay off Jaylen."

"All right." Grinning, Charlie raised her hands. "I'll ease up."

"Why don't you go find Abel and fill him in?" Trevor

said to Annie and Jaylen. "I'm sure he wants to know how the game went, and I need to get some food in your sister since I'm sure she hasn't eaten all day."

Charlie opened her mouth to lie but her grumbling stomach betrayed her. "I forgot." Not a lie. "It's been a day." Also not a lie.

"Sounds like a plan." Jaylen hooked an arm through Annie's and steered her toward the stairs. "You can tell him how you're gonna kick our asses in the tourney next month."

"I promise I won't be too hard on you."

Charlie barely contained her laughter. Annie's competitive streak was as fierce as Trevor's and—

Charlie blocked the mental image before it fully formed, focusing instead on the here and now. Her family, and the case that had eaten up more than half her day. "Jaylen," Charlie called after him. "Once Annie is on her way, find Diego and get up to speed on the new case."

He nodded. "Yes, ma'am."

They disappeared down the stairwell, and Charlie retreated into her office, Trevor on her heels. He sank into one of the visitor chairs in front of her desk. "Seems like love is in the air for those two."

She swiped the box of Raisinets from the tray and dropped into the chair beside his. "Doubly good I wasn't there cheering for the wrong team."

"Please." Trevor took a swig from his soda bottle. "Jaylen's been here a few years now. He knows the drill."

Rolling her eyes, she traded the box of candy for a hot

dog, unwrapped it, and took a bite. Doctored with ketchup and cheese, just the way she liked it.

"Heard them making plans for another date next week," Trevor said. "What's that bring the tally to? I've lost count."

Charlie hid her prideful smirk behind a napkin. "Me too." She was happy Annie and Jaylen were getting closer, especially since she'd been the one to set them up. But her pride was tempered by recent events and events in the near future. "Do you think she'll be okay?"

She didn't have to say more for Trevor to understand where her thoughts had gone. Annie was a primary concern for both of them as they'd each considered the move to DC. "I hope so," he said. "I hope it's the fresh start she needs too."

Annie would be out of any other Henby shadows and on her own two feet with Jaylen by her side. Abel would still be in town—Annie wouldn't be totally without family—and Charlie and Trevor would only be a six-hour car ride away. She was a grown woman. Charlie shouldn't worry, but turning that instinct off where her little sister was concerned was impossible.

Trevor set his empty bottle on the desk and angled toward her. "Have you heard any more from the feds?"

She paused midlift of her hot dog. She appreciated the shift in conversation away from the hard one to something else, but she was cautious about having this particular conversation at the station. Her work on the Salazar case had caught the attention of the organized crime unit at the FBI. Joining the Bureau would be a giant leap for her career, but every time she thought about the opportunity, every time she let herself get a little excited about it, the next instant her stomach would churn. Yes, she'd taken down Hector Salazar, but her father and brother had died in the process. Yet somehow, she was the one climbing the LEO ladder when they'd only been in the ground a mere month? Nothing about the situation seemed fair.

And nothing about joining the organization where Sean Hale worked as an assistant legal attaché seemed wise either. But Sean was a legat at The Hague, and she'd made damn sure he'd had nothing to do with her recruitment. He'd said he was going to let her live her life, and this was another door opening. To a possible future of her own in DC. Exactly when she needed it. But, fuck, would the guilt that roiled her stomach and burned the back of her throat ever go away?

Trevor grasped her knees with both hands. "Charlie."

Would the sparks Sean had reignited ever go away either? Fire burned where Trevor laid his hands, same as warmth still heated her cheek where he'd pecked it earlier. They knew where this led, or rather didn't. They'd tried and failed after Sean's first disappearing act. But then Sean had returned and reignited an attraction that wasn't so easily snuffed out. She fought through the emotional storm to focus on Trevor's words.

"You earned this," he said. "It's okay—"

"What will Annie think? I just got her back." Somehow the hard conversation had become the easier one. "What if this pushes her away again? For good?"

"How will working to put away more criminals like

Hector Salazar, saving other families the pain ours has gone through, push her away?"

The bile receded a little. Trevor always knew what to say to comfort her. "I just don't want to be disrespectful, to the department, to them"—she covered his hands—"to any of you."

Hazel eyes bored into hers. "You're not, Charlie. You'll be doing good work. Abel got that when you told him the other night. Annie will too. And just like moving to DC, you'll be doing what you need to move on."

Hearing those words, Charlie tore her gaze from Trevor's as she mentally weathered a barrage of bittersweet memories.

Sean's grief-stricken face, absent too long from Hanover. Trevor's livewire reaction to his presence as well as her own more simmering one. The ever-present connection between her and Trevor that had caught fire, Sean the spark. A bottle of scotch, a long overdue apology, and then an explosion of tangled limbs and bodies.

A cold, empty side of the bed the next morning.

A glimpse at what the three of them could have been, the future they could have had, but never would.

A final goodbye. The one they should have had ten years ago, the one a part of her still refused to acknowledge. Refused to let go of and move on, despite her own words claiming to do just that. The anger that had been supplanted by grief then keeping the pain fresh now.

The lingering temptation to try again with Trevor, just the two of them, despite the near certainty they would crash and burn like the last time. The critical piece missing. And then where would they be?

Unable to meet Trevor's gaze, sure he'd see some of what she was thinking, she aimed her own eyes toward the bullpen as her mind continued to vault and spin over the possibilities. Until the ringing desk phone interrupted her mental gymnastics. Standing, she stepped around the desk and picked up the receiver, the display flashing an internal extension from downstairs. "Talk to me."

"Jaylen's gonna bring Annie back upstairs," Abel said. "You need to get her and Trevor out the front door. Quickly."

"What's going on?"

"Feds are here."

Her spine stiffened. "They're early."

"One of 'em is here to interview you."

"Here? But I'm supposed to meet Agent Conder in Wilmington."

"Seems he's here. The other..." Abel cleared his throat. "The other is here about Professor Marshall."

"Already?" There was no way Agent Marshall could have gotten there so fast. Which meant what? The feds had gotten wind of the case and sent someone to steal it? On what grounds? She might be considering a job with them, but for now, she was still HPD's deputy chief, the lead detective on this case, and the professor's death was not a federal matter. She glanced at Trevor, who was moving around the room, cleaning up, while keeping a worried eye on her.

"I'll explain when you get here," Abel said.

"Explain now."

"Charlotte." His voice was stern, clipped, brooking no argument. "Get Annie and Trevor out of here, now, then meet me in the back alley."

Her eyes cut to the stairs where Jaylen and Annie appeared. "Give me five."

"And, sugar," Abel said, his voice grim, "brace."

The line went dead, and she jerked the phone from her ear, staring at it as her stomach churned once more, this time with apprehension.

"Everything okay, sis?" Annie asked from the doorway.

Concealing her anxiety, Charlie replaced the receiver in the cradle and circled her desk. "I'm sorry, but we're going to have to cut the party short." She hated the disappointment that slashed across her sister's face, but maybe she could make up for it. "How about we pick the party back up tonight? I'll swing by Pier Point for burgers and meet you at your place?"

"Sounds good." She turned to Jaylen. "Want to join us?"

He grinned. "I'd be delighted." Then abruptly seemed to remember his boss was also in the room. "Unless I'm needed here," he said to Charlie.

Charlie didn't make him sweat. "Don't think the debrief will take that long." She shifted her attention to Trevor. "Can you give Annie a lift home?"

"No problem. Okay if I stay for the party too?"

She shoved his shoulder. "Of course it is."

He leaned in and kissed her cheek, setting off another flicker of heat. "Later, honey."

Once they were clear, Charlie made her way to the back alley and was surprised to find her uncle sitting on the station stoop. Elbows propped on his knees, head hung in his bear-claw-sized hands, he was the picture of misery. What the fuck was going on? She stepped outside, the station door banging shut, and Abel shot to his feet. He spun and Charlie nearly gasped, his expression almost as grim as the night her dad and brother had died.

"What's going on?" she asked as she descended the steps and stopped in front of him. "Where are the agents?"

"The agent here to interview you went back to Wilmington. He'll meet you there on Monday as scheduled. I explained the sensitivity of meeting here."

"Good, thank you," she said with a nod. "You said there was another agent asking about Professor Marshall. You got a name? If I'm headed into a jurisdictional pissing contest, I'd like to know who I'm up against."

"It's not like that, sugar."

"Then what's it like, exactly?"

Abel repeated his earlier warning. "Brace, Charlotte."

An angry, frustrated *What the fuck is going on?* died on her lips when a smooth, deep voice called out from the shadows behind Abel.

"Charlie?"

Eyes widening, she rose on her toes to peer over Abel's shoulder, confirming the unbelievable truth her ears had told her. The owner of that familiar voice stepped out of the shadows into the strip of afternoon sun lighting one half of the alley.

Brace.

BRACE.

Except there was no bracing for this.

Same as there'd been no bracing a month ago when she'd glimpsed her ex-lover across the cemetery at Mitch and Cal's funeral. Only then she'd been seated and numb with grief. Now, though... Now all of that buried anger and resentment bubbled and collided with longing and panic as she laid eyes again on Anderson Sean Hale.

Not a lifetime later, not ten years later.

A month later.

She and Trevor had agreed not to tell anyone about Sean's presence at the funeral and at the house after. Why would they? It was a blip on the what-might-have-been radar. In reality, Sean was supposed to be in Europe. So what the fuck was he doing here? And why was he interested in *her* case?

She sidestepped Abel and took in the sight of her ex. His dark hair was cut short, neater than it had been the day of the funeral. Bureau regulation, she supposed, though nothing else about him, other than the holstered gun at his hip, appeared FBI issued. His gray V-neck tee stretched temptingly across his arms and chest, and the dark wash jeans and motorcycle boots were a far cry from his funeral suit and oxfords, but his eyes... His eyes were the same breathtaking shade of blue she'd looked down into and found brimming with tears, with the same longing and despair that permanently occupied a corner of her heart. She hadn't been able to get those eyes out of her head since he'd left for the airport the next morning.

Eyes still on Sean, she lowered her voice and spoke to

Abel. "You need to lock down the files. I don't care who he is or why he's here. This is our case."

"Diego's on it already." Abel squeezed her shoulder and stepped the rest of the way around her, headed for the door. "I'll leave you to it."

Her ears followed his retreating steps while her eyes remained locked on Sean, who was moving toward her. She spread her legs, squared her shoulders, and crossed her arms, assuming a defensive position. Sean froze midstep, hurt and surprise streaking across his face. She didn't give him an inch, for her own sake and the department's. "What are you doing here, Sean?"

His body jerked, his eyes slammed shut, and his face twisted as if he were in pain.

"Sean?" she called again when he didn't reply, and his face contorted further.

"Fuck." He raked his hands through his hair and laced them behind his neck, head bowed. "I shouldn't have come back here."

"Why did you?"

"Jefferson Marshall."

"Is a local matter. My town, my citizen, my case."

"No one's disputing that." He dropped his arms and lifted his chin. His eyes were wary, the brow above them furrowed, and his lips pressed together in a thin line. Whatever his reason for being here, he didn't want to tell her. "I owe him, Charlie."

Now there was the Sean Hale she knew. Duty-bound, except apparently when it came to her and Trevor. Regardless, that was then, this was now, and as she ran class schedules through her memory, she couldn't make the equation work. "Jefferson Marshall? He was never one of your professors."

"No, not him."

"Then who?" she demanded. "Who did you fly across an ocean for?" Who was that important to him? More important than she and Trevor had ever been.

"I'm back in the States now."

She rocked back a step, barely catching the *Since when?* on the tip of her tongue. Same as he'd promised a month ago, she hadn't checked up on him either. As far as she'd known, he was still at The Hague—

Wait, The Hague.

"Him? Emmitt Marshall? Professor Marshall's son?"

Sean nodded. "He's a colleague. One who's saved my ass on more than one occasion." Pink slashed across Sean's cheekbones above his neatly trimmed beard. "Marsh is on assignment and delayed a few days. He wanted eyes on the case, and we need to see to his father's estate."

A nickname, a blush, an entanglement in the other man's affairs. Charlie wondered how close Agents Hale and Marshall were and why that made her back straighten and her voice harden. "I spoke to Agent Marshall this morning. He didn't mention sending you."

"It took some convincing, considering." He shrugged and ran a hand over his nape. "I'm not here to interfere with your investigation or your life, Charlie. I'm just doing a favor for a friend, then I'll be out of your hair." He dropped his arm with a sad half smile. "Like I promised I would be."

Except he was there now—in Hanover—and not an ocean away. Ignoring all that, and ignoring her curiosity as a detective and as his ex who wanted to know more about his involvement with Agent Marshall, Charlie focused instead on reading his expression and explanation. The contrite, conciliatory look on his face indicated he was sincere. He wasn't there to cause trouble, but after his last visit, Sean Hale in Hanover was bound to stir some up nonetheless. Her best play was to cooperate, give him the info he wanted, then send him on his way before keeping their promises became impossible. No matter how much her heart recoiled at the notion of him leaving a third time.

"Let me brief the team, then we'll bring you up to speed." She turned on her heel, climbed the stoop, and opened the station door. "You can wait in my office."

"Much appreciated." One corner of his mouth tipped up, and she immediately questioned her decision. Her gaze drifted to his high cheekbones still flushed pink, his strong, square jaw covered with stubble, his full lower lip she'd never forgotten the taste of. Had been reminded of a few short weeks ago. Electricity sparked through her veins.

She distracted herself from the charge by reminding him, "This is HPD's case."

"Understood, Deputy Henby." He grinned and raised three fingers as they stopped at the top of the stoop. "In and out, I promise."

And there was the jokester she remembered, the one who'd been absent earlier in the month, none of them in the joking mood then. She shouldn't be now either, but that grin, when Sean let it out, had always been infectious. "Boy Scout, my ass," she said with a smirk.

Laughing, he stepped past her into the station. Coffee, Irish Spring, and a singular Sean Hale scent tickled her senses, and she wondered how many promises would be broken by the time this was all over.

CHAPTER FOUR

Trevor leaned partway out the door to check on Annie and Jaylen. They'd scooted closer together on the bench swing at the far end of the screened-in porch, and Jaylen's arm was stretched out behind her. Trevor bit the inside of his cheek to stop from smiling too wide. "You two good?" he asked when he was sure he could talk without cartwheels in his voice.

Annie made no such attempt, her voice as bright and lively as it had been throughout dinner. "Just let us know when the pie is ready."

"Ten minutes or so," he said, judging by the aromas of baking crust and simmering peaches wafting from the kitchen. "We'll shout."

He ducked back inside and up the two steps to the raised galley kitchen where Charlie was washing dishes, her hips swaying to the blues album he'd put on the turntable after dinner. He wrenched his gaze away from temptation, even as his mind rewound to the night four weeks ago he still couldn't believe was real. When Charlie's entire body had writhed against his, when his fingers had slipped between her folds to tease her, when his dick had slid through her tight fist, against her hip, then into—

Finally the mental brakes kicked in, stopping the burgeoning memory of the *last* person he should still be thinking about, no matter how many times he'd gotten off to the replay of that night over the past month. He focused instead on the here and now, the lines of Charlie's back and shoulders, thankfully a bit more relaxed than when she'd first arrived at the house. The burgers from Pier Point, Annie's good mood, and the pie he'd made from scratch that afternoon had worked their magic. Sort of. Whatever had gone down at the station after he and Annie had been shooed out—because he damn well knew that's what had happened—had riled Charlie up. And not in the heckle-the-umpire good way.

"You might have Annie fooled—"

Charlie raised a brow. "Fooled or distracted?"

He leaned a hip against the counter next to her. "Either way, she's not caught on to the Charlie-sized ball of nerves who couldn't sit still on the barstool beside her all through dinner."

"But you noticed."

"Impossible not to." Trevor snagged the dishtowel off her shoulder. "Tell me what happened at the station after we left. Is it the case?"

"No, the case is fine," she answered sharply, then cringed. Trevor snickered at her self-awareness, and she let out a breath on a chuckle of her own, more of her tension leaving with it. "We've got it handled."

"Something else, then?" he asked as he put the dishes away.

Charlie removed the stopper from the sink but didn't respond.

He ventured another guess. "City hall giving you a hard time?"

She scooted the coffeemaker out from under the cabinet and filled the pot with water. "Our illustrious mayor left a voicemail. Usual political bullshit." She poured water into the machine, then replaced the pot under the drip. "With the election coming up, Craig needs to appear in control. Otherwise, the fixed results will be obvious. He demanded a meeting on Monday."

Hanover's mayor, Craig Rowan, was Trevor's least favorite human in all of Hanover. Had been since high school. They'd had a brief reprieve from him in college, Craig partying hard at Wake Forest like the frat boy he was destined to be, but then he'd returned home and followed his family's footsteps into local politics. He was like the shit that stuck to the bottom of your shoe that you could never get off; always causing a fucking mess.

Trevor retrieved four mugs from the cabinet, set two aside for Annie and Jaylen, and doctored the other two, one sugar in Charlie's, two plus cream in his. "But you've got your FBI interview Monday."

Charlie bobbled the scoop of coffee grounds.

He shot out a hand, steadying hers, and they poured

the grounds into the filter together. "So that's what this is about?"

"Trevor."

He tugged the scoop from her hand, set it aside, and pressed Brew on the machine. He clasped Charlie's shoulders and angled her toward him. "You'll get the job."

She stole the towel back and folded it, avoiding his stare. "Are you sure you want me there? In DC with you? I don't want to hold you back."

He trailed a hand down her arm and snagged one of hers. "I wouldn't have made the offer if I didn't want you there with me. I could be in a new town all alone or there with my best friend." He squeezed her hand. "I'd choose the latter every day."

He'd choose more if it had worked between them after the first time Sean had left, but it hadn't. They loved each other, no doubt, but without Sean, it had felt like too much was missing. Like they couldn't be all they were meant to be without him. But after their recent night together, after he'd fallen back into Charlie's arms and into the something more they could be that was always right there beneath the surface, he couldn't help but wonder if maybe it would work this time, just the two of them. Without Sean. The attraction was constant as was the yearning for something more, but he was loathe to risk the most important friendship in his life, especially when he knew the likely outcome was failure. It was more important to have Charlie in his life as a friend, as a roommate in DC, than to not have her in his life at all. Sean had moved on, and they would too. Always together, but in a way that worked for them.

"What about Tracy?" Charlie said. "Is she gonna cause an issue?"

He laughed out loud. "That assumes she comes up for air from the Julian-haze long enough to notice I'm gone."

The ink was barely dry on their divorce and his ex-wife had already married the man she'd had a two-year affair with. An affair that hadn't needed to have been an affair at all, but there lay the crux of the irreconcilable differences that had doomed his marriage, at least as far as he was concerned. As far as Tracy was concerned, well, that was a different matter, most of which had to do with the woman Trevor stood beside now.

"She'll get her share of the house proceeds when I move out." The profit from the sale of the home he'd bought for Tracy as a wedding gift were being held in escrow, pending the end of his short-term leaseback. "She'll be glad to get rid of me."

And of Charlie.

Who, he realized, was trying to distract him. "Stop dodging."

"Sean is back."

Her right hand was still in his, but Trevor could've sworn she'd punched him in the gut. "What did you say?"

Her gaze darted past his shoulder, toward the patio, and Trevor realized he'd raised his voice. How else was he supposed to hear himself over the ringing in his ears? He lowered it when he spoke again, hissing through his teeth. "Sean has been gone for ten years." Except for that one night after Mitch and Cal's funeral. A night they'd didn't talk about in earshot of anyone else. The night Trevor clearly couldn't get out of his fucking head.

"He's here now," she said. "About the case."

He snatched back his hand. "Bullshit."

"Hey," a voice called behind him, and they both whipped around to find Annie standing in the doorway. "Is that the oven timer going off?"

Not just ringing in his head, then.

"Shit," Charlie cursed.

He reached the oven first, turning off the heat and blocking Charlie's path. "Where's he staying?"

"Trevor."

"Where?" He needed to see this—*Sean*—for himself. Needed to find out what the fuck their ex was playing at because Trevor's warning had been crystal fucking clear. Charlie did not deserve to get her heart broken again.

And neither did he.

"Where, Charlotte?"

Dark conflicted eyes held his, same as they had that morning a month ago when he'd walked out of the beach house bedroom to find Charlie huddled in the corner of the couch, wrapped in a blanket, quietly crying.

The answer then had been "The Hague."

The answer today was "The Sand Dollar Inn."

A whole hell of a lot closer.

The Sand Dollar Inn had seen better days. A twenty-room motor lodge, it stood at the south end of Hanover's beachfront peninsula, one half of the U-shaped complex fronting the Atlantic Ocean, the other the Intracoastal Waterway, and the lobby, pool, and patio in the middle riding the inlet. Between the two motel wings, the pot-hole-ridden parking lot was full of cars, weekend summer travelers who were willing to overlook chipped paint and rusty gutters for spacious rooms and water views.

Trevor didn't give a damn about the view. His sole focus was on room twelve at the end of the beachfront wing. Because of course Sean would pick the room with that number, Charlie's favorite, and somehow manage to snag it on a busy weekend. He charged down the covered walkway from the lobby, still not believing Sean was back in Hanover. Just thinking the other man's name made Trevor's heart race and his blood boil, made him fist the jewelry in his hand so hard his nails dug into his palm. He needed to see for himself before he could believe the one man who should've never returned to Hanover had done so.

Again.

He reached the last room and rapped his knuckles against the wooden door. "Sean, if you're in there, open up!"

When no one answered, Trevor sidestepped the door and peered inside the room through the gauzy curtains. One look at the form standing in the middle of the room and Trevor had to grasp the window frame to steady himself, anger warring with relief warring with the spark of desire that flared anytime he laid eyes on Sean Hale. And there was no denying that's who was inside the room. Trevor would know that body anywhere. Head bowed, hand on his nape, Sean appeared to be stuck, unsure whether to answer the door or not.

Trevor didn't give him an option. Seizing on his anger, Trevor raised his fist and pounded the door again. "Sean!" he bellowed. "Open this goddamn door right now, or I swear to God, I'll break it down."

"Cool it, Trev!" Sean hollered.

Trevor's jaw clenched. He'd banished that nickname, but he'd be lying if he said a shiver didn't race up his spine at hearing Sean shout it again. Ignoring the trill of excitement, he held firm to his anger, banging the door until Sean came unstuck. The lock clicked, the door swung open, and Trevor charged inside, shoving the jewelry against Sean's chest. "Fuck that. And fuck you too."

Sean gasped, and since Trevor, back to him, didn't hear metal hit the floor, he guessed his ex was getting a good look at the items he'd forced him to catch. Two necklaces on leather bands—Sean's with two hammered metal charms, a heart and a baseball bat; Trevor's, a matching heart and a catcher's mitt. Charlie's gifts to them after they'd won the CWS. Trevor had contemplated banishing the keepsakes after Cal, that night after their police academy graduation when Sean had left the first time, had given him Sean's necklace, along with Sean's ring he'd proposed to him and Charlie with that morning. But Trevor hadn't been able to part with the necklaces and Charlie, through tears that night as she'd handed him her ring, had asked him not to part with those either. He'd tucked the jewelry in a satchel in the back of a drawer until he'd recently debated whether to pack them for the move to DC. But he hadn't wanted to upset Charlie, and he still couldn't part with the mementos from the best period of his life. He'd left the rings at home, but the necklaces... In Sean's hands, Trevor hoped the damn things felt more like a couple tons than a couple ounces, that Sean would understand the heavy heart Trevor had never been able to banish either.

The door clicked shut and Trevor spun. Sean pocketed the necklaces, then lifted his hands, palms out. Like he'd done that day a month ago when he'd made a promise he clearly hadn't kept. Incensed, Trevor closed the distance between them and did the one thing Charlie had kept him from doing after the funeral. He let his right hook fly, right into Sean's jaw.

Bending at the waist, Sean braced a hand on his knee and cradled his face with the other. "Fuck, you hit hard."

"You bet your sorry ass I do," Trevor seethed over his hunched form. "And there's more where that came from if you don't get the hell out of town."

"Trev, calm down."

"Fuck calm, and stop calling me that. You made a promise, and I told you what would happen if you broke it. I'm not gonna let you hurt her again. You need to leave. Now."

"Let me explain."

"Wrong answer." Trevor lifted his knee and rammed it into Sean's chin.

Head flying back, Sean slumped against the closed door. "Fuck, man, if you'd stop hitting me for five seconds, I'd explain why I'm here."

"I don't care." Trevor crowded him against the door. "You left. Twice. And both times, *I* made a promise to myself and Charlie to always take care of us. *I* keep my promises."

"Trev, I didn't mean—"

"A decade we've been here, never quite moving on, never quite making it work, neither one of us, and when we're finally ready for a fresh start, here you are. The past thrown in our faces. Again."

"Like I told Charlie, I'm here as a simple favor for a friend. I'm not here to cause trouble. I'll just be in and out."

Trevor laughed, an unhinged cackle, because what the fuck else was he supposed to do when faced with such a blatant lie. "In and out, my ass, and you wouldn't know *simple* if it punched you in the fucking face."

Sean pushed off the door and straightened to his full height. "Are you mad for her or for you?"

Trevor didn't back down either, leaving less than a foot of space between them, every inch of it vibrating. "Both of us. But yeah, me too, asshole. I loved you, and you also made it possible for me to love my best friend. We had it all, Sean, and then you fucking left. Both times without telling me goodbye. How the fuck is that supposed to make me feel?"

Sean's body swayed toward his, a hand coming up as if to cup his face. "I couldn't—"

Trevor stopped him short, hand around Sean's wrist, holding on to his anger and resisting the promise of Sean's touch. "Whatever you're gonna say next, don't, because you don't know if you *could* or *couldn't*. You didn't give us a fucking chance."

Sean's fingers curled, deflating with the rest of him. "Trevor, I'm sorry."

He wished that was enough. Wished it was enough to wipe away the pain of the past ten years and of that morning a month ago when he'd been left behind again without so much as a word or parting kiss. But it wasn't. He couldn't trust Sean not to leave again. *In and out* he'd said. No pretense of staying this time. Why the fuck had he even come? He released Sean's wrist and stalked the opposite direction of the tempting past toward the open sliding glass doors. "I've been picking up the pieces after you for ten years, Sean, and I'm fucking tired. We all are."

Direct hit, judging by Sean's sharp inhale behind him. Good, he deserved to—

Trevor drew up short next to the table in the middle of the room. He'd seen his share of crime scene photos over the years—he'd practically been raised by the Henbys—but they were more disturbing when they were someone he personally knew. As with Mitch's and Cal's murders, the photos from the scene of Jefferson Marshall's death were no easier to see. There were shots of how they'd found him —hanging from the barn rafters with a thick rope noose around his neck, face bloated and discolored. He was clothed in dress slacks, a button-down shirt, and a sports jacket, wrinkled and torn in multiple places. The pictures of him in a body bag were no better—vacant eyes open in his mangled face; deep, red ligature marks scoring his neck; hands and nails scraped and bloodied.

There was one photo in the file not of Jeff, and Sean had placed that picture in the middle of the table. A thin strip of paper with a handwritten note on it. A quote Trevor recognized immediately. He'd highlighted and underlined it in the worn paperback he kept in his desk. "Cordelia."

"What?"

"The note. The photos..." Taken together, the picture —the scene—resolved. "It's Cordelia's death from *King Lear*."

Sean hustled to his side. "Explain."

Trevor picked up the photo of the note. "This quote is from the original text." He handed Sean the picture. "King Lear says it after he finds his daughter, Cordelia, murdered—"

"In a barn. I remember now. You were in that play our senior year." A flicker of a smile, then his brow furrowed. "She was hung in a barn."

Trevor nodded. "Falsely accused of treason."

"Treason? An HU professor?" Sean's gaze darted from the photo to the table and back. "Jefferson was slight of build. Easy snatch and grab from campus. Two points for convenience. He was also insanely well connected. Ten points for treason." He tossed the photo on the table. "Any idea how Jeff might be connected, falsely or not, with treason of some sort?"

"No, but I can ask around. He's on my tenure committee, but otherwise, I tried to steer clear of him. He was a colossal asshole."

Sean chuckled. "Consistent with what I've heard. Any info would be helpful, but be discreet. We don't know who or what we're dealing with yet."

Trevor leaned a hip against the table and crossed his arms. "I may be a professor, but I've spent most of my life around cops."

Sean inclined his head in acknowledgement. "I'll also talk to Marsh."

"Marsh?"

"Jeff's son, Emmitt Marshall. He's a colleague and the friend I'm here for. Charlie didn't mention him?"

"She said, 'Sean is back' and everything kind of went red." Grinning ruefully, he circled a hand in front of his face, then did the same in front of Sean's. "Sorry about the hits."

Sean playfully batted down his hand, caught it, and held it between them. "No, you're not, and I deserved them."

"Yeah, you did."

"I meant what I said to both of you." The fingers around his tightened, and Trevor's emotions warred again —stay mad or stay close. "I'm not here to cause trouble."

"And yet you always do."

"Not this time."

"Sure, Sean." Fighting the good fight, staying strong for himself and Charlie, Trevor withdrew his hand and turned for the door. "I'll ask around campus, discreetly, and get back to you."

"Thanks. I'd appreciate it." He was halfway to the door when Sean called after him. "Hey, Trevor, what could—"

Trevor didn't want to hear the end of that question. Didn't want the dozen more it would plant inside his head. He blocked out the words and slammed the door shut behind him.

CHAPTER FIVE

Charlie turned into the station parking lot and almost dropped her thermos. Parked between a police cruiser and her uncle's Jeep were Trevor's monster truck and a sweet-ass Harley. Recalling Sean's boots from yesterday and the roar of a bike cruising past the beach house last night, her mind raced and her hand trembled as she lowered the thermos and parked. No one in Hanover had a bike that nice. Vintage, mint condition, expensive. It had to have been Sean who'd driven by the house, taking a trip down memory lane. Unable to sleep after the day's roller coaster, she'd done the same, finishing the leftover bottle of Ardbeg and drowning in mental snapshots of their night together.

And now the bike was at the station. Sean was at the station. In the same place as Trevor. *Fuck.* She'd hoped the inevitable explosion between those two would've happened last night, after Trevor had left Annie's house. Or maybe Trevor and Sean were at the station because the explosion had been that bad. Which one had been arrested? Both of them? Why hadn't anyone called her? In any event, she didn't relish tiptoeing through an emotional minefield as she tried to solve a case.

Her apprehension grew with each step, increasing exponentially when she reached the main floor. A group was gathered in the large conference room on the other side of the bullpen. Sean and Trevor stood side by side, their backs to her, as the former pointed to something on the conference room table. Jaylen, Abel, and Diego stood on the other side of the table, similarly engrossed in whatever was laid out before them.

Taking a deep breath to calm her tumbling stomach, Charlie crossed the bullpen floor, wrapped her hand around the conference room doorknob, and said a silent prayer. She pushed open the door, and five sets of eyes swung her way. Hers went straight to Trevor's hazel ones. "What are you doing here?"

Trevor opened his mouth to answer, but Sean beat him to it. "Trevor stopped by to see me last night."

Her gaze darted between them, noting Sean's bruised jaw and Trevor's swollen knuckles. They'd fought, yet now they stood side by side, relatively calm. She sensed an undercurrent of tension, but at least they weren't still tearing each other apart. What had transpired to warrant a ceasefire?

Before she could ask, Sean explained, "Trevor identified the quote from the crime scene."

"'A plague upon you, murderers, traitors, all,'" she recited.

"It's Shakespeare," Trevor said. "From *King Lear*."

Sean pushed the photo of Jefferson Marshall hanging from the barn rafters her direction. "Lear says it when he finds his daughter, Cordelia, hung in a barn."

She picked up the photo and studied it anew. There were some similarities, but from what she recalled, it was a young princess in the play versus an older professor in their crime scene. She needed more. "Why?" she asked Trevor.

"Why Jeff, or why Cordelia?"

"Either. Both." She shrugged and tossed the photo on the table. "You both know I was a math major, not English lit. Someone enlighten me." She walked to the rounded end of the conference table and braced her palms on the tabletop, tapping her nails on the wood. When no explanation was offered, she glanced at Sean, recognizing a detective's morbid glint in his eyes. "You've obviously got a theory, so out with it."

He grinned wide, so much like that morning he'd proposed to her and Trevor, a secret he couldn't wait to share, that Charlie slammed her eyes shut against the suddenly spinning room. She clutched the edge of the table and fought the two-fisted attack of vertigo and nausea.

"Charlotte," her uncle called, his shout muted by the blood whooshing in her ears. "Sugar," he said a beat later, closer, his big hand on her arm.

Warmth spread across her lower back from the other side, and the familiar scent of Old Spice wafted around her. The rushing noise faded, the nausea receded, and the world steadied. She opened her eyes to Trevor by her side, right where he always was whenever her life was thrown into chaos.

"Hey there," he said. "You okay?"

She took a deep breath, released her death grip on the table, and straightened.

He dipped his mouth to her ear and whispered, "Good to know you find Shakespeare so swoonworthy."

She smiled at his teasing words. "Thank you."

"Anytime." He winked, then dropped a kiss on her temple, an extra shot of calm, before returning to his place beside Sean, who was stretched over the table, pointing something out to Diego and Jaylen.

To her left, Abel remained close, his dark eyes full of concern. "All good?"

"Good," she assured him.

Sean's discerning gaze snapped to hers. He cocked his head, silently asking for the all-clear.

"Talk to me about this theory of yours," she said.

As if sensing what had set her off before, he didn't smile as he began again. "Two things. First"—he held up his index finger—"Trevor reminded me Cordelia was hung in a barn, falsely accused of treason."

"Treason? Professor Marshall?" Charlie scanned the crime scene photos again. "Guilty or falsely accused?"

"We're looking into it," Jaylen answered.

"Does make murder seem more likely than suicide," Diego added, then glanced at Sean. "If it *is* murder, I don't think he's a victim of convenience."

Charlie's gaze followed her detective's. "You thought he might be?" she asked Sean.

"It has to be considered," he said. "The stables are owned by HU, close to campus, and Jeff was dressed for lecture."

"But?"

"He was well connected, and his son, a fed, thought the least of him."

"Guilty, then?" Jaylen said. "Of treason of some sort?"

"I'd stake my Harley on it."

"That bike is a thing of beauty," Abel said. "But even I wouldn't take that bet."

"You always were a smart gambler." Charlie smirked, then began assigning tasks. "Dig deeper into Professor Marshall," she ordered Diego and Jaylen. "The crime scene didn't give us much, so let's focus on the victim. Friends, enemies, debts, the full work-up. Psych too. While I agree murder seems more likely, we can't rule out suicide yet."

"We're on it," Jaylen replied.

She turned to Trevor. "Can you ask around campus?"

"Already on it, and he"—Trevor jutted a thumb at Sean—"already gave me the 'be discreet' lecture. I'll see what I can find out."

"You said there were two things, Agent Hale," Jaylen prompted.

"Yeah." Sean's face took on a decidedly darker expression. "We should prepare for the possibility of more victims."

Charlie had worried about the same, another thing that

had kept her up last night. "The number written next to the quote," she said. "You think we could be dealing with a serial?"

Sean nodded. "If it is in fact murder."

"Diego, Jaylen," Charlie said, "double-time it on Professor Marshall's background. Give Abel all the financial results."

Her uncle was HPD's best forensic investigator. His sister, Charlie's mother, had been a high school math teacher. Charlie could have gone the same route had the station not called more loudly. Math genes ran in the family.

"If you run into any roadblocks, let me know," Sean told Abel. "Marsh can clear the way for you."

"Obliged," Abel said, then followed Diego and Jaylen out.

Charlie returned her attention to Trevor. "Will you make it to Annie's in time for dinner tonight?"

Growing up, their mother had insisted on Sunday family dinners. They'd carried on the tradition with barely any misses, save for the month following their dad's and brother's deaths. Now, though, they were back on schedule, with dinners moved to Annie's since the beach house was packed up and Charlie was as terrible at cooking as she was at sports.

"Might be late." Trevor slid his hand across her back again, and while the gesture, the casually affectionate nature, was typical Trevor, same as he'd used to comfort her earlier, something about it now sent a tendril of heat unraveling in her belly and weaving along that connection between them. "But I'll be there in time for dessert." His hand lingered on her hip before stepping away. "Sean," he said, clipped but not murderous, on his way out the door.

"Trevor," Sean returned, his voice so falsely polite, his frame strung so tight Charlie almost laughed out loud.

Whatever détente they'd struck was a fragile one. Shaking her head, Charlie turned to the table and gathered the crime scene photos into the case file.

"I talked to Marsh," Sean said. "Nothing rang a bell for him as far as treason."

"He'd tell you the truth? He is the victim's son."

"I'd know if he were lying."

"Are you sure?"

"I'd know," he repeated curtly.

He knew Agent Emmitt Marshall, all right—as more than just a colleague.

"Fine," she snapped, then immediately chastised herself. She had no claim on Sean, no right to feel jealous, even if she were still in a relationship with him. They'd talk and figure out how to make it work.

Make it work.

Same as she needed to do if she wanted to solve this case. She took a deep breath and reined herself in. "I'll take your word for it, but I'd still like to go over a few things with him when he arrives."

"He's happy to help."

Charlie pushed off the table. "Thank you."

Sean, however, made no move to leave. "What time's your interview with Agent Conder tomorrow?"

"Ten, at the office in Wilmington."

"Congrats on that. Mitch and Cal would have been proud."

"Thanks," she said around the lump in her throat, then repeated the rationalization she was still struggling to accept. "I'd be glad for the opportunity to spare others the pain we had to go through."

"It's good work." He angled his face away, and if Charlie wasn't mistaken, he was fighting back emotion as well. He cleared his throat and was all business when he spoke again. "Watch out for Conder. I spoke with him yesterday, and he's impressed, but he's so far up the Bureau rulebook's ass, I'm surprised he hasn't gotten stuck there."

"Not your favorite person?"

"I was glad to be an ocean away from him." Sean returned her teasing smile. "Pretty sure if he'd seen more of me, I'd be near the top of his shit list."

"Won't be listing you as a reference, then."

He smiled wider. "Probably a good idea."

She turned abruptly to the door, needing to get far away from his tempting smile and fast.

"I'm sorry." He caught her wrist in a gentle hold. "Just then I said or did something to upset you. And earlier too."

She waved him off and avoided his gaze. "It's nothing."

"Charlie." Sean tightened his fingers around her wrist until she looked him in the eye. "I meant what I told you and Trevor yesterday. I don't want to interfere with your plans to move on. I mean to keep that promise. I'm only here for a few days to help Marsh with his dad's case and estate. He needs that closure. I'll assist HPD as little or as much as you need. It's your call." He released her hand and headed for the door. "Abel has my number."

She watched him leave, her mind racing again. How was she supposed to respond to that? Tell him the truth? That his mere presence in Hanover was an epic interference. That she and Trevor still needed him—then, now, always—if they were ever going to be as happy as they'd once been. That she was scared to death to make that kind of bet on him again.

CHAPTER SIX

S ean made another circle around the dining table covered in crime scene photos, and when no great insights revealed themselves to him, he walked right on past to the bottle of Ardbeg on the coffee table.

He was an assistant legal attaché for fuck's sake, not a profiler. He'd been assigned to one serial case his entire time abroad as a legat, and his responsibility on that case had been to broker information sharing between agencies. Serial Killers 101 had been a long time ago in Academy, and most of what he remembered from that class was the fuck-hot professor. And all that conjecture assumed this was a serial case at all. Yes, he'd raised the possibility at the station today, but that may have been premature. There was only one victim so far and a cryptic numbered clue. At this point, based on statistics, it was still as likely a suicide as a murder and an even slimmer chance it was a serial.

Why had Marsh thought he could help? Yes, he could assist with the estate matters—he'd handled enough of that himself lately—and he could be a friend, which was the least Marsh deserved, but the case itself... Marsh could probably hack more clues than Sean could find. Another mystery, why had Sean practically leapt at the chance to intercede? Especially knowing one, this wasn't his area of expertise, and two, the pain and heartache it would stir up.

No mystery, not really. He couldn't resist seeing Charlie and Trevor again, despite all his better instincts, despite his promise to Trevor, despite the fact he was due to turn in his badge next month, despite the fact he was expected at Paxton Industries after that, and despite the fact he'd made a different promise to a dead man a decade ago. If it had been a bad time to bring attention to the Henby family then, it was an even worse one now, and yet, here he was. Again. But he had convinced himself he needed to know Trevor and Charlie were happy in order to move on. Selfish Bastard 101. He could teach that course.

Scotch in hand, he opened the sliding glass door and stepped onto the small cement patio. He dragged one of the plastic chairs to the edge, dropped into it, and dug his toes into the sand. It wasn't home—home was five miles down the road with a For Sale sign still in the yard—but the sand between his toes and the salty sea breeze reminded him of the comfortable years he'd spent here, the most comfortable he'd spent anywhere.

He lifted a hand to the charms on the necklaces around his neck—both of them—and let the memories crash into him like waves on the shore.

Falling into Charlie, literally, his first day on campus as

he barged into his, Trevor's, and Cal's dorm room carrying an unwieldy stack of boxes.

Being hauled up and off the stunning girl in jean shorts, a tank top, and an oversized baseball jersey by an equally stunning boy, his skin tan, his hair long, and his hazel eyes sparkling with interest. The owner of the jersey.

Stripping Trevor out of that jersey after a game one early spring night when Cal had been off campus and the tension between him and Trevor had finally boiled over.

Admitting to Trevor later that spring that he was attracted to Charlie too, and for the first time in his life, someone fucking getting it. Not judging him for it.

Watching the friendship between Trevor and Charlie bloom into something more over that summer. Being there for their first kiss that began with a tentative brush of the lips and exploded into a moment of such hunger and relief that Sean considered himself the luckiest man alive to witness it.

Lying sweaty, panting, and tangled in the bedsheets with them after they'd made love, then... and a mere month ago.

He took another swig of the scotch, the alcohol nowhere near as searing as the memories. And nowhere near enough to numb the burn.

His phone vibrated in his pocket, and he was grateful for the distraction, until he saw the name onscreen. He owed her a call. It was Sunday night, and the number of Sunday night calls were ticking down, but fuck, the last thing he wanted to do was think about what was next, about what had drawn him away from Hanover in the first place. The ringing stopped, then started right back up. Not a good sign, and not a call he could risk putting off.

He lifted the phone to his ear. "Hey, Aunt Marie."

She wasn't really—both of his parents had been only children—but Marie and Saul Paxton had been their best friends, and when Sean's parents had died in a plane crash, Saul and Marie hadn't hesitated to take in their ten-year-old son, even though they were forty-two and had never planned on having kids. And even though Saul had just started his own company. A company that had thrived beyond their wildest dreams. Dreams that took a nightmarish turn when strapping and seemingly healthy Saul was diagnosed with cancer at fifty-five. He'd beaten it twice, prolonging Sean's stint with the feds, but this latest bout had been too much for his worn-out body to beat. "How is he?"

Marie sniffled. "The doctors say any day now."

"Do you need me to—"

"No, dear," she said. "You saw him last week, thankfully. He's so pumped full of drugs now, he's no longer lucid."

"Better than the pain." The cancer had gotten into his bones, and despite Saul's effort to hide it, Sean had seen the grimace every time his adoptive father moved. Just squeezing Sean's hand had made him nauseous and dizzy.

"Stay and finish your work," Marie said. "I'll need you more after."

"If that changes—"

"I'll let you know. You should get to enjoy the last few weeks of the job you love before you have to give it up."

And wasn't that just the kicker. When Marie had called him that day ten years ago and explained why she and Saul had missed his police academy graduation—that Saul was in the hospital fighting for his life—she'd told him not to come. But *someone* had overheard the conversation and urged him to go. Had promised to tell Charlie and Trevor why he'd left. And that he'd be back.

When Saul had recovered, Marie had urged him to return to Hanover and law enforcement—they didn't need him to take over the family business yet—but that *yet* was always there. Waiting and threatening. At the time, he couldn't imagine Charlie and Trevor ever leaving Hanover. He wouldn't ask that of them. But maybe he could steal a few more years with them.

He was intercepted at the airport. *Someone* had never told Trevor and Charlie why he'd left. *Someone* had intercepted his other attempts to make contact. The two people he loved the most thought he'd abandoned them. And once the same *someone* explained why extra attention was the last thing the Henbys needed, twenty-three-year-old Sean had been swayed by the duty he felt to the Paxtons and the Henbys. By the words of someone he considered a friend. Family.

He'd joined the FBI instead, and as soon as he was qualified, he'd requested an overseas assignment, putting himself as far away from Hanover as possible. But he'd also lost valuable time with Saul and Marie.

"You are my family," Sean said. "You need me, you call me."

She hemmed and hawed but eventually agreed, just as

the line beeped with another incoming call. *Marsh*, the screen read. "Marie," he said, "I need to take this other call. It's about the case. Keep me posted on Saul."

"I will, dear. Love you."

"Love you too." He ended one call and answered the other. "Hey, sorry," he said to Marsh. "I was on the other line with Marie."

"How much longer?" Marsh asked, cutting straight to the point as was his way. His Texas drawl soothed the slice a bit but not as much as having a friend there with him would. A friend who knew all his secrets.

"How fast can you get here?"

"Shit, Hale, I'm sorry."

He took another gulp of the scotch. "Don't be sorry," he said, lowering the bottle. "Just fucking get here."

CHAPTER SEVEN

Charlie swiveled on a padded barstool in her dad's old house, now Annie's. Their second family home was in a quiet neighborhood of older homes closer to town and HU with a private marina on the waterway where the family boat was docked. Charlie was glad her sister had kept the house after their father's death. Even happier that Annie had started updating the place. As a librarian at HU, Annie's salary limited major renovations, but while she saved for the big things, she'd already begun making some of the easier fixes. Painting the dark wood wainscoting white, stripping the wallpaper above it and painting the walls a warm buttery yellow, cleaning out the attic, ripping up the carpet to expose the hardwood floors underneath.

She was making the place her own, further evidence Charlie didn't need to worry about leaving her little sister. Annie was almost thirty and a smart independent woman.

Plus she had Abel, Jaylen, and her friends from the softball team and HU. She deserved her time in the spotlight.

"Nice pick on the wine," Annie said, drawing Charlie out of her thoughts. "It was perfect with the tapas. I'm sorry I couldn't drink more than a taste. Headaches lately."

Charlie swiveled back around to the kitchen. "It's fine. And bravo to you on the food." She clapped for her sister, pleased when Annie's face lit with pride. "The tapas were delicious, and I needed the escape."

"The rumors are true, then?" Annie rounded the bar and climbed onto the stool beside her. "Sean is back?"

Charlie drained the rest of her wine, then rested her head on her sister's shoulder.

Annie chuckled. "I'll take that as a yes."

"He's here about the case."

Delicate fingers smoothed over her shoulder, squeezing tight, reminding her so much of their mother. Charlie may have been the spitting image of Alice Henby, but Annie had the same big heart that had made their mother a beloved teacher. "At least it's just the one case," Annie said.

"Except that part where I might also be working for the feds."

Annie dropped her hold with a "*What?*" and Charlie cursed the wine-laced slip.

"Is that why you're going to DC?"

Charlie reared back, the crack of her sister's voice like a whip. Annie had their mother's heart, but she also had the same temper they'd all inherited, for better or worse. "No, it's a recent development," she explained. "They're recruiting me, and it's not a done deal. I have an interview tomorrow."

Annie hopped off her stool, rounded the bar, and began furiously scrubbing the kitchen counters. "How did this happen?"

"Annie—"

"Is it because of Salazar?" As she feared, Annie had taken no time to put the pieces together. "Which division, Charlotte?"

She was busted. Annie would know between being a librarian and always having half an ear on police conversations. "CID," she admitted.

"Criminal Investigative Division. The organized crime unit?"

Charlie nodded.

Annie cursed and scrubbed the counters harder. "How could you do this?"

Charlie slid off her stool and stepped around the bar. Removing the towel from Annie's grasp, she placed her hand on top of her sister's. "Annie, I—"

As quick as her sister's temper had flared, it waned. Her shoulders slumped, and her head bowed. "How could you do this to me? To Trevor? How could you be so selfish?"

Charlie sucked in a choked breath, Annie's question a direct hit. She *was* being selfish. She was thinking of herself, thinking about moving on, and in doing so, hurting those she loved in the process.

"There're my girls."

Both of their heads whipped up and to the side, eyeing

the front door where Trevor stood balancing a green and white box of doughnuts.

Observing their standoff, his smile vanished. "What's going on?"

Before Charlie could answer, Annie bolted for the back door, yanking open the sliding glass door and practically running down the steps.

"What's wrong with A?" Trevor asked as he stepped into the kitchen and set the box on the end of the counter.

"She'd heard about Sean." Charlie stared out the open door. "And then I let slip about the FBI opportunity. Things went sideways from there."

"Sean Hale strikes again." Trevor grunted, unamused, as he flipped open the box. "Give her a few minutes to cool off."

"Because that worked so well for you?" Charlie flicked the side of his hand, just shy of his swollen knuckles.

He flicked her hand away with a grin and grabbed a powdered, jelly-filled doughnut out of the box. "I have no idea what you're talking about."

Charlie couldn't help but laugh when he shoved half the doughnut in his mouth and jelly spurted out the other end. Unfazed, he shoved in the rest, chewed, and swallowed. His satisfied smile and powdered-sugar–covered face was a welcome respite from the long, wonky day. It felt normal. It felt like home. She snagged a dish towel and wiped the sugar off his face. "You'd think after thirty-three years, you'd learn how to eat these things without making a mess."

He grinned wider and licked the jelly off his fingers. "Where's the fun in that?"

"You didn't answer my question."

"What question?"

"You do know I interrogate people for a living, right?"

His eyes widened in mock surprise. "I had no idea." Laughing, he swiped another doughnut. "But *I* might have a lead on Jeff."

"Yeah?" She snatched the original glazed from him and chomped it in half.

"I see how it is." He narrowed his eyes, going for pouty betrayal but failing miserably to contain his laughter. She finished her doughnut as they fell into their normal after-dinner coffee routine. "So, I overheard an interesting conversation at the summer staff potluck."

"I can't believe y'all still had that two days after Jeff died."

"Best time for gossip, and it seems Jeff's death is likely to clear the way for several tenure candidates."

"To fill his spot?"

"No, others. I don't know why I didn't think of it before." He pushed the Brew button, then leaned a hip against the counter. "He's been the logjam on my tenure committee. Apparently, he's made a habit of it over the years."

"But would that amount to treason?"

"Depends on how seriously your killer takes academic integrity. I'll dig around some more tomorrow, see what else I can find out."

"Am I going to have to deputize you?" she teased, lightly shoving his chest.

He caught her wrists and leaned in. "Learned from the best, honey."

Before he could move back, before she could think better of it, Charlie rotated her wrists, locking him in and holding him close. Wanting to soak in more of the easy comfort. She lifted her eyes, meeting Trevor's wide hazel ones. Greens and browns morphed from surprised to confused to heated. His lips parted on a shaky gasp, such a vulnerable, luring tell from such a large man. She couldn't deny the relief she'd felt falling back into his arms after the funeral, couldn't deny how naturally the kisses between them had come, even after ten years apart. Couldn't deny being tempted to chase after that sweet relief again. They were older now. Maybe they could make it work this time.

"Charlie, if you want this..."

She fingered his open collar, then sighed and tipped forward, forehead to his chest. "Even if I wanted that, I'm terrified to lose this."

He curled an arm around her back and nuzzled her temple. "Me too."

Her weary chuckle was cut off by a gasp and crash of plastic behind them. Startling apart, she shifted to Trevor's side to find a red-faced Annie by the back door, a tipped over laundry basket at her feet.

"I'm sorry." Annie bent to gather the scattered clothes. "I didn't mean to interrupt."

Trevor rushed to her side. "It's okay, A." He laid a hand on her shoulder and knelt beside her. "Here, let me help."

Charlie switched off the coffeemaker on her way to them but stopped a foot short when her cell chimed with an emergency alert from the station. She glanced at the screen. "It's an SOS from Abel."

"Go," Trevor said as he helped Annie gather the scattered clothes. "I've got this."

"You always do." Closing the distance, she squeezed Trevor's shoulder with a whispered "Thank you" and coasted her other hand over Annie's head. Her sister flinched, curling her fingers around the edge of the basket. Fuck, she needed to handle that, needed to bridge the gap before it opened into another chasm like the one after the funeral. She'd just gotten her sister back.

The phone beeped again, and she cursed aloud.

"Go," Trevor said, then mouthed, *It'll be okay, I promise.*

Holding on to the comfort of that promise—if there was anyone she trusted, it was Trevor—she grabbed her keys and hustled out the door, dialing Abel on the way. "What've you got?" she asked as soon as he picked up.

"Someone drunk at the cemetery."

She halted midstride. "Why can't the duty officer handle that?"

Abel sighed. "It's Sean."

Shit.

The cantankerous old groundskeeper was waiting for her at the gate to the cemetery. "Where is he?" she asked.

He slapped the picked padlock into her palm. "Your mama's grave." No kind words, no steadying hand. Just the blunt truth and the padlock that half of Hanover had picked at least once in their lives. She'd picked it more times than she could count, including Halloween night her sophomore year with Trevor and Sean by her side. The pick sticking out of the lock tonight, however, was professional grade, a far cry from a sparkly purple bobby pin.

She stood there remembering that night. How what had started as a dare, Sean worked up by town ghost stories Trevor had goaded him with, had turned into a conversation with her mother. Albeit one-sided, she frequently visited and updated Alice about what was going on with her, the family, and Hanover. She'd introduced her to Sean that night and told her how she and Trevor had finally become more than friends. Something Alice had always teased her about, something Charlie knew Alice had always wanted for them. Trevor and Sean's back-and-forth as they'd filled Alice in on baseball and Charlie's terrible cooking had had her rolling with laughter, then later that night, rolling between the two of them, never having felt closer.

"Your mama's grave."

What was Sean doing there now? Like he'd promised, he'd stayed out of her way at the station that afternoon, working with Jaylen and Diego. But now he was directly in her path again. What did he have to say to Alice?

She walked her usual path through the cemetery, no need for a light despite the darkness of the hour. She stumbled to a stop at the edge of the Henby and Champion plots, brought up short by the heart-crushing sight of Sean slumped against the base of the stone angel atop her mother's grave. His head was tipped back, his eyes closed and lips moving, his hands hanging loose around an empty bottle of scotch between his legs. She laid a trembling hand on a nearby gravestone, struggling to center herself in the hurricane of emotions.

Surprise that Sean was there, in her family's final resting place.

Anger that he was back in Hanover after he'd left twice before.

Fear that he would one day learn all her secrets, including about her mother's death, and that it would paint any of the good memories he had of the Henbys, memories that had led him there tonight, in a different, darker light.

And above all else, a desperate longing to run to him, to comfort him, to beg him to stay and try again with her and Trevor.

But how could she ask him to stay when she and Trevor were leaving? How could she ask either of them to go back when they were supposed to be moving forward? Annie's earlier words rang in her ears. *"How could you be so selfish?"*

Her sister was right. About more than just the job. No matter where things were headed with the FBI, Charlie had to leave the past behind, for everyone's sake. Turning the way she'd come, her feet and mind propelled her away from the past, logic and reality moving her toward the future. Three steps later, a branch cracked beneath her foot and her past called out.

"Charlie, 's 'at you?"

Halting, she closed her eyes and breathed deep, grasping at her quickly fading resolve. "Yeah, Sean, it's me."

"Did that old asshole call the cops on me? How is he even still alive?" Groaning, he shuffled to his feet. "I told him *I* was a fucking cop. Oof!"

She spun in time to see Sean tumble headfirst toward Mitch's gravestone, arms flailing, destined to miss and break something. She lunged, catching him by the arm and wrestling his tall, muscled frame against hers. She wrapped an arm around his waist and guided him back to the ground in front of the angel. "Maybe stay there."

He grinned sheepishly. "Yeah, don't mind me." He slouched against the stone base and closed his eyes again. "Just pretend I'm not here."

She hesitated, caught between what Charlie the ex and Charlie the cop should do. In his present condition, she doubted he'd make it back to the motel on his own. He'd probably fall asleep here, and the station would receive another complaint in the morning. But what if he did try to get back on his own? She shivered at what might befall him in his current state—stumbling in front of a moving car, another altercation with Trevor, an unannounced visit to God only knew where. Caution winning, she lowered herself to the ground next to him, taking up another side of the angel's base. "What were you talking to them about?" she asked.

"Scandalizing your dad with stories about the red-light district in Amsterdam," he answered with a roguish grin.

She laughed at her father's imagined affront. Despite all he'd seen as a cop, Mitch Henby was easily embarrassed when it came to such matters, perhaps because Alice was the only person he'd ever been with. Childhood sweethearts, married right out of high school, devoted to each other and their family, inseparable until the day—

Charlie cut off the thought and covered by flashing Sean a sideways grin. "Visit it often, did you?"

"Once. For a case."

"Only once? Cal would be so disappointed in you."

He didn't respond, and Charlie glanced his way again. He swallowed hard, fighting a lump in his throat or fighting to keep words down; she couldn't tell. And couldn't resist asking. "Why'd you come here tonight?"

"Saul's dying."

She pitched forward, shifting onto her hip toward him. "Fuck, Sean, I'm sorry." It was the last thing she expected him to say, and her heart instantly hurt for him. She'd only met Saul and Marie Paxton a handful of times, but she knew they loved Sean like a son, and he loved them like the second set of parents he'd been blessed with after losing the first. He'd lost so much family already and now to lose more... She reached out a hand, aiming for his arm, but he blocked her with the whisky bottle.

"Here," he said. "Drink this."

"It's empty, Sean."

Retracting the bottle, he held it an inch from his nose and squinted. "Hmm, I guess it is." He set the empty bottle between his legs and spun it. "Sorry. Didn't mean to drink it all."

She suspected that's exactly what he'd meant to do. She reached over his leg, snagged the bottle, and set it out of his reach. "Tell me."

"Cancer. Terminal this time."

"This time?"

He lifted a hand, three fingers raised.

"Since when?"

He slumped back, eyes closed. "Feels like forever.

What did that mean? Before he'd come to Hanover? No, he would have told them. They would've known. Wait, was that—

Sean interrupted her speculation with a bitter groan. "Marie's holding up better than me."

She laid a hand on his shoulder. "I'm sorry, Sean."

Sean covered it with his own, clutching her fingers. When he spoke again, agony and regret were etched in every word. "I'd blocked it out, everything about Hanover, about the family I'd lost here. And I avoided my other family too, lost how many years with them because if I couldn't have both of you, it was easier to just be gone." The next instant, Sean rocketed to his feet, and Charlie vaulted to her knees, bracing him with a hand to his hip, holding him steady until his wobbling ceased and his pacing began. "Fuck! What am I doing here? In Hanover, talking to a family that's no longer mine, putting you and Trevor through hell. Why am I not with Marie and Saul? Fuck!" He plowed his fingers through his hair and yanked on the ends. "I just want to do right by all of you, and all I seem to do is make the wrong decisions and let all of you down."

Her heart stopped, stuttered, then hammered double time. She was right. When Sean had left Hanover that night after graduation, she'd suspected he hadn't done so voluntarily. It didn't square with the man she loved. But if Saul had been sick, the Sean she knew would rush to his side, especially after all the Paxtons had done for him. But why hadn't he told them? Why hadn't he made contact or come back? Why, when Cal went after him, did Sean say there was nothing to come back to? That didn't square with a man who put duty and obligation first, who, unable to sacrifice his duty to one for the other, had thought he had to run from both families he so clearly loved.

Charlie rose the rest of the way and cut in front of Sean, halting his swerving circuit. "Sean, why didn't you tell us? Trevor and I would have been there for you." She laid her hands on his chest like she'd done that morning a month ago. Except this time there was something under his shirt. No, two somethings. She pushed aside his collar and lifted out not one but two necklaces—his and Trevor's CWS gifts from her. She gasped. Nothing about this fucking squared. "Why didn't you come home to us?"

"It doesn't matter." His chest rose and fell under her hands, his breaths heavy and ragged. "All that matters is I left you and Trevor and Saul and Marie. Both my families." He closed his eyes and shook his head. "Nothin's been right since."

But it *did* matter, Charlie was beginning to sense. Maybe more than any of them realized. Another mystery on her plate to unravel, one that had nagged at her for a decade. But Sean, the other investigator she needed, was in no shape to get into either case tonight. He was too caught up in regret and despair, past and present.

He let out a long, shuddering sigh before he lifted his arms and covered her hands with his, holding them to his chest, holding her close. Same as she'd done with Trevor back at Annie's, the three of them inextricably linked. "I'm so sorry, Charlie. For leaving, for coming back, for being a coward."

Like she had with Trevor earlier, Charlie leaned forward and rested her head on his shoulder, offering comfort more than taking it this time. Thinking about the choices she'd made to protect her own family and considering the choices Sean had had to make too, choices until tonight she'd never known about. "We all made the only decisions we could. I'm sorry too." If she had any hope of Sean forgiving hers, she needed to work on also understanding—and forgiving—his.

CHAPTER EIGHT

J ulian Hirsch eased open the well-oiled back door of his home and peered inside, checking for any signs of life in the darkened house. Cocking his wrist, the glowing digital face of his watch read half past two in the morning. As it was Monday, his wife's shift at the hospital didn't end until five, so he should be in the clear. But he had to be careful, considering.

"Darling, are you home?"

Hearing no response, he continued across the threshold and flipped on the overhead lights in the mudroom. He braced a hand on the built-in organizer, toed off his shoes, tucked them into a cubbyhole, and dropped his wallet and keys into the catchall drawer. Phone in hand, he scrolled through his contacts until he found the fictional name he was looking for.

He tapped out a quick text message. **Need to see you again.** He thought for a moment on when his wife's next graveyard shift fell. **Wednesday night?** He hoped the extra touch of desperation would be enough to convince her. He didn't have to wait long.

See you then, Professor, came her reply.

His cock stiffened at the prospect of another few rounds like tonight. Wednesday couldn't come soon enough. Smirking, he deleted the incriminating text messages, slipped his phone back into his pocket, and pulled off his shirt. He was about to toss it in the laundry basket when a shimmer of pink lip-gloss on the collar caught his eye. He attempted to rub the stain out with his thumb but only made it worse.

"Damn it."

He turned on the hot water in the utility sink and held the shirt collar under the faucet. After a few minutes of scrubbing with detergent, the damning stain was hardly noticeable, but his wife's well-trained eye would probably see it. He spotted a few mounds of sorted dirty clothes, then glanced at his watch again, quickly doing the math in his head. He had enough time to do a few loads before she got home—one might look suspicious, but three would look like a good husbandly deed. Starting with the load of towels, he tossed the shirt in with them, added an overflowing cup of detergent, and set it to run on heavy duty.

Problem solved.

Wiping his hands on his pants, he turned off the lights and left the laundry room, padding barefoot through the moonlit first floor of his refurbished Southern colonial. His foot landed on the second step of the curved staircase and a loud *click* rang out behind him. Whirling, his stomach lurched as he stared into the shadows.

Had his wife come home early?

Was there someone else in the house?

His eyes and ears frantically searched for the source of the noise. Seconds later, he jumped out of his skin at another loud *click*.

He reversed a step, his fingers white-knuckling the banister. "Who's there?"

His question was answered by a *whoosh* of water filling the washing machine. Breathing a shaky sigh of relief, he released his death grip on the railing and chuckled at himself for getting worked up over the washer's safety lock.

He shook his head at the silly fit of paranoia and climbed the stairs the rest of the way to the second floor. In the master bedroom, he discarded his phone on the bedside table and shed his pants and undershirt on the way to the bathroom. Under the bright vanity lights, he inspected his appearance in the mirror, looking for any scratches or hickeys, an unfortunate side effect of bedding coeds who often got carried away. Finding none, he cranked on the shower, turned it to hot, and hopped in, rinsing off any evidence his wife might otherwise detect. He indulged in the spray a couple extra minutes before turning off the water and toweling dry.

He swiped clean the vanity mirror to make one last examination.

This time, he wasn't alone.

"You do like 'em young, don't you, Julian?" sneered the

visage standing behind him. "And only a few months back from the honeymoon. Guess that's over."

He struggled to find a voice for the questions swirling in his mind. Too late. The reflection rushed him, aiming a gloved fist at his neck, a silver needle glinting in the light. Spinning, Julian raised his hands. Too late again. The needle punctured his throat and cool liquid rushed into his veins. He batted the needle away and his assailant scurried past him, out of the bathroom. Julian moved to chase—one step, two steps—before his legs gave out, dropping him to his knees on the slick tile floor.

A cold, hard cackle sent chills down his spine. He'd never been more terrified in his life. Crawling into the bedroom on his hands and knees, his fear multiplied tenfold as he watched through increasingly hazy eyes as his attacker removed several thick ropes from a duffel and expertly knotted one to each bedpost.

"What're you...going to do...to me?"

He collapsed onto his side as the world spun, his heart beating like a jackhammer, but the pumping blood did nothing to stir his immobile limbs. It was a struggle to lift his head, to force his eyelids to stay open so he could stare up at the person who, he realized with startling clarity, was going to end his life.

"Only what you deserve, Julian." The reaper fluffed a pillow between gloved hands. "Only what you deserve."

CHAPTER NINE

Sean woke reluctantly, the pounding in his head amplified by the pounding on his motel room door. Groaning, he cracked open an eye and glanced at the bedside clock glowing six on the dot. Way too fucking early after a long night and a bottle of scotch. Rolling onto his stomach, he covered his head with a pillow and attempted to ignore the world.

The world knocked again.

Did everyone in Hanover know where he was staying?

Probably. He had forgotten how fast word traveled in a small town. Even with much of Hanover's population rotating each academic year, the homegrown locals gossiped. But would any of the locals wake him at this ungodly hour? With that authoritative knock? He didn't think so, which meant either Trevor or HPD.

Possibly Charlie.

It had been late when she'd dropped him off at the hotel last night. There were still questions that needed answers and a similar conversation to be had with and an apology to be made to Trevor. But despite the dark circles under Charlie's eyes last night, they'd seemed warmer, a touch brighter when they'd left the cemetery, and an immeasurable weight had lifted off Sean's chest. He'd given her the apology she deserved, and she'd offered an apology of her own. For what, he had no idea, but he was sure her sins could be no worse than his.

The past ones, at least.

Charlie's voice floated out of the dark. "Sean, it's me. Open up."

He tossed aside the pillow and levered onto his elbows, listening intently, not sure if what he'd heard was real or a dream. But then the knocking came again, closer, against the sliding glass door of the bedroom, followed by Charlie's words, also closer... and louder. "I know it's early, Sean, but wake up."

Grimacing, he rolled to the side of the bed, switched on the lamp, and swung his feet to the floor. Padding to the door, he pulled aside the slatted blinds and, squinting into the dark, saw Charlie standing on the tiny patio outside, her face illuminated by her phone light. She looked as tired as he felt, but there was a giant cup with a coffee logo on it in her free hand.

He pushed back the blinds, opened the door, and beckoned her inside. She entered and thrust the cup in his direction. "Drink," she ordered, then moved around him and his motel room, pulling clothes out of the dresser and tossing them on the bed, then flipping on lights and running water in the bathroom.

Caffeine waking his brain, he was on the verge of asking what was going on when the telltale rattle of the ibuprofen bottle he always carried greeted his ears. Sweet relief. Charlie returned, exchanging the coffee for a glass of water and three tablets. He downed the water and pills, handed the glass back to her with a mumbled "Thanks," then reclaimed the coffee.

With each sip of brew, the fog cleared more, and he noticed Charlie was dressed impeccably for the hour. Not police blues but professional—heels, pant suit, a green silk top—and as she moved, her shiny badge and holstered weapon were visible on her hip. Looking beyond her attire, Sean observed her rigid posture, the deep crease between her eyes, and the precise and methodical way she invaded his space. Efficient yet vibrating with anxious energy.

"There's been another death," he surmised. "A murder." No shying away from that now. If there was another death, and if she was involving him, then it was connected to Jeff's case, which was no longer a suicide.

"Shower and dress." She took the coffee from him and downed a giant gulp, scowling. She'd never been a fan of it black. "We're needed at the crime scene." Confirming his speculation. But that didn't explain the strange, edgy energy radiating off her. This was more than professional Charlie; something had triggered a personal response.

"You knew the victim." When she didn't respond, he asked, "Who was it?"

"Julian Hirsch."

"Who's Julian Hirsch?"

"A professor at HU and Tracy Hirsch's husband."

"Who's Tracy Hirsch?" he said, sensing he wasn't going to like the answer. Which came to him the next second. "Wait, *Tracy*? As in—"

Charlie nodded. "Trevor's ex-wife."

Sean trailed Charlie up the steps of a massive Southern colonial style house, the morning sun glinting off the wide white columns. Abel stood on the porch beside Tracy, a petite brunet dressed in nurse's scrubs. Sean recognized her from the engagement photos of her and Trevor he'd downloaded in one of his check-up sweeps before he'd stopped doing them. Tracy's smiling face in those photos was nothing like the expression she wore now. As her red-rimmed eyes cut to Charlie, *grieving widow* and *spitting mad* both played across her face, and Sean would bet every last cent in his bank account that Charlie was the last person Tracy wanted to see right then.

"What are *you* doing here?" she spat in Charlie's direction.

Definitely not who Tracy wanted to see.

"Now, Tracy," Abel cajoled. "Charlie's the best detective we've got. You want her on this case."

"I'm sorry for your loss, Tracy." Charlie's genuine sympathy in the face of Tracy's contempt was admirable. "We'll find out who did this."

And did nothing to blunt the harsh edge of Tracy's anger and grief. "You can start by talking to my ex-husband."

Sean stepped forward, next to Charlie. "What's Trevor got to do with this?"

Tracy's blue eyes cut to him. "Who are you?"

He withdrew is badge and flipped it open, flashing his credentials. She looked impressed, until he said his name. "Agent Sean Hale."

Sean didn't think eyes could roll that hard. "Ah, *the* Sean Hale, I presume. Of course you're here too." She swung a weary glare back at Abel and Charlie. "My life is ruined. Again. I'm sure Trevor and your lot have something to do with it." She turned on her heel and stormed inside, shoving her way through the solid wall of Diego and Jaylen. She hurried through the brightly lit foyer and into what Sean guessed was a powder room under the stairs and slammed the door shut.

"Well," Charlie said, "that went about as well as I expected."

"Bad blood?" Sean asked as they crossed the threshold into the foyer.

Abel half laughed, half choked. "Understatement of the year."

Sean would have queried further except Diego and Jaylen had joined them and additional gossip seemed inappropriate, given the circumstances.

"How bad?" Charlie asked the officers.

Jaylen covered his mouth and gulped behind his fingers.

Diego patted the younger officer's back. "About like the last one." Which Jaylen had only seen in crime scene photos. This case was probably one of the more gruesome in his time with the department, considering. "Maggie's up there with the techs."

"When did the call come into the station?" Sean asked.

"Five thirty, when Tracy got home from work." He shifted his attention to Charlie and Abel. "You mind if we step outside for some air?"

"Go." Charlie waved them out, then turned a grim face to her uncle. "Go get Trevor. Bring him to the station."

The chief shifted on his feet, a far more subtle movement than Sean spinning around, slack-jawed. "You don't think he had anything to do with this?" He'd been gone a while, but surely Trevor hadn't changed *that* much.

"No, of course not," Charlie said. "I just don't want him hearing about this from anyone else." She glanced around his shoulder to Abel. "He's got a class at eight. He should be up and about."

"You got it, sugar."

"We should call city hall too. Mister Mayor will want an update."

"I'll get Wally on it," Abel said, departing with the phone to his ear already.

Sean inhaled deep, cracked his neck, and tapped his toes like he would at the baseball plate. Getting ready for whatever pitch was thrown their way. He started for the stairs, but Charlie's hand in the crook of his arm stopped him. It was the first time she'd touched him since last night, and heat cascaded from the spot. "I need to make a call," she said, and he struggled to focus on anything but that simple touch. "I'm not gonna make it to Wilmington by ten. Any pointers for dealing with Conder?"

That snapped him out of it. Fuck, her interview was this morning. She was right; there was no way she was going to make it. "Explain it's for a case," he said. "He values commitment to the job. He'll understand."

"Thank you." She released his arm, the warmth lingering, continuing to smolder, stoked by the fact she'd asked him for help with Conder and with the crime scene. He'd take those nuggets of trust. Would work for more. While she detoured into the dining room off the foyer, Sean busied himself inspecting the front door. No sign of forced entry. He walked down the hallway to the back of the house. No damage to the patio door either. Off the kitchen, the mudroom was a mess to tiptoe through—the washer had overflowed, and sudsy water covered the floor—but there was no sign anyone had tampered with that door either.

So a window... or a key... or a lock pick. Or Julian had left a door unlocked. On his way out of the room, Sean noticed the alarm panel and made a mental note to request records.

"Sean!" Charlie shouted from the foyer.

"Sorry," he said, hustling back to her. "Was just checking the doors." With a pair of duty officers milling around the living room, he carefully worded his next question. "All good with your appointment?"

"Moved it to tomorrow." She climbed the stairs ahead of him. "You find anything?"

"No signs of forced entry. We should get the alarm company records."

"I'll get Diego on it."

"Laundry room was flooded. Looked like the washer overflowed. Maybe someone trying to hide something?"

"Zero trace evidence left at the first crime scene," Charlie said. "Just the note."

"Which they left here too?"

She nodded. "Assuming it's the same perp, I doubt they'd be that sloppy with the washer. It was probably Julian trying to hide *his* misdeeds."

Sean almost missed the next step. "You think he was cheating on Tracy? Already? They've been married, what, six months at most?" He knew from his snooping that Tracy's divorce from Trevor had only been finalized in November.

"Five months. Married on Valentine's Day." She dug two sets of surgical gloves out of her coat pocket and handed a pair to him. "She'd been sleeping with Julian for two years."

Sean focused on the next step to make sure he landed it. "Did Trevor know?"

"He knew." They crested the top of the stairs, and Charlie halted several feet from the crime scene techs gathered outside the master bedroom. "Even offered to bring Julian into their marriage, despite the complications it would cause."

Sean raised a brow as he snapped on the gloves. "What complications?"

"Julian was a classics professor at HU and dean of the Humanities Department."

"Trevor's boss." Sean whistled low. "This Julian guy sounds like a piece of work."

"You don't know the half of it."

"Was Trevor in love with him too?"

Charlie shook her head. "No, but he would have tried to make it work. I doubt Julian would have objected either."

"So Tracy decided she wanted to be married to Julian instead?"

"Only to Julian, for numerous reasons." Charlie could pull off the *spitting mad* face too. "And the fact she wasn't poly was at the bottom of the list."

"Charlie, that you?" a woman called from the direction of the bedroom.

It had been years since Sean had heard that voice, but it hadn't changed much. Maybe a little hoarser, probably from bossing everyone around, a husband and three kids added to her list of cats to herd.

"Yeah, Mags, it's me," Charlie returned.

A freckled face popped out from behind the door-frame, and Maggie Perez, née Reardon, smiled wide, her green eyes bright and her auburn curls bouncing despite the early hour and reportedly gruesome crime scene. Her pleasant demeanor, however, vanished as soon as her gaze landed on him. Eyes widening, she yanked off her gloves and barreled toward him, five and a half feet of blistering Southern fury.

Charlie moved to intercept, but Sean stepped in front of her and held out a hand, aiming for polite, same as Charlie had done with Tracy downstairs. "Hey, Maggie, good to see you again."

Worked about as well on Maggie as it had on Tracy.

"Hey?" Her open palm connected with the side of his face, right where Trevor had decked him on Saturday. "Hey yourself, asshole."

Okay, worse than the run-in with Tracy. He flexed his jaw and held a hand over the aching spot. The whole side of his face was going to be a rainbow at the rate things were going. "I probably deserved that."

"You bet your sorry ass you did." She crowded into his personal space and stabbed his chest with a manicured nail. "You wrecked the lives of two people I care about."

And just like that, he was back in the graveyard, regret and remorse rushing back in. He had to work twice as hard to keep his shoulders and spine straight, to stop from deflating on the spot for everyone to see.

As if sensing his deterioration, Charlie stepped around him and lightly clasped her friend's elbow. "Maggie, let it go."

"I will not." Maggie shrugged her off and came at Sean again. "You left them on a night that was supposed to be a celebration. Just left. You deserve a whole lot worse than a slap and a few bruises."

He ran a shaky hand through his hair. "Believe me, I know."

"And just because she's tolerating your presence on this investigation doesn't mean I have to. You've got a steep hill to climb, mister." She shoved him hard, two hands to his chest. "One more fuckup, even a tiny one, and it'll be my fist next time. You got me?"

Sean held up his hands. "I got you."

"All right." Charlie slipped all the way between them,

facing Maggie. "Now that you've said your piece, can we please get back to the crime scene?"

"Sure," she replied brightly as if a light switch had been flipped. "Fair warning, it ain't pretty." She snapped on another pair of gloves and headed toward the bedroom. Sean marveled at how easily she'd swapped the best friend hat for her medical examiner one.

"Show's over, folks," Charlie said to the crowd that had gathered to observe the ruckus. "Clear out." She waited for the last tech to descend the stairs before turning back to Sean. "You okay?"

"Yeah, I'm fine." He rubbed his hand across his cheek again, trying and failing to reduce the sting. "She still scares the shit out of me."

Smiling, Charlie brushed aside his hand to inspect the damage herself, her fingertips lightly grasping his stubbled jaw and setting off a totally different kind of sting. "Some things never change."

"No, they don't." His response was low, husky, and it drew her gaze to his lips. Not intended but unmistakable, and a rush of warmth spread up his neck and down to places he had no business thinking about at a crime scene.

"Yo!" Maggie called, shattering the charged moment. "There's a dead body in here."

Charlie removed her hand, and Sean reined in his careening desire. Pulling up his agent persona, he willed his id to behave and stepped into the room.

Diego wasn't kidding, and Sean was in the same boat as Jaylen. He hadn't seen worse than this either. The sight would replay in his nightmares forever.

Stripped naked, Julian Hirsch had been positioned spread-eagle on the bed, a limb tied to each post. Blood coated the ropes, the bedposts, and his thighs and groin that had been scored. Blood was smeared around his mouth, red on his pale, slack face, like someone had covered his mouth and pinched shut his nose.

"Smothered," Maggie confirmed. "By hand, then pillow."

And to think, Tracy had come home from the hospital to find her husband dead in their bed, bloodied and butchered. Based on first impressions downstairs, Sean wasn't a fan, but he wouldn't wish this discovery on anyone. That thought, more than the scene itself, made his stomach lurch. He turned his back on the room and braced a hand against the bathroom doorjamb. Eyes closed, he struggled to catch a breath, afraid the deep inhale he needed would make his stomach churn worse.

Beside him, Charlie snapped her fingers Maggie's direction. "Vicks."

Pocket contents jangled, then a moment later, Charlie shoved a travel-sized metal can into his hand. "Under the nose," she said.

He stripped off a glove, popped open the canister, and dabbed the strong-smelling balm beneath his nostrils. He handed the canister back to Charlie and breathed deep, letting the menthol do its work. Charlie settled against the wall to his left, giving him space to pull himself together but letting him know she was there. Sean wrestled his gut and mind into check, and when all was stable, relatively, he glared at Maggie from beneath a raised brow. "'Ain't pretty'?"

"Sorry." She tossed them each a new pair of gloves. "I might have understated that a bit."

Charlie joined him beside the bed. "Just a wee bit."

"You got the note?" Sean asked.

The ME withdrew a plastic bag out of the evidence case on the dresser and handed it across the bed to him.

"Where was it?" Charlie asked from over his shoulder.

"Tacked to that pillow"—she jutted her chin at a bagged bloodied pillow on the other end of the dresser—"over his face."

Sean studied the newest note. Same paper, same red block letters, but with the next number and a new quote:

#2 – *SO SWEET WAS NE'ER SO FATAL.*

"Desdemona," Charlie said.

Sean whipped around, brow raised even higher.

"HU's Repertory Theatre put on *Othello* last year," she said with a shrug. "Annie and Trevor dragged me with them. Desdemona was falsely accused of adultery."

"Nothing false about this one," Maggie quipped. "That man was the walking definition of can't keep his dick in his pants. Now"—she gestured at the bed—"no pants."

Sean groaned.

"Sorry, sorry," Maggie said.

"I don't know how Diego does it," Charlie said with a chuckle. "Speaking of, can you go downstairs and tell your husband and Jaylen to gather everyone in the dining room for a debrief? Looks like we've officially got a serial case."

"Sure thing." Maggie covered Julian's body with a

sheet and removed her gloves. She paused halfway to the door and pointed at Sean. "I'm watching you."

Sean waited until she left the room to shiver dramatically. "Yep, definitely hates me." Charlie didn't smile at his joke, which meant she was taking this one harder than usual. "You okay?"

"It's hard seeing someone I know butchered like that." Her eyes flitted to the bed and back. "You okay?"

"Just don't tell anyone I cracked."

That got him a half smirk. "Pretty sure Mags will tell everyone."

He hung his head back and groaned, drawing a fuller smile from Charlie. She only wore it as far as the hallway, though, as Jaylen came rushing up the stairs, alarm written all over his face. He careened to a halt in front of them, and Sean clasped Charlie's shoulder, preparing for another hit. She didn't shrug him off; she sensed it too. "What is it?" she asked the officer.

"Abel called. Trevor's in the wind."

Curveball.

Done with his records search on Diego's borrowed computer, Sean perched on the corner of the officer's desk, taking advantage of the bird's-eye view into Charlie's office. Jacket and heels gone, she made another circuit around her desk as she tapped the screen of her phone. At the rate she was circling, she was going to wear a hole in the floor. He'd still be wearing his own in the conference room floor if he hadn't needed a break from the gruesome crime scene photos. Unfortunately, his searches had proved fruitless, and with mounting frustration came mounting worry for the person who no doubt had Charlie worried too.

Following the report that Trevor was missing, he and Charlie had left Jaylen and Diego to brief the other officers while they'd sped through the streets of Hanover Oaks. Julian's refurbished house was at the center of the subdivision. Trevor's house was among the smaller, well-kept homes toward the back of the neighborhood, an addition built five years ago. According to Charlie, Trevor had bought the house as a wedding gift for Tracy.

Sean's sympathy for the other woman had waned. He still hated that she'd come home to that awful sight, but he'd hate that for anyone. Tracy, though, from what he'd gathered, had practically rubbed her affair with Julian in Trevor's face. No wonder Trevor had wanted to move on. The move to DC, the job at Georgetown, suddenly made a whole hell of a lot more sense.

What didn't make sense was the state of Trevor's house that morning. The bulk of it had been packed up, similar to the beach house a month ago, but in the kitchen, a half pot of cold coffee and damp coffee grounds left a bitter smell in the air, and upstairs, in Trevor's bedroom, a set of luggage was thrown open on the unmade bed, the smallest size missing. Several drawers were open, clothes rummaged through, and his travel kit, like the middle suitcase, was nowhere to be found, even though his toothbrush was still in its holder. He'd left in a hurry sometime early that morning, and all calls—from them, from HPD, from HU when he didn't show up for class—were going straight to voicemail. He'd either switched off his phone or had no service wherever he'd taken off to.

Or been taken to.

Sean didn't want to consider either possibility and mentally mounted evidence against each. If Trevor had been taken, if he were the killer's next victim, why would he pack a suitcase? If Trevor had taken off, if he were the killer, why would he get sloppy all of a sudden? He knew enough about police work to cover his tracks like at the crime scenes. Why leave that morning in a way that made him look guilty? Not to mention Sean hadn't detected any guilt the other night in his hotel room when Trevor had first glimpsed the crime scene photos. Only surprise. And he fucking knew Trevor. Yes, he'd been gone a while, but there was no way someone that empathetic, with that big a heart, could commit cold-blooded murder. All that said, Trevor's connections to the case couldn't be dismissed— Jeff was stalling his tenure; Julian was fucking his wife; and the murders were fitting—poetic, even—for an English lit professor.

Trevor was involved, whether he knew it or not, and every second he was gone was a second he was potentially in danger, and fuck if Sean would let anything happen to him, selfishly and for Charlie's sake. Even if he couldn't be with them, he owed them that much, their chance at a new life in DC, one Sean was coming to realize how much they both needed.

"Can't take your eyes off her, can you?" Abel's deep

voice and the acrid scent of station sludge jostled Sean out of his thoughts. The older man handed him a mug, then sank into Diego's chair with a cup of his own.

"Of course I can't." Sean took a swig of the bitter brew. "She's the girl—the woman—who held half my heart."

"Past tense?" Disbelief colored Abel's voice. "According to Maggie, it didn't look past tense at the crime scene today. It sure doesn't with you sitting on the corner of this desk, watching Charlotte pace around her office."

Sean sipped his coffee. "Any hits on the APB?"

"Nothing yet."

"I know I've been gone a while and a lot has happened, but I don't see Trevor as a murder suspect."

"Neither can I nor can Charlie." Abel took a long swallow from his mug. "She's worried more than anything. We all are. Somethin's not right here." Sean couldn't agree more, but before they could talk it out further, a commotion at the reception desk drew their attention, and Abel cursed. "Ah, hell."

Petite, blond Rachel was arguing with a bruiser of a man in an ill-fitting suit, looming over her in a clear attempt to intimidate. Add to that the air of self-importance, and Sean immediately clocked him as a politician. "Mayor Rowan?" he asked Abel as the visitor bullied his way through the waist-high swinging reception door.

"The one and only." Abel lowered his mug, stood, and stepped into Craig's path.

Sean remained on the desk corner, not wanting to draw attention to himself yet. He also wanted to get a measure of the windbag. He'd heard stories, never the full one, but so far Craig Rowan was living up to every bad word Sean had ever heard about him, directly and indirectly.

"What kind of circus are you running here?" Craig lobbed at Abel.

"Now, Craig, if you'll calm down," Abel said, always the mediator. "I'll get Charlie, and she'll brief you on the case."

The mayor wasn't interested in rational conversation. Just more ranting. "I've got two dead professors and a campus crawling with press. My phone is ringing off the hook with calls from the media, university officials, and concerned parents, and I've got a line of constituents out the door at my office."

Constituents.

Sean wondered if there was a word in the English language he hated more. Every politician he'd ever known, personally and professionally, used that word as an excuse for being a coward or a jackass. Or both. When Marie and Saul had backed, and matched, his decision to donate his inheritance to LGBTQ shelters in their hometown of Kansas City, *constituents* had blocked them at every turn. There was a reason they and Paxton Industries were head-quartered in DC now, and it wasn't only because Saul's doctors were there. And when his legat office had lobbied for more cross-agency cooperation, *constituents* had blocked the funding. He'd lost a colleague, a friend, in a terrorist attack the next year that might have been averted with better local training and cooperation. Craig Rowan, if Sean had to guess, was a bit of both—jackass and coward—

and he had no qualms about using his *constituents* to get what *he* wanted. Judging by Charlie's determined stride out of her office, she was about to make sure that didn't happen today.

"You idiots over here are sitting on your hands doing nothing," Craig continued to rant, oblivious to the fury closing in. "I want to see everything you have on this case, and I want to see it right now."

"That's enough, Craig," Charlie snapped.

"That's Mayor to you."

"I don't care what you call yourself," she said from a good two inches above him with her heels back on. "If you disrespect my chief or my officers, then don't expect me to show you any respect in return."

"This is ridiculous." Craig stepped back, clearly uncomfortable having to look up at her.

Sean shifted off the desk, uncomfortable for an entirely different reason. Charlie was stunning with that temper on full display.

"Wallace called first thing this morning, did he not?"

"Well, yes," Craig stammered.

Charlie crowded into his space, forcing his gaze up again. "Then I'll tell you what's ridiculous. *You* barging into this station, wasting time that could be better spent on the investigation."

"I'm the mayor of this town." Craig fumed, his face growing redder by the second. "When I request a meeting with the police chief and the detective in charge of this case, that's who I want to speak to. Not some minion."

Sean sensed a loaded, angry undercurrent running

between them that involved more than just this case. Seeking to diffuse the tension, he stepped forward. "Abel and Charlie were at a crime scene this morning, then all of us were chasing down leads. There hasn't been time for a call, much less a meeting."

Craig's gaze shot to him, and his eyes grew wide when they landed on the sidearm at his hip. "Who are you?"

He dug his badge out of his pocket and flipped it open for the other man. "Special Agent Sean Hale."

An ugly Cheshire cat grin split the mayor's face. "Well, I'm glad the FBI is involved since I can't trust local law enforcement to handle things properly."

This guy had no business calling anyone an idiot if he was fool enough to think Sean would take his side. Shoving his badge back into his pocket, Sean retreated a step behind Charlie and Abel. "This is HPD's case. I'm only observing, and from what I've seen so far, Chief Champion's department is more than capable of handling it."

Stymied, the mayor's beady blue eyes bounced between the three of them. "I want hourly updates."

"You'll get updates as new information is available," Charlie said. "Feel free to direct all press inquiries to me. We wouldn't want to overtax city hall."

Craig took a menacing step forward. "If your last name wasn't Henby, I'd have your ass out of here so fast."

Charlie didn't flinch. "And if your last name wasn't Rowan, yours wouldn't be in city hall either."

"Craig," Abel said, interrupting the escalating hostilities. "You'd best leave now."

"I want updates," he persisted.

"And as Charlie said, you'll get them as they become available."

"Fine." He gave Charlie one last murderous glare, then stormed out.

The front door had barely closed behind him when the station erupted in applause. With a tight grin, Charlie gave her colleagues a half bow before Abel ordered everyone back to work.

"Wally," Charlie said, "Call Nadine in Craig's office again now and every hour with an update."

Across the bullpen, Officer Sylvan hung his head in his hands. "Fuck me."

"With any luck, they'll get as tired of it as you. Wear 'em down good," she said with a wink, then turned to Abel, all humor fading. "You think we'll ever be rid of that asshole?"

"You said it yourself, sugar. His last name's Rowan." He reclaimed his coffee and took a long swallow. "Before too long it'll be his son's ass in that chair."

"Fuck me," Charlie said, repeating Wallace's sentiment.

"You handled him well," Sean commended.

"I've had a lifetime of dealing with that man's shit. I'm a pro." More than weary frustration flashed in her black eyes, but then it was gone a second later. "The only one who handles him better is Trevor. Speaking of, I'm going to try him again, then I'll meet you in the conference room."

Sean nodded and waited until she was in her office to ask Abel for more of the story. "What was that all about?"

"Things are tense between city hall and HPD."

"You don't say." This was more than politics, though. Sean could see it in the grim set of Abel's mouth and the thinly veiled hate in Charlie's eyes. "They go back, Charlie and Craig? I heard vague rumblings, but our paths here never crossed."

"One date in high school. Didn't end well."

Sean's own hostility toward the mayor escalated. "Did he hurt her?"

"No, Trevor got to her in time," Abel replied. "Doesn't help that Craig's younger brother, Adam, gets dragged in here routinely. He's out within the hour, thanks to a judge in his daddy's pocket. Zero consequences. Frustrates the hell out of Charlie."

Sean glanced across the bullpen to where she was pacing in her office again. "Not the only thing that's frustrating her at the moment."

"No, it's not."

Abel's phone rang an office over, and once it became clear the call was going to take a while, Abel throwing his feet up on the desk, Sean headed back to the conference room. Break over, and wouldn't you know it, the case and crime scene photos were preferable to thinking about Charlie and Craig. Diego and Jaylen had set up a whiteboard, a black line drawn down the middle, separating it into two halves. One side was covered in notes and photos from Jeff's crime scene. On the other side, they'd started to collect the same for Julian's.

Sean rested against the end of the conference table, studying the photo of the note from *Othello* and the photo of where the note had been found.

"Desdemona, for sure," Charlie said behind him. "Double-checked it." She stood in the doorway, shoulder to the jamb.

"We used to have to drag you kicking and screaming to plays," he said. "And you'd only go to the ones Trevor was in."

"Trevor and Annie dragged me to this one." She moved toward the whiteboard and flipped it over, blank side facing out so their investigation notes and photos weren't visible. "Speaking of, Annie's on her way."

"Why's Annie coming in?"

"She's a librarian at HU. She overhears more about what goes on there than anyone."

"Makes sense," he said. "You said a couple reasons. Something else?"

Charlie's high heels tapped a staccato rhythm against the floor. "She's close to Tracy and Trevor. I need to tell her what's going on. In person."

Sean fought his traitorous eyebrow that threatened to lift, but before he could ask why Annie had remained close with Trevor's ex-wife, the object of his curiosity appeared in the doorway. Sean smiled, waves of forgotten brotherly affection washing over him. The years had been kind to Annabelle Henby. Her long white-gold hair was held away from her face by a pair of oversized sunglasses atop her head, her big blue eyes shone bright, and dressed in a pink button-up, pressed black slacks, and black flats, she was the picture-perfect stylish librarian who could also pelt you with a wicked fastball.

Her fingers fidgeted with the strap of her messenger

bag as her eyes zoomed between him and Charlie. As a teen, she'd been shy around him at first until he'd conspired with Trevor and Cal to make her laugh at every opportunity, which was why he couldn't help contorting his face right then, crossing his eyes, wrinkling up his nose, and letting his tongue hang out the side of his mouth.

Annie tried to hide it, but the corner of her mouth twitched. "So it's true, Odie, you're back?"

He barked in jest, and Charlie backhanded him with a slap to his gut.

"That was fast," Annie mumbled.

Charlie stepped ahead, hugging her sister. "What was fast?"

"Nothing." Annie returned the embrace somewhat stiffly, her eyes staying locked on him over Charlie's shoulder. "What's going on? Abel didn't give me any details over the phone. He just said I should come to the station ASAP."

"Let's have a seat." Charlie led her sister toward the chair at the head of the table. Sean closed the conference room door and took the chair on Annie's other side.

She glanced back and forth between them. "You two are making me nervous."

Charlie scooted closer. "Something's happened, and I wanted to tell you in person"

Annie instantly went from curious to concerned. "What's wrong?"

"There was an incident this morning at Julian and Tracy Hirsch's home."

"Oh no, Trace." Tears welled in her eyes as she covered her mouth with a hand.

Charlie slung an arm around her sister's shoulder. "Tracy's safe. She wasn't home, but Julian's dead."

Annie's eyes grew huge, skittering to him, then back to Charlie. "Does Trevor know?"

"We can't find him to tell him," Sean answered, laying a hand over her shaking one. "We went to his house this morning, and it looked like he'd packed and left in a hurry. And he's not answering his cell."

Oddly, Annie relaxed, unclenching her hands and shrugging out of Charlie's hold. "Oh! That's probably because he's in the mountains by now."

"Mountains?" Charlie asked. "You know where he went?"

"Apex, Virginia. He called me early this morning and said he was headed to Apex University. He got an email overnight from someone there about a case he was helping you with. The contact wanted to meet with him in person, and she was only available until noon, so he had to book it. I assumed he called you too."

Charlie's eyes were a turbulent mix of betrayal, concern, and doubt. She stood abruptly and walked to one of the windows overlooking Main Street, her back to them.

Giving her a moment, Sean carried on with Annie. "Why did he call you?"

Annie's attention swung from Charlie back to him. "He left a voicemail for his assistant and sent her an email, but he wanted me to follow up to be sure his classes were canceled. Good thing, as I called, and she was a no-show today. I'm headed over there next."

Sean breathed a sigh of relief at the same time he cursed Trevor for taking off without calling either him or Charlie. Probably because he knew if he did, they'd both tell him not to go.

"Trevor's not in trouble, is he?"

"No." Sean squeezed her hand again and smiled. "We've been worried is all."

Annie smiled in return before looking to Charlie, who'd turned back to them. "Julian's really dead?"

The swirling storm of emotion in Charlie's black eyes was gone, replaced by compassion. Same as she'd banked her own feelings at Tracy's that morning. Took a special person—a special cop—to be able to do that. "Yeah, sweetie, Julian's really dead."

"How's Trace?" Annie asked, compassion and concern something the Henby women shared.

"Not good."

"I should go." Annie moved to stand. "I need to check on her and see if I can help somehow."

Charlie's hand on her shoulder kept Annie seated. "I know you two are close, but she was distraught when we saw her this morning, blaming everyone, including Trevor and anyone connected to him."

Something else Charlie had said earlier nagged at Sean. "Annie?"

"Hmm?"

"Charlie told me about Julian's..." He struggled to find the right word under the circumstances. "Extracurricular activities. You wouldn't happen to know who he was currently seeing, would you?"

One corner of her mouth hitched. "'Seeing'?"

"You really gonna make me say it, A?"

"I knew what *fucking* meant when I was thirteen." She patted his hand in perfectly patronizing fashion. "I definitely know what it means now."

Even Charlie laughed at that, and Sean bit back his own smile. He didn't mind the laugh at his expense if it lightened the dark day for the Henby sisters.

"Sarah Barnett, last I'd heard," Annie said. "That might have changed by now, but start there. I'll keep an ear out too."

"We appreciate it," Sean said as Diego opened the conference room door.

"Deputy, we need you in the bullpen."

"Give me a second," Charlie told Diego as they all stood. She wrapped Annie up in another hug. "Thanks for coming in, A. It helps a lot that we don't have to worry about Trevor now."

"Happy to help. Now go, duty calls."

With obvious reluctance, Charlie released her sister with a "Be good," then exited to the bullpen where Diego and Abel waited.

"Thanks again for coming in," Sean said as he and Annie trailed behind. "If you hear from Trevor, you'll let us know?"

"Sure thing."

"Everything will be okay. Your sister's on the case."

"I know," she said with a small smile.

"Everything good with you two?"

"It will be," she said with a nod. "It's good seeing you again, but I need to go. I'm supposed to be at HU Med in an hour to read to the children's ward."

He gave her a half hug before she turned on her heel and hurried out.

Charlie strode back into the conference room less than a minute later. "Jaylen and Diego are headed to campus to find Ms. Barnett, a rising sophomore."

He rested against the windowsill and whistled. "Julian liked 'em young?"

"Julian liked them all."

"Are you talking from experience? He ever try anything with you?"

She grimaced, causing him a momentary flare of anger. First Craig Rowan and now Julian Hirsch.

"Once. Hit on both me and Rachel the same night. We were out with Trevor, Cal, and Annie at Pier Point. Julian made certain overtures. Trevor decked him."

"Sounds familiar."

She laughed and rested back against the window ledge. "I'm just glad Trevor's okay."

"Me too." He debated his next question, ultimately deciding to ask what had been on his mind all morning. "You want to tell me about you and Tracy? Seemed like you were the last person she wanted to see this morning and not just because her husband was murdered."

Her gaze drifted out the window. "I was always the last person Tracy wanted to see."

"You want to talk about it?" He told himself he was

asking as a friend and investigator, not as the man who desperately wanted to know if there was still something between Charlie and Trevor, something Tracy couldn't accept. Something Sean could pin his hopes on if not for himself then at least for them. Charlie looked at him like he was crazy for wanting to wade into the middle of it. He laughed, a hand raised. "I unloaded some heavy stuff on you last night. Just returning the favor."

She smiled, tension easing from her shoulders. "Thanks, but I'll be fine. Nothing I haven't dealt with for years." She pushed off the windowsill and moved directly in front of him, reexamining his face. "I'd stay out of Craig's way unless you want to add more bruises."

"You want to talk about that?"

"Fuck no." She handled his face the same as she'd done that morning at the crime scene, and her fingers were just as scorching now. He held his breath and curbed his impulse to reach for her. "You are quite the rainbow."

"Seems maybe Hanover isn't good for my health."

"You're still breathing," she said with a wink and a gentle pat to his jaw.

Sean rapped his knuckles on the closest piece of wood.

CHAPTER TEN

The backdoor of the station had barely closed behind Trevor when Sean cleared the bottom of the stairs and came barreling toward him.

"Trev, glad you're back," he said, not slowing one bit. Trevor held his hands up to block, only to have Sean slice his forearms between them and obliterate the defensive position, knocking Trevor's arms aside. Hands to Trevor's chest, Sean slammed him against the wall. "If you ever take off like that again without telling us, I'll kick your fucking ass."

What exactly did he think he was doing now? Sean certainly had the upper hand. Trevor was still struggling to catch his breath from the physical jolt to his body and from the emotional jolt of Sean's words and actions. Anger and worry swirled in Sean's eyes, and *us* rang in Trevor's ears. "Where do I even start to unpack all that?"

"Better question," Sean said, not giving an inch, "why

the fuck didn't you tell us where you were going? Or answer your goddamn phone all day?"

Us.

Ignoring how good, how familiar that sounded, even in Sean's angry growl, even if the context was strictly professional, even if his twice-burned heart knew better, Trevor lowered a hand and dug his phone out of his pocket. He turned the darkened screen toward Sean. "It's dead. I left in a hurry and forgot the charger." Sean's eyes—tired judging by the lines of red running through the whites and the bags beneath them—flicked to the phone. "And I didn't tell you or Charlie I was going because you'd just tell me not to go."

Sean's gaze whipped back to him. "Damn right."

"Proving my point."

Sean stepped closer, his fingers curling in the front of Trevor's shirt. Trevor's breath stuttered, flashes of their recent night together careening through his mind. "Sean, what—"

"Sean, back off." Charlie's clipped command shattered the suddenly toasty bubble in the hallway. "That's enough."

Sean's weary blues flashed with the same heat coursing through Trevor's veins. Trevor immediately missed it when Sean heeded Charlie's warning and retreated. But not without a final warning. "Don't do it again."

Trevor straightened and pocketed his phone. "Message received." All of them. But with Charlie approaching, they'd have to get into unpacking all that later. And he meant to. "Thank you," he said to Charlie.

"If you think I'm gonna go any easier on you…" She smirked, and despite the weariness he could see in his best friend too—her skin paler than usual, her hair hastily pulled into a bun, the divot between her brows and the same dark circles under her eyes as were under Sean's—it was impossible to deny how attractive she was in her element, magnified standing next to Sean.

He waved off the fight, chuckling. "I know better."

"Fess up," she said.

"I followed a lead."

She crossed her arms and leaned against the wall, knee hitched and foot propped. "I know you think you're a cop, but you're not. You're a professor."

"Exactly." Which was why he'd gone to Apex as a fellow professor without a cop on his arm. "A cop wouldn't have gotten what I did."

"Which was what?" Sean asked.

If they were going to question him, he had a question for them first. Possibly related to the information he'd obtained. "First, tell me why the press is still out front?" He'd had to park around back because Main Street was completely blocked by press vans and reporters. "I figured that would have died off some by now, unless there's been a development in Jeff's case."

Sean stepped closer. "You haven't heard?"

Trevor ignored the tingle at the bottom of his spine and patted his pocket. "Dead phone, remember?"

The tingle raised goose bumps on his arms as Charlie also drew closer, her expression shifting. Gone was the smirk, vanished was the hard-ass detective and best friend who gave him shit. Instead, she wore the *I'm about to deliver bad news* face. Serious but compassionate. He knew that face. Had been on the receiving end of it a few times—the most recent the morning earlier this month after Sean had left again. There could be only one explanation for it now. "There's been another murder," he surmised.

She laid a hand on his forearm.

A full-body shiver joined the tingles and goose bumps. "Who?"

Sean closed in on his other side, and he remembered this move too, how the two of them had talked him down their senior year after the Pirates had been eliminated from the CWS. "Why don't we go upstairs into the conference room?" Sean suggested.

Fuck that. If his pinging instincts were right, which they usually were with these two, the last thing he wanted was to be on the main floor when they delivered whatever news they were so skittish about. "Who, goddamn it?"

Charlie held his gaze and grasped his wrist. "Julian."

There was a second where he didn't believe what his ears told his brain, but the look on Charlie's face, on Sean's, punched the truth through the layer of disbelief. "Holy fuck." Despite Charlie's grip, he wrenched his arm free and stumbled around them to the nearest wall, slamming a fist against it. Warmth flanked him from either side— Sean's "You okay, Trev?" close and quiet, Charlie's hand on his back soothing, but he kept his eyes closed, trying to sort through the barrage of emotions and questions that were pummeling him, one hitting the hardest. He angled his face to Charlie. "Who found the body?"

She coasted her hand down his spine. "Let's get out of the hallway."

Fuck, that meant only one thing. "Oh God, Trace." He flipped his back to the wall and sank to the floor, head held in his hands.

Sean's boots echoed the direction of the stairs, making the hall as private as he could, while Charlie knelt beside him, her voice close and on his level, confirming the worst. "Tracy found him this morning."

He remained quiet for several long moments, hands wrapped around the back of his neck. When he finally lifted his face, he settled his gaze on her. Steadiness in the storm that had unexpectedly swept him up. "I have no love lost for either of them, but Christ, I wouldn't wish that on Trace."

Charlie took his hand in hers and squeezed. "None of us would."

"Was there a clue again?"

"'So sweet was ne'er so fatal,'" Sean replied as he walked back their direction.

Trevor glanced between them. "Desdemona from *Othello*, falsely accused of adultery."

"Which Julian was not," Charlie said. "He was smothered, in a manner of speaking."

"It's Shakespeare's *Four Tragedies*." He'd bet anything on it, including Sean's bike. "First, *King Lear*, now *Othello*. Was the new clue numbered?"

Sean nodded. "With a two."

He was right. "*Hamlet* and *Macbeth*. Those are the other two plays in that collection."

"I should have asked Annie about those when she was here," Charlie said.

Fuck, Annie. He shot to his feet, then regretted it immediately, wobbly from the shock and probably the fifth can of Mountain Dew he'd guzzled on the drive home. He put a hand to the wall to steady himself and ignored the double dose of concerned looks. "Is she okay?" he asked. "She and Trace are tight."

"Annie's fine," Charlie said. "A little shocked but okay."

"I should check on her." He dug his phone out of his pocket, and seeing the darkened screen, cursed himself again for running off without a charger. "*Fuck*."

Charlie slipped the device from his hand, saving it from imminent destruction in his fist or against the wall. "You can use my office phone, but first we need to hear what you found out in Apex."

He shifted so his back was to the wall again, Charlie and Sean in front of him, and inhaled deep, fighting to calm his racing heart and mind. "You remember when I mentioned Jeff had caused difficulties with some tenure candidates?"

"Your own included," Sean said.

"Yes, he's been stalling mine, which was part of the reason for Georgetown." Georgetown. DC. "Fuck, Charlie, the interview." His heart raced, fueled by nitrous-powered guilt. "It was this morning?"

"Pushed it to tomorrow."

He let out a relieved breath, but Sean didn't let him

savor the victory long. "Let me guess, someone at Apex was a victim of his stalling?"

Trevor nodded. "When she got tired of waiting and accepted a position at Apex, Jeff held her letters of rec up too. She had to threaten a formal complaint to finally get the letters."

"A complaint for what?"

"Discrimination. Ten women have come up for tenure since Jeff was appointed to the tenure committee. He's only approved two."

"That's the treason," Sean said. "A traitor to the academic institution, someone who systematically denied HU talented academics because of their gender." He angled toward Charlie. "It fits."

"As *one* possible motive," she said. "We still have Barnett and Julian to consider."

"Wait!" Trevor sliced a hand between them like a field ref would. "Barnett. Why does that ring a bell?"

"Julian was having an affair with a student, Sarah Barnett."

Trevor shot off the wall, anger re-infusing his limbs. "She was in my freshman lit class last semester."

"Are you surprised?" Charlie said.

"No, but still, a nineteen-year-old? And for fuck's sake, he and Trace have barely been married five months."

Julian liked younger women. Tracy was almost twenty years younger than him, but students were off-limits as was sleeping around in a supposedly closed marriage. He growled and continued to pace the narrow hallway,

Charlie and Sean staying out of his way, neither trying to contain him.

But Sarah... Julian sure could make a mess. "Do you know who her father is?"

"Whose?" Charlie said.

"Sarah Barnett's?" Sean said, then a split second later, his eyes widened, clearly making the connection Trevor was leading him to. "Duncan Barnett?"

"Bingo."

Sean scowled Charlie's direction. "Conservative front-runner for Missouri's senate seat. Saul hates him."

She let her head fall back and stared at the ceiling. "As if Jefferson Marshall and Craig Rowan weren't enough."

"Possible political motive?" Sean said.

Charlie tapped her heel. "But from a political stand-point, wouldn't it be easier to just let the affair run its course unnoticed?"

Trevor suppressed the disgusted shiver that fought its way through him. As blood boiling as all this was, there were also now more leads for him to follow at HU. He needed to get to campus. "Can I borrow your phone charger?" he said to Charlie. "I'll charge my phone in the truck on my way to campus."

Compassionate Charlie vanished as did contemplative Charlie who was just talking about the case with Sean. Hard-ass Charlie, the one who helped keep the department in line and who used to keep him and Sean in line, moved between him and the stairs, her arms crossed. "I think maybe you should stay here."

"Why?"

Following her lead, like always, Sean stepped behind him and blocked the other exit.

"We're still working out possible motives," Charlie said. "Possible connections too, and along with the political one, the other connections we have to work with are HU... and you."

CHAPTER ELEVEN

Charlie dropped the red-and-white plastic bag and sweating gallon of sweet tea on the break room table Maggie stood beside. "Talk fast. Rachel's flirting with the new delivery guy. He looks eager, so it shouldn't take her long to get his number. Five minutes max. What've you got?"

Laughing, Maggie snagged plates and cups out of the cupboard. "Heaven forbid we violate Rachel's no-discussing-dead-bodies-while-eating rule," she said as she filled the glasses with tea. "And thanks for the early dinner."

"Or late lunch." Somewhere in the middle, and in any event, the first food Charlie had had all day. After the crime scene that morning, then Craig's tantrum and Trevor's arrival, it had taken until now for her to even get hungry. She unloaded the bag, spreading the boxes of fried chicken, barbecue, red slaw, and hush puppies on her desk. "Four and a half minutes."

Maggie, however, seemed determined to focus on anything but work. She swiped a hush puppy and packet of honey butter, opened the latter, and dredged the fried dough through it. "It confounds me how you eat like this with no consequences." She plopped into a chair, then popped the hush puppy into her mouth with a satisfied hum. "Don't care, mind you, but it confuses the inner scientist."

"This is stress eating," Charlie said as she loaded plates. "And there are consequences. Five miles every night." She handed a plate to Maggie, left another on the table for Rachel, then sank into a chair across the table. "Four minutes."

"Fine." Maggie snagged her plate and ate another hush puppy before launching into her report. "I'm still examining Julian. Don't expect prints, tox screen tomorrow, won't have DNA until the end of the week if any."

"And Professor Marshall?" Charlie asked as she dug into the barbecue. "His son will be here tomorrow and wants the body released for the funeral."

"He's good to go."

"Evidence?"

"No prints, no trace fibers, nothing on the body or at the scene that didn't belong to Jeff. Perp knew what they were doing. Jeff's neck and hands were scarred from the rope but no other defensive wounds."

"Toxins?"

Maggie pointed at her neck with her fork. "Diprivan, injected."

"Preliminaries on Julian?"

"Similar injection mark on the neck, so I'm guessing he'll also test positive. Otherwise, on first glance, the body is clean except..."

Charlie paused with a drumstick halfway to her mouth. "Except?"

"Whoever the killer is, in both cases, they waited for the victim to wake before actually killing him."

"The bloodied ropes?"

Maggie grimaced and set aside a forkful of barbecue and slaw. "For starters. There was also a gag on the ground in the stables that tested positive for Jeff's saliva. He must have gotten that off after he woke but before he was hung. As for Julian, the blood on his face and pillow was smeared. He struggled."

Appetite waning, Charlie abandoned the drumstick and her plate. Maybe there was something to Rachel's no-discussing-dead-bodies-while-eating rule.

"Hey!" Rachel appeared in the breakroom doorway, her honey-colored eyes narrowed in mock offense. "You started without me."

"Trust me, you're right on time." Maggie pushed the third plate toward her. "You get the new guy's name and number?"

She picked up the plate and claimed the open chair. "Sure did, but I won't be using it."

"Why's that?"

Blissfully unaware of their previous discussion, she attacked a chicken thigh with gusto. "I've got my eye on someone else."

"Anyone we know?" Charlie asked.

"May-be," Rachel drawled in a way that clearly meant *yes*, but then added, "I don't want to say more yet. Things are... unsettled. Enough about me, though. Now that we know Trevor is safe and sound and snoring on your office couch, what's going on with Sean?" Before Charlie could object, Maggie launched into a play-by-play of the incident at the crime scene. Rachel's eyes grew wider with every word, her ponytail of blond ringlets swinging as her gaze swiveled between them. "Is he back back? Like for good?"

"No." Charlie ignored the disappointment and heaviness in her gut. *In and out*, he'd said. "He's a friend of Jeff's son, who's also a fed. He's stationed overseas with Sean. Sean's just keeping an eye on things until he gets here."

Maggie fixed her with a patented disapproving parent stare, one that Charlie had only ever seen bested by her dad. "Then why was he at this morning's crime scene with you?"

And just like the time Mitch had caught her at Pier Point on senior skip day, Charlie didn't have a good explanation. She could argue she'd brought Sean along because he was a LEO, another trained set of eyes couldn't hurt, but her reasons were also personal. She knew Julian; she knew Tracy better. She hadn't wanted to face that crime scene alone, and Sean had been there for her, exactly how and when she'd needed him.

"Uh-oh," Maggie said. "I don't like that look."

"What look?"

"The wistful one that just floated across your face," Rachel answered.

She feigned ignorance, but neither of them was buying

it. "Don't, Charlie," Maggie said. "He's not back for good. This will not end well if you go there."

"Think about Trevor," Rachel said, adding her unfinished plate to the others. "You two are supposed to be moving on. To DC and all that might offer."

"I heard Trevor laid Sean out night before last," Maggie said. "Serves him right for leaving you two without so much as a goodbye."

Charlie drained her tea. "At least I got one earlier this month."

Rachel gasped, her arms flailing and sending her barely balanced plate flying, splattering slaw everywhere. "*What?*"

Maggie grabbed a stack of napkins and held them out to Rachel. "What the fuck happened earlier—" She cut herself off with a sharp inhale. "The funeral?"

Charlie nodded. "He was there. And at the beach house after."

"Trevor too?" Rachel asked.

Charlie nodded again.

Maggie snagged the last napkin on the table, balled it up, and hurled it at her. "Way to bury the lede, Henby."

"There's a lot going on if you hadn't noticed." Maggie winced, and Charlie immediately regretted her more-biting-than-intended tone. She reached across the table and grasped her friend's wrist. "I'm sorry."

Maggie smiled and rubbed a comforting hand over hers. "You're right. There's a lot, babe. You all were together again?"

Charlie withdrew her hand and closed her eyes,

leaning back in her chair, face to the ceiling. "Yes, and for the first time in ten years, things felt right. But fuck, things were already so complicated. Now they're a million times worse."

"What's so complicated?" Maggie asked, logical and brutally honest to a fault. "Sean's left. Twice. Probability is high for a third time. Versus Trevor, who let's all be honest, still loves you, and you still love him, right?"

"I've always loved Trevor, but romantically, it didn't work last time. Not without Sean. I couldn't be with Trevor that way and not feel like a piece was missing. And with anyone else, it feels like two pieces are missing."

"You sure there's not enough there? With Trevor?" Rachel asked, her gaze downcast as she tossed her plate and napkins into the trash. "There's a lot to love there."

Charlie snagged her trailing hand before she sank all the way back in her chair. "I'm sorry. Is this awkward?" Caught up in her own conflict, she'd forgotten that Trevor and Rachel had dated in high school. Charlie suspected Rachel still held a torch for Trevor, but it had never stopped Rachel from telling her to go for it with Trevor in college and being there for them both after Sean had left.

Rachel squeezed her fingers. "That was a lifetime ago. You two were always meant to be."

"Exactly, so back to what I was saying," Maggie pressed. "What's more important? A friendship—possibly more—with the man who's been by your side most of your life or taking a flyer on a guy who's left twice already?" She popped another hush puppy into her mouth and swiped her hands together in a 'that's that' gesture. "Seems like easy math to me, Miss Math Team."

Easy math. Not even. There were equations from the past that didn't add up. New variables in the present. And a future unknown to solve for. This wasn't easy math. It was the hardest fucking problem of her life.

And that wasn't even counting the dead bodies.

Charlie clocked Sean from fifteen feet away, strutting across the bullpen floor toward her office. He wore a cocky grin and thumped a rolled yellow paperback against his palm. Her insides were no less settled after the meal with Maggie and Rachel, but when faced with a mound of paperwork and a stack of press calls to return, she welcomed the interruption. She held a finger to her lips as Sean strode into her office and cut her gaze to where Trevor still slept on the couch. Sean's face softened, fondness and longing written all over his handsome features, and Charlie reached for her phone. She wanted to snap a picture so Trevor could see that look for himself, so he could better understand why Sean hadn't been able to bring himself to say goodbye to him either time he'd left before. It would have ripped them both to shreds.

She wasn't fast enough. Sean wiped the expression away before she got the camera app open. He dropped into one of her visitor chairs and threw his feet up on her desk. She lifted her heels to the opposite desk corner, mirroring his relaxed posture. "Make yourself at home." She spoke softly so as not to wake Trevor, but the way he slept, hard and deep, it would take more than just her and Sean talking to rouse him.

Smirking, Sean nodded toward the perilously leaning stack of pink message slips. "How's that backlog of press calls going?"

"I got halfway through before Rachel brought in another stack. Please tell me this isn't my future if I—" She cut herself off before she spoke out of turn and before she spoke too loudly. "If things go well tomorrow."

"Higher-ups usually handle the press, though I might have caused a few stacks like that."

"Speaking for your superiors, you owe them a shitload of whisky."

He tipped his face to the ceiling and laughed out loud, the warmth of it filling her office and waking the slumbering man behind them on the couch.

"Could you be any louder?" Trevor grumbled.

Sean twisted in his chair. "You said the same thing to me that first day on campus."

Trevor straightened and ran a hand through his messy hair. "Because I could hear you and Charlie howling from halfway down the hall."

Charlie remembered that day with the same kind of fondness Sean had just looked upon Trevor with. She'd been unpacking crates in Cal and Trevor's dorm room when Sean had barged in. A dangerously high armload of boxes blocked his face and his view of the rolled rug in the middle of the floor. Racing across the room, she'd stretched out her arms and yelled for him to stop, but it was too late.

Caught in the avalanche of falling boxes, she'd tumbled backward, headed for the floor, but at the last second, a strong arm banded around her waist and cushioned her fall.

Pinned beneath an attractive stranger with messy dark hair and bright blue eyes, she'd found herself at a loss for words. But only for a moment. Once she got her breath back, she smiled up at him and asked, "Anderson Hale?"

"*Sean* Hale. Leave my father out of it." He'd raked those captivating eyes down her body, hotter than any fumbling high school fooling around she'd done with guys. When his eyes returned to hers, they were several shades darker, and a blinding white smile split his handsome face. "Or you can just refer to me as your future husband," he'd declared with complete confidence.

The absolute arrogance of his statement had prompted her to respond with an equally absurd rebuttal. "I hope you like handcuffs."

He'd growled playfully. "Kinky. I like it."

"I'm your roommate's sister, the other one's best friend, and the police chief's daughter," she'd said. "Keep making ridiculous declarations and either they'll beat the shit out of you or my dad will have you in cuffs."

His eyes had widened comically. "Friend zone for you."

"Probably the safest place for *you*," she'd said, biting back laughter.

Sean hadn't, laughing out loud, and then so had she, the two of them cracking up on the dorm room floor, which was exactly how Trevor had found them. Sean had stayed in that friend zone for almost a year, even as he'd become more with Trevor. But the following summer, before their sophomore year, they'd become more, all of them together, and four years later, Sean's prediction had almost come true. And damn it all to hell, the disappointment that it hadn't happened still stung.

Sean didn't give her long to dwell on her lingering heartache. He shot out of his chair and stood in the middle of her office, sniffing the air like one of the K-9 shepherds. "Where're the goods?"

"The goods?"

"Barbecue, fried chicken, and hush puppies if I'm not mistaken."

"You're not mistaken," she replied, amused at his single-minded focus.

"Corner fridge," Trevor said, and she shot him a glare for conspiring with the enemy. He waggled his brows at her. "I call a drumstick."

Sean had the door of her mini-fridge open before she could stand. "This is perfect." He settled back in the visitor chair with the bag of leftovers and jug of tea. "Mark this one off the list."

"Do I even want to know what list you're talking about?" Charlie asked.

He took a slug of tea straight from the jug and hummed in pleasure. "The Hanover gastronomical tour. Still need to hit Krispy Kreme, Bojangles, and find fried okra."

"You said you were back in the States." Trevor moved to the chair beside Sean and swiped the drumstick from the box in his lap. "Where are you, California?"

Sean choked on his tea, then recovered and split a glare between them. "It's not the same, and you know it." He popped two hush puppies into his mouth at once. "Really," he mumbled around the mouthful of food. "I'm disappointed in both of you. Bad, bad Southerners."

Charlie tossed a stack of napkins at each of them to hide her smile. "I was saving that for tomorrow. It'll be a miracle if there's any left."

"I'll tell you what'll be a miracle," came a third voice, and Charlie looked beyond Sean and Trevor to Jaylen standing in her doorway. The officer's step faltered at seeing Trevor there, and Diego, behind him, nearly ran into his back.

She waved them both in. "It's fine. He's read in," she said. "Now, what'll be a miracle?"

"If we can get a hold of Sarah Barnett's phone records," Jaylen said as he and Diego claimed the couch Trevor had vacated.

"She's not cooperating?" Sean asked, setting aside his food.

Diego ran a hand through his hair. "She's willing to cooperate."

"So what's the problem?"

"She's on her parents' cell plan."

Charlie shrugged. "So they have to consent. It's nothing we haven't run into before."

Sean leaned forward, resting his elbows on his knees. "But will Duncan Barnett allow that?"

She hung her head and cursed. "Back into the sea of politicians we go."

"You might be on to something," Sean said.

She righted her face. "You've got a theory?"

"Hold that thought," he said. "First things first, I can swing the phone records."

"FBI?"

"Marsh is a cyber legat. Best hacker I know and has a knack for trouble."

Charlie shook her head, not at all surprised. Sean had already hinted at not being the most straitlaced of agents, and it sounded like his friend was no better.

He twisted in his seat toward Diego and Jaylen again. "How long were Sarah and Julian sleeping together?"

Trevor growled and munched on his drumstick.

Jaylen snickered and Diego fought not to as he answered Sean. "About a month. She's in his summer Intro to Mythology class."

A fifty-year-old married man seducing nineteen-year-old girls. Julian was handsome, powerful, and had a way with words, but anyone with half a brain would recognize him for the philandering bastard he was.

Swallowing her disgust, Charlie asked her detectives, "Did she have any connection to Professor Marshall?"

Jaylen shook his head.

"What about her parents if they found out about the affair?" she asked Sean.

"Can't be dismissed." He adjusted in the chair and crossed an ankle over his knee. "But I think you were right yesterday. Easier to let the affair run its course. And I'd be surprised if Duncan had anything to do with Jeff's murder. They were both GOP, but I don't think they knew each other personally. I'll ask Marsh, though I don't think it fits the pattern."

"And we're back to your theory," Charlie said.

He grinned wide, something she was getting more used to, for better or worse. The better part—that despite what was going on for him with Saul, with her and Trevor, and with the gruesome case, Sean's confidence and humor were bubbling to the surface. The worse part—said confidence and humor had always been a fucking turn-on, had always kept her and Trevor from being too serious.

Seeing that confidence in a professional context was even sexier. He held up the yellow book, a ragged Cliffs-Notes guide for Shakespeare's *Four Tragedies*. "Bought it off a kid on campus."

Trevor tossed the cleaned drumstick into the trash can and wiped off his hands. "You know I have like ten of those in my office."

"He'll have a nice dinner out."

Trevor's eyes widened. "How much did you pay him?"

"Boys." She crossed her arms and waited for them to settle. "Sean, what did you learn from Mr. Cliffs?"

"What Trevor said about Shakespeare's *Four Tragedies* earlier got me thinking." He flipped to a dog-eared page in the book. "The clue from Jeff's crime scene and the way he was killed pointed us to Cordelia's death in *King Lear*. Cordelia was falsely accused of treason." He flipped farther in the book to another dog-eared page. "And Desdemona was falsely accused of adultery."

"Nothing false about Julian committing adultery," Trevor said.

"Exactly," Sean concurred. "And after your trip to Apex, sounds like there might be something to Jeff being guilty of academic treason. So, assuming the numbers before each clue represent Shakespeare's *Four Tragedies*, what if the killer is avenging what they perceive as the wronged heroines from those four plays?"

"Four," Jaylen said, following the train of thought she, Trevor, and Sean had worked out earlier in the day. "Two more to go?"

"Ophelia in *Hamlet*," Trevor replied. "Falsely accused of conspiring with Hamlet."

"And Lady Macbeth," Sean said. "That one's the rub." He tossed the CliffsNotes on her desk and braced his forearms on his knees. "Lady Macbeth *is* guilty. She goads Macbeth into killing the king. She's ruthless, ambitious, power hungry. I can't figure out how that one fits, but Ophelia is obvious."

"Let's start there." She kicked off her heels, stood, and paced the area behind her desk. "We're looking for someone actually guilty of conspiracy."

"The victim would be a man," Sean said, "if the pattern holds."

"Makes sense," Trevor said. "Killing men who are guilty of crimes the women unjustly died for. Pretty fucking poetic actually."

"And the killer?" Jaylen asked.

"Still up in the air," Sean answered.

"Jeff was a skinny fella," Diego said. "But he was

strung up good. And Julian wasn't a small guy. Either would be hard for a woman to handle."

"There was a pulley for bales of hay in the barn," Charlie reminded them. She paused in her circuit and slid the case file across her desk to Sean. "And Jeff's tox screen was positive for Diprivan, a fast-acting anesthetic. Maggie suspects the same will show up in Julian's panel."

"So focusing on the potential vic," Jaylen chimed back in, "likely a male, guilty of conspiracy of some sort. Where do we go from there?"

"The common threads between Jeff and Julian," Sean replied.

"HU," Trevor said.

"The iffy political connection," Charlie supplied.

"Duncan could be Ophelia," Sean said. "According to Saul, he's crooked as sin."

"Can we talk to Saul?" Trevor asked. "Might be he gives us something to go on."

The investigative high Sean had been riding popped like a bubble, his face falling along with his chin, a hand skirting up to his nape.

Charlie stepped in with the rescue. "Saul's not really an option."

Trevor opened his mouth to no doubt question further, but after a sharp shake of her head, he caught on, moving to the next possibility. "Craig too," he said. "After the incident with the cheerleaders last year—"

Diego huffed. "You mean how he covered up the date rape of those three young women by his buddy Teller's football players?"

Charlie nodded. "Conspiracy."

"Same way," Trevor said, "he and Teller covered up slipping *you* a Mickey and trying to do the same to you our senior year of high school."

Sean lurched to the end of his chair. "He did what?"

"He didn't succeed," Charlie said, though the fallout from the attempt—the tragedies that had ensued—made bile churn in her stomach. That night had included Trevor's fist in Craig's face, Craig busting his nose, and Teller, who's dad was the HU baseball coach, threatening to torpedo Trevor's baseball scholarship.

And her mother's death.

As if sensing the direction of her thoughts, Trevor helpfully brought the conversation back to the present. "It fits for Ophelia." He yanked his hair back into a bun with the rubber band from around his wrist. "Plus, Craig's younger brother is at HU, barely hanging on by his D average, and Craig guest lectures from time to time."

Charlie choked out a bitter laugh. "On what? How to be a dick?"

"Local government." Trevor framed his head with his hands, then made an exploding motion complete with sound effects. "Feeds his enormous ego. Only makes him a bigger dick."

"There's another possibility," Sean said. He wore an expression similar to the one he'd worn in the alley last week. He didn't want to say the thing he had to say.

She braced. "Out with it."

"Trevor."

The room instantly went wired. Trevor scraped back

his chair to stand, looming over Sean, and Diego and Jaylen bolted up from the couch to form a solid, threatening wall of muscle behind him. Charlie appreciated the show of support for one of their own, but Sean was only giving voice to the troubling connections she'd also made. The connections that had led her to keep Trevor at the station all day. "Guys," she said, "let him finish."

Trevor's betrayed glare stung, but then Sean lifted his hands and drew an even icier one his direction. "Obviously you didn't do this. You weren't even in town last night. But the facts can't be ignored." He lowered one hand and began ticking off fingers with the other. "You're a professor at HU, Jeff held out on your tenure, and Julian stole your wife. We might want to think about protective custody for you. Officially."

"You think he's a potential victim," Charlie surmised, at the same time Diego asked, "Guilty of conspiracy? Accessory to murder?"

As soon as the words left Diego's mouth, Charlie's eyes shot to Trevor. He knew the truth about her mother's death. Was that enough to make him guilty of conspiracy? And who else would know that?

It took a half second for Trevor to make the same connection, and he deflated instantly.

Ignoring Sean's quizzical expression, Charlie addressed the others. "Tell Wallace he's been upgraded to protective detail on Craig. Put him in a room at The Sand Dollar Inn. Book one for Trevor too. Should be vacancies now that the tourists are gone for the week. And keep digging into Jeff and Julian. Focus on the HU connections and note any other potential victims. Wally can help us there too."

Jaylen and Diego nodded, then booked it out the door.

"I'm going to go help," Trevor said. She opened her mouth to protest, but his pleading eyes stopped her. "Let me do something. Kill some time. If I have to spend all evening in a room next to Craig, you'll have another murder on your hands."

She circled her desk and clasped his hands. "I need to keep you safe."

"We both need to," Sean said from behind them, his voice full of the same alarm and concern as Charlie's. "As a precaution."

Trevor leaned forward and kissed her cheek, a bright flare of warmth zinging through her. His warm hands squeezing around hers magnified the effect. Until they were gone and cold rushed back in. He turned for the door and shot Sean a smirk over his shoulder. "You can drive me to the motel when you're ready to go. Safe and sound."

"I guess that leaves me to follow up on the Barnetts," Sean said, once it was just the two of them left in her office.

Charlie rested back on the edge of the desk. "Do you think Marie might know something? About Duncan?"

"Maybe. If she doesn't, I've got no problem confronting that asshole myself." His voice had an edge to it that made her think he wasn't just talking about Duncan's possible connection to the case. "But promise me one thing."

"What's that?"

"Have bail money on hand," he said, grin returning.

"I can do you one better." She dug in her pocket and withdrew a set of station keys. "I have the keys to the cell."

"Well, all right then," he drawled. "I'll call if there's trouble."

"You do that." She chuckled, turning around to gather the files on her desk. "Oh, Sean." She waited for him to stop and turn back to her over the threshold. "I didn't get to ask the other night. Where are they? Saul and Marie? I'd like to send a care package, but Paxton has offices all over. I didn't know which—"

He locked eyes with hers. "DC is the home office."

"Are you serious?"

After a moment's hesitation, he turned his back, took a step, then paused. And dropped a bomb that would've taken her legs out if she weren't still leaning against the desk. "I moved there last week."

CHAPTER TWELVE

———————————

Trevor yanked his hair into a knot and glared across the cab of his own fucking truck to the smug bastard in the driver's seat. "Tell me again why protective custody requires you to drive me, in my own ride, to the motel."

Sean shrugged. "You're the one who offered."

"I didn't mean it literally. Is this payback for not calling?"

Sean slapped his shoulder. "Now he's getting it." Trevor batted him away, and Sean put both hands back on the steering wheel. "You had to know it'd freak Charlie out."

It hadn't sounded like only Charlie was freaked out earlier—sure as hell didn't feel like it with Sean crowding him against that hallway wall—but Trevor didn't call him on that half-truth. He rolled down the window and propped an elbow on the ledge, head in his hand. "It wasn't intentional, and I didn't know Julian was gonna turn up dead." They hadn't yet made the *Four Tragedies* connection when he'd left. Maybe if they had, he would have pegged Julian for the next victim, but he sure as shit wouldn't have pegged Julian as having an affair, *already*, with a nineteen-year-old. He shivered, despite the hot and humid night air blasting his face. He shifted the conversation in a less unpleasant direction. "And Charlie was supposed to be in Wilmington this morning for that interview. I thought I'd be back—" Trevor cut short his explanation when Sean hung a right three streets too early. "Did you suddenly forget where the motel is?"

"Nope," he said. "Just remembered where something else was."

There wasn't much else on this road at all. There was only one place Sean could be headed. Face back toward the breeze, Trevor closed his eyes and tried to *woosah* himself to chill, to build a wall against another barrage of memories that were sure to pummel him when they reached their destination.

A barrier between him and the too-tempting man to his left.

Together with Charlie, Sean had expertly calmed him in the hallway when he'd learned of Julian's death. Then this evening in Charlie's office, Trevor had woken to the sound of much-missed laughter and fallen into the easy, familiar banter that had been a hallmark of their time together. With those old feelings primed, being out here with Sean now was like throwing a lit match at gasoline. One spark and all his good intentions—to protect Charlie, to protect himself, to move on—would go up in flames. And Sean Hale was always that damn spark.

Maybe grabbing hold of anger again would be easier. Countering the good memories with the aftermath of Sean leaving—Charlie withdrawn and unreachable, their one and only attempt to be together that had ended in tears and a week of radio silence during which he feared he'd lost his best friend. It was the longest they'd ever gone without talking, and it had been the most painful week of his life. All because of the asshole pulling Trevor's truck to a stop in the empty parking lot of the rusty, run-down batting cage that used to be "their spot."

Well, fuck him. "This is protective custody?" Trevor sneered.

Sean was already halfway out the door. "Get out of the fucking truck, Trev," he tossed over his shoulder. "We both need to hit something, not each other, or Charlie will kill us both."

Despite Trevor's souring mood, Sean's eager eyes and unvarnished truth were enough to get Trevor moving. He followed Sean toward the small clubhouse at the front of the fenced-in structure that stood among the grove of magnolias. Bad game, bad day, this was where they'd always gone to clear their heads. Where Trevor had been going to hide out long before Sean ever came to town. "You're lucky this place is still here."

"Not sure I'd call it luck considering you hold the deed to the land and rent it to your uncle for a dollar a year." They stopped outside the clubhouse, and Sean peered inside the glass door. "It's dark."

"It's nine o'clock at night and only open on the weekends anymore." Owing to his uncle's arthritis and because most kids nowadays seemed to always have a phone in their hands. Didn't leave much time or space for a baseball bat.

"You got a key, or do I need to pick the lock?"

Trevor nodded at his keyring still in Sean's hand. "Third one from the end."

Sean grinned. "Still a sentimental romantic."

Trevor's fingers ached to form a fist, but he forgot about that ache as soon as he stepped across the threshold and his heart ached worse. He came back here once a year to commemorate the day he, Sean, and Cal had won the College World Series. And now one of them was gone way too fucking early. He rubbed a hand over his chest, which did little to ease the pain. Neither did Sean's question about a different source of heartache. "Are your parents still in town?"

Sean didn't know about Trevor's visits to this place after he'd left. But he did know why Trevor had started coming here as a kid, his uncle letting him hang out whenever his parents came home from a months' long bender, usually still drunk, usually still fighting. He'd slept on the floor behind the counter where Sean stood loading balls into a bucket more than a few times.

"Gone," Trevor answered as he turned off the alarm and flipped on lights. "Somewhere." He joined Sean behind the counter, collecting a bat and bucket. "It's been years now. One good thing Tracy did for me." He flipped the big handle for the cage lights and led Sean outside. As the overhead flood lights flickered on, Trevor carried the bucket of balls out to the rickety old pitching machine. He loaded it up, turned it on, then returned to the line of batters' boxes with the empty bucket, shedding his dress shirt on the way. Down to his undershirt, he rejoined Sean in the middle batter's box just as the first pitch sailed by. Sean didn't pay it any attention, his gaze locked on Trevor, who leaned back against the dividing fence. "Been a while, Hale?"

As if his voice had broken the trance, Sean blinked fast a few times, then seemed to remember where he was... and what they'd been talking about.

"You wanna tell me about Tracy?" he asked as he stepped up to the plate, his stance as perfect as it had been a decade ago. A natural behind the plate.

"Nope."

Sean whiffed at the next pitch. Maybe not so natural anymore. Trevor lifted a brow. "Strike two."

He stepped back and started over. Tapped one toe in the dirt, then the other, then the tip of the bat against the plate. His usual routine. He lifted the bat over his shoulder, then flicked his eyes at Trevor. "Answer the question, Caldwell."

"She moved to town three years after you left." The machine pitched the next ball and Sean hit it clean, the crack of the bat an arrow of joy through the bubble of anger Trevor had been trying—and failing—to hold on to. Popped, it even allowed him to recall the joy of those early days with Tracy when he'd thought love was possible again. Because Sean was right; he was a sentimental romantic. "Annie met her first, at the hospital. Introduced us. We hit it off."

"I'd say so. You married her." Another hit, a ground ball that skirted over the packed-dirt infield and bounced off the base of the machine. Sean readied for another. Toe, toe, bat, lift. "When'd it go wrong?"

"Probably the first Henby dinner I took her to."

"Tough crowd?" He swung and missed the next pitch, the ball clanking off the fence behind Sean. He kicked it and the other missed balls over to Trevor.

Trevor gathered them back into the bucket. "The opposite actually. They welcomed her with open arms."

Pitch. Hit. A scorcher to center field. "I don't follow."

"She never believed that it wasn't Charlie's arms I wanted to be in."

Sean's piercing blue gaze cut to his as the next pitch sailed between them. "Was she right?"

"To a degree. What she didn't get was that Charlie's arms weren't enough."

Pitch, hit, a gorgeous arc all the way to the back fence.

Fuck if watching Sean Hale at bat wasn't still a turn-on.

"What happened with Julian?"

The interrogation, not so much, but the fact Sean could carry it on while still hitting most of the pitches was impressive. And fascinating enough that Trevor kept answering. "Neighbor told me. I told Tracy we could bring Julian in. I wasn't attracted to him, but she could be the connection that made the polycule work. I just needed the relationship with her. She could also have a relationship with him. But by then, she wasn't in love with me anymore."

"Charlie said she wasn't poly."

"That too. She always thought it was Charlie I wanted *instead* of her. She couldn't wrap her brain around the notion I could love and want them both. Or that I could be poly and be in a monogamous relationship if that's what she wanted."

"Most people don't get it." The next ball sped past, and their eyes clashed again over the plate. "Trev—"

He stepped up to the plate. "My turn." He connected on the first pitch, ground ball to short, and then Sean threw a fastball of his own.

"Why didn't you and Charlie try to find a third? If Tracy didn't work, someone else?"

Anger gone, joy depleting as the conversation wore on, Trevor was too exhausted to hold back the truth. He mentally collected all the balls and blitzed Sean with them. "Because *we* were all connected. Without you, something was always missing. And who the fuck else would've had the self-confidence to encourage two best friends to fall in love and be sure enough in themselves to know they'd still have a place among them." He slammed the bat into the next ball, a line drive to third. "Only you, Sean. Only you're that arrogant."

He didn't sound arrogant at all when he spoke. "I'm sorry, Trevor." His voice was soft, pained as if all those balls had pummeled him.

Trevor pitched another. "Why'd you leave us?"

"Jesus, you don't pull your punches."

"I thought that's why you liked me."

"Loved you."

Trevor hit a homer to center field.

Sean ended the game. "Saul's dying."

The bat fell from Trevor's hands. "Repeat that."

"I got a call from Marie right after police academy graduation. Saul had collapsed and was in surgery. Cancer."

If Trevor thought his heart had ached before... "Is he better?"

Sean whipped his head to the side and his Adam's apple bobbed. "Third time's gonna get him." He cleared his throat. "Any day now."

As soon as the next ball blew past, Trevor bolted across the plate, grabbed Sean by the arm, and dragged him to the other side of the fence and into his arms. "Fuck, baby, I'm sorry. I know how much he means to you." One orphan to another, Trevor knew how much it meant when someone else opened their arms and home and invited you into their family. Knew how much it hurt when you lost those people who were your second chance, your hope.

"I'm the one who should be apologizing."

"You forget I know how this mind works." Trevor cupped the back of his head, fingers threading through the short hairs, as so many pieces of the puzzle fell into place. "You ran to your family. You thought you'd have to stay and take over Paxton and you wouldn't ask us to leave *our* family."

All the breath, all the fight, rushed out of Sean and he melted into Trevor. His arms circled Trevor and his hands scorched a path up Trevor's back. "Fuck," Sean mumbled into his shoulder. "How do you always do that? Know exactly where my head's at."

Trevor had a good idea where it was now too. "If Saul's dying, that means you have to take over. Marie never wanted to. That's why you're back in the States?" Sean nodded, and Trevor could only laugh at fate turning the screws. Again. "Right when Charlie and I are finally ready to leave. Fucking timing." He drew back enough to see Sean's face, and when he noticed the tears gathering in the corners of his eyes, he gently cupped his cheeks, thumbs wiping away the moisture that escaped, savoring the familiar weight in his hands and the rough scrape of stubble under his palms. "KC? Is that where you need to be?" That's where Sean was originally from, where Paxton Industries was based, last he'd checked.

"No."

"Where then?"

"DC."

Trevor froze. "Are you fucking kidding me?"

"Saul's doctors are there. Better politics too." He swallowed hard and forced out an "I'm sorry."

He angled his face, trying to look away, but Trevor held firm, fingers tightening around his skull. "Stop fucking apologizing. Why didn't you tell us?"

"Because you're supposed to be moving on. I didn't want to stand in the way of whatever that looked like."

"Oh, baby." He leaned forward and rested his forehead against Sean's. "That plan got fucked the minute you showed up after the funeral." Out of balls, the pitching machine died, quiet descended, and Sean's rapid breaths were all Trevor could hear.

All he wanted to taste.

It would burn. Giving in to whatever this might be. Whether it was a good burn or a bad one, Trevor couldn't predict, but Sean was a fire he'd never been able to look away from. He slid his hands into Sean's hair, drawing him closer.

Rough lips ghosted across his. "Trev."

"Yeah, baby."

"Fucking kiss me."

The spark caught fire, and he crashed his mouth against Sean's, tongue diving between those rough lips and sweeping inside, tasting everything he couldn't get out of his mind the past month. The past ten years. Coffee and Sean and hunger. Sean's lust rivaled his own, his mouth greedy and his hands clutching at the back of Trevor's shirt. A groan rumbled from Sean's chest that vibrated against Trevor and sent an arrow of need straight to his dick. He needed to feel more of Sean, starting with his cock. He shuffled them back against the fence and thrust a thigh between Sean's legs, rubbing against Sean's erection. As hard as his own.

Sean rolled his hips and tore his mouth away on another groan. "Fuck, you feel good." He thrust again. "More... Fuck."

Trevor countered, but Sean's words had shaken loose Trevor's favorite memory from a month ago. Charlie writhing between them, begging for more. And on the heels of that one, a less pleasant memory from a decade ago. Charlie curled in the bed beside him, frustrated because there was more she—they—needed. Same as he and Charlie hadn't been able to get Sean out of their heads then, she was in Trevor's now, and as much as he wanted Sean, as much as he wanted to drop to his knees and take Sean's cock into his mouth, he also wanted to look up from that position and see Charlie's lust-darkened eyes watching from over Sean's shoulder, wanted to hear her voice directing him and Sean how to make it good for all of them.

He tore his mouth away, panting. "We need—"

"Charlie," Sean finished on a pant. Seemed she was on Sean's mind too. "I know."

"Does she know? About DC?"

He nodded, then skimmed his lips over Trevor's jaw, little nips and licks that kept him on edge. "I told her this evening."

"Good." He sighed and held Sean close, enjoying the gentle attention as his breaths slowed. "We'll talk. You need to tell us everything, including why you didn't come back."

Sean skated his hands around Trevor's sides and to his front, resting over his chest. "That's also a conversation we need to have with Charlie."

Trevor sensed it would be an unpleasant one, but if it got them to the pleasant part, to a place where maybe this would work, they owed it to themselves to try. The stars had aligned in their favor for once, and the romantic in him couldn't look away.

He covered Sean's hands with his and leaned forward

to press his lips to Sean's forehead. "We'll talk about it. We'll make it work. We have to."

"What are you doing down here?"

Trevor turned his head and squinted Charlie's direction. "Migraine."

"Lack of sleep and too much caffeine?"

He nodded, then slowly pushed himself to seated, pleased to find the throbbing headache he'd woken up with mostly gone. "Needed the quiet and darkness down here" —he gestured around the station's shadowed holding cell, even more so owing to that morning's rain—"while I waited for the meds to kick in."

She kicked off her heels outside the cell door then crossed the box on quiet feet, lowering herself next to him on the bench. "Wouldn't the hotel or my office couch be comfier than this?" She patted the narrow strip of cold cement between them.

"Ixnay on the hotel. That whole I might murder Craig thing. Ixnay on your office as it was Grand Central yesterday."

"Picky, picky." She rolled her eyes and bumped a shoulder against his. "Just be glad I'm not officially locking you up for that disappearing act you pulled."

The guilt that had been shoved aside yesterday by the twists and turns of the case, then by the twists and turns with Sean, made itself known again. He covered Charlie's hand on the bench. "Hey, I'm sorry I worried you, and I'm sorry I put more stress on you when there's enough already. It wasn't intentional. I was going to call."

She shot him a knowing side-eye. "After you got to Apex."

"After I got to Apex." No use lying. She had him dead to rights. Because she was a good cop and because she knew him better than anyone. "In fairness, I didn't know another body was gonna drop. And I thought you were going to be in the interview most of the day."

Her side-eye twinkled with humor. "Excuses, Caldwell." They both laughed, their soft chuckles reverberating around the quiet corner of the station, and when Charlie lifted her fingers, Trevor slid his in between them.

After the roller coaster of the past three days—fuck, the past month—the simple touch, the comfortable silence, was a balm. He enjoyed the easy quiet another minute before following up on the topic of conversation he'd left open. "Speaking of, tell me how the FBI interview went this morning. You're just back?"

She nodded. "Traffic to and from Wilmington was heavy for a Tuesday."

"Summer vacationers."

"Rain didn't help either." She leaned against the wall and closed her eyes. "It was kind of like an Internal Affairs interview, retreading the details of the Salazar case. Sean warned me the interviewing agent liked his rule book and no joke, we walked through every step of that op."

"Including what happened to Mitch and Cal?"

"He said the takedown was textbook."

"Like we keep telling you. It wasn't your fault." Maybe

she'd believe it now, hearing it from an impartial third party. He didn't press, though, wanting to hear how the rest of the meeting went. "And after that part of the interview?"

"We ran through a few case sims and discussed how I would approach them. Then he explained the training process and how assignments in CID work."

Like those times when he used to be in the dugout, checking his equipment or reviewing the stats for the next inning, and the crack of a well-hit ball would draw his attention back to the diamond, his heart raced with excitement. With the promise of a home run. "Wait, so you're in?"

"Pending clearances, yes."

"Holy shit, Charlie." He yanked her off the wall and into his arms. "I mean, I knew you'd get it, but... Holy shit!"

When she opened her eyes, her face scant inches from his, a potent mixture of pride, hope, and concern swirled in her dark gaze. "But it's real now."

"Take the job, Charlie," he implored. "You deserve this. We'll work everything else out. With the department, with Annie, with—" He cut himself off, still not quite believing last night at the batting cage with Sean was real. The hope and prospect he offered. But judging by Charlie's wide eyes and pink cheeks, her mind had gone to Sean too. And that look on Charlie's face only made other mental pictures crowd his mind. Charlie astride Sean's lap, head thrown back, lips parted, a flush creeping up her chest and neck. Of Sean's lips stretched around his cock and his body, sweaty and naked, beneath them. Of Charlie's lips colliding with his own, over and over, neither of them able to get enough, groaning against those lips as he'd come down Sean's throat.

Fuck. He shook himself out of the fantasy and back to reality, which also included the third person in those memories, but this wasn't the time or place. And they were missing a critical piece of the conversation. He shifted the conversation a different direction for now. "FBI offer aside, how are you?"

"Honest answer?"

He squeezed her fingers. "Always."

She tilted to the side, erasing the distance between them as she leaned her head on his shoulder. "Fucking exhausted."

The guilt returned and along with it the urge to shield her from the worst of whatever was to come. Never mind she was the one with the sidearm. He looped an arm around her shoulders, hugging her gently. "We'll get to the bottom of this. Then we'll sort out where we go from here."

He reconsidered—not regretted—his words as soon as they were out. Was he being too presumptuous? He knew what he wanted, what Sean wanted, but what about what Charlie wanted? But as she reached again for his hand and threaded her fingers through his, hope—and more— returned, the intimacy more than their usual casual affection. More like what they used to be. But maybe it was only comfort that she needed, given the enormity of the circumstances, including the fear Charlie voiced. "What if it has to do with Mom?"

"Then we'll deal with it. I'm not gonna disappear again. Promise." Curling his fingers around hers, he lifted their hands and kissed the back of Charlie's. "But Jeff and Julian had no connection to that night, then or now."

"We can't dismiss the possibility."

"In that case, you should be at the Sand Dollar too."

"Not if the killer is targeting men—"

He bumped her chin with their clasped hands, forcing her gaze up. "Charlie."

Defiant eyes glared right back. "I'll consider it."

"I need to keep you safe."

"You do remember I'm the cop, right?" She smiled softly, and he couldn't resist unfolding his index finger to trace the corner of it. Charlie's stuttered breath skated over his knuckles.

Followed by her lips.

It was a risk, putting all that was on the line for what could be. A risk he'd avoided taking after the last time Sean had left and he and Charlie had had to dig themselves out of heartbreak and claw their way back to friendship. A risk he shouldn't take after putting himself out there with Tracy and getting burned again. But damn it, this was Charlie, her eyes darkened, her head tilted invitingly, her warm breath rushing over his lips as her eyelids fluttered shut.

"Charlotte! You down here?"

Abel's shout from around the corner startled them apart. Except for their hands, which remained clasped.

"Coming!" Charlie called back, then cast him a half-hooded, half-embarrassed look.

He spared her the latter, standing and pulling her up. "Duty calls, Deputy Henby."

She squeezed his fingers with a smile. "You want in on this meeting?"

"Think I'll skip this one. Need to catch up on some work."

"Can't say I blame you. It only seems to get worse."

She started for the door, but with her hand still in his, he stopped her midstep. "I need to keep you safe too." With the future potential he'd glimpsed with Sean last night, then with her just now, he needed that more than ever. "For whatever this might be."

She lifted his hand and kissed the back of it. "For whatever this might be."

CHAPTER THIRTEEN

Charlie leaned a hip against her desk, making a quick call to Annie while Abel gathered everyone in the conference room.

After four rings, she was about to hang up and try again when Annie finally answered. "Hey, sis. Sorry about that." She sounded out of breath, and the background noises weren't the usual library ones.

"Everything okay there?"

"Yeah," she said. "I was just in the laundromat. Dryer's busted at home again, and of course the only machines open here were the top ones. Why God denied me the extra few inches you got, I'll never know."

Charlie chuckled. "Not how you wanted to spend your afternoon, I'm sure."

"Honestly, it's better than the slower than slow library today." She dragged out the second *slow*, and Charlie's chuckle became a full laugh. "Too nice out. The only folks who came in this morning were those who had to, and they made quick work of it." A door opened and closed in the background and Annie excused herself, probably stepping out of the way. "How's Trevor?" she asked once it quieted again. "He texted he was back, but we've been playing phone tag since."

"Safe and sound."

"Oh, thank god." Annie's relief carried over the line as did her concern. "How'd he take the news about Julian?"

"Not well. He's worried about Tracy."

"I was dropping a book off for a patient at the hospital and swung by to check on her. You were right. She didn't want to talk to me."

Charlie wished there was a way to ease the hurt apparent in her sister's voice. No matter her own opinion of Tracy, she didn't want Annie to lose a friend. They'd lost enough lately, and it would be a shame for that friendship to have survived Tracy and Trevor's divorce only to end now. "I'm sorry, Annie. I know you two are close."

"She didn't look good, Charlie. I heard her say the funeral is Thursday. Are you going?"

"I'll watch from a squad car. You?"

"I'm going to try to make it."

Charlie wasn't surprised. Her sister was fiercely loyal that way. "I'll be your backup," she teased, hoping to lighten the mood but also wanting Annie to know she was more than ready to come to her defense if Tracy caused a scene.

"Thank you," Annie said, and Charlie was glad to hear the relief again. "Was there something else you needed?"

"I was hoping you could swing by Trevor's place and

pack him an overnight bag." He'd had a change of clothes leftover from the trip to Apex, but she couldn't be sure he had another, and she knew Annie had a key to his place, same as her.

"Why?"

"We're keeping him in protective custody."

"Why?" her sister repeated.

"We're taking precautions since he's connected to both victims."

"Isn't that kind of extreme?"

Charlie cringed, then ran a hand down her face to wipe it away. This was not a conversation she wanted to have over the phone, especially from the station. It wasn't a conversation she ever wanted to have with Annie, but she had to. Her sister didn't know the truth about their mother's death, and finding the right time to share it was proving impossible. Things had been so strained after the funeral that Charlie hadn't wanted to throw another log onto the fire. Hell, at the time, she was still processing the letter—the confession—herself. Annie's mood had improved since, and so had things between them, and Charlie hadn't wanted to disrupt that. And now with the move and the potential job, things between them were more like a roller coaster. Conversations like the one now were pleasant; the one the other night at Annie's, not so much. She was having a harder time than usual getting a read on her sister, but would there ever be a good time to have this conversation? Annie deserved the truth, and Charlie would rather she hear it from her than anyone else.

"I'll explain everything, I promise, but for right now, I need to focus on keeping Trevor safe."

"Of course. You love him."

"I do," she said. A year ago she would have qualified that with *as family, as a friend*, but after the past month, all her caveats where Trevor was concerned were on shakier ground. Only one reason for that.

As if hearing her thoughts, Annie asked, "Is this about Sean?"

"I don't know," she admitted. "He's back, and things are different."

"But also the same?"

"I think his being here is reminding us both how we felt all those years ago."

"What happens when Sean leaves again?"

That was the million-dollar question. Would she and Trevor crash and burn again? Did they have to with Sean in DC too? They were all leaving, yet all going to the same place. A first. But if they gave it a shot, what happened years from now if something happened to one of them?

"Hey, sis," Annie said. "Where'd you go?"

Charlie sighed and ran a hand through her hair. "Trying to find the answers."

"Good thing you're an awesome detective. The FBI would be lucky to have you."

The smile in Annie's voice both pleased and confused Charlie. "You mean that? You seemed upset with me the other night. About DC and the job."

"I'm sorry about that," she said. "I'm doing better since

everything, but sometimes the emotions still get the better of me. I got scared about possibly losing you too."

Like she had Mom, Dad, and Cal.

"Annie—"

"But we can't let fear hold us back. That's what my therapist says. We move forward, the best we can."

Her upbeat certainty helped put Charlie at ease. As did Maggie cutting across the bullpen toward the conference room and flagging her down with a stack of papers. Time to go to work, to be the detective Annie was proud of. "Speaking of moving forward, Maggie just got here and looks like maybe she has something helpful on this case."

"Go," Annie said. "I'll finish up here, then I'll swing by Trevor's and throw some stuff in a bag."

"That'd be great. He's at the Sand Dollar."

"I'll get it to him."

"Thanks, A."

"Sure thing, sis. Bye for now."

Charlie ended the call and slumped in partial relief. At least that conversation had gone well. The nugget of relief evaporated, though, at seeing Sean following in Maggie's footsteps. Clean-shaven and dressed in a dark suit, she couldn't deny how well he still wore one.

The case, Henby, focus!

If she wanted any future with Trevor and possibly Sean too, she had to solve this case and get them all on the other side of it—alive.

Charlie entered the conference room where Sean and Maggie were gathered with the rest of her team. "Talk to me."

The ME slid a folder across the table. "Tox screen results on Julian confirmed Diprivan. Same as Professor Marshall."

"Anything else?"

"Clean. He took a shower when he got home, so no fluids or fibers. Unfortunately, I don't expect much more."

"Diprivan is a controlled substance?"

Maggie nodded and pushed another document across the table. "I called the manufacturer and got a list of all the recent orders in Hanover and the county."

Sean peered at the document over her shoulder. "There's only one buyer. HU Med."

Charlie's head shot up, her gaze split between Abel and Maggie. "You don't think?"

"It's an anesthetic," Maggie said.

Sean snagged the list and reviewed it more closely. "What am I missing?"

"Tracy Hirsch is a surgical nurse at HU Med," Abel told him.

"Wasn't she on shift at the hospital when Julian was killed?"

Charlie pointed at Jaylen. "Call the hospital and double-check that. Now."

"On it."

He ducked out of the conference room as Sean tossed out another question. "Does Tracy have any connection to Jeff?"

"None that I know of. But Trevor does."

"Revenge?" Abel speculated. "A frame-up?"

"I wouldn't put it past her," Maggie said. "Especially if she'd found out what her ass of a husband was up to."

Diego rolled his eyes toward the ceiling as if asking God for patience. When he righted his gaze, Charlie laughed. "What else you got?"

"Another possible lead." He withdrew his phone and tapped the screen, glancing down at his notes then back up. "We caught up with Sarah Barnett yesterday outside her French class. The lecturer, Beth Martin, let us use her classroom to talk."

"Go on."

"Sarah called us about an hour ago. She had a class in the same building this morning, and Professor Martin was waiting for her afterward."

Sean rested against the edge of the conference table. "That's odd."

"Not necessarily," Diego replied. "Beth, by Sarah's own account, seems to genuinely care about her students. Sarah didn't think much of it at first."

"I'm sensing a *but*," Abel said.

"*But* today, Beth asked more pointed questions. Not the how-are-you sort but more the what-did-the-officers-ask-you-about sort."

"Female. Connected to HU." Sean raised two fingers, then a third halfway. "She look like someone who could maneuver Jeff and Julian?"

"About Charlie's height and build."

Sean finished raising the third finger.

Charlie went for four. "Any connection to Jeff or Julian?"

"We're looking into it now."

"Did Beth know about Sarah and Julian?"

"We asked Sarah," Diego said. "She didn't tell Beth about Julian, but the professor did confiscate her phone for texting in class a couple weeks ago."

"Let me guess," Abel said. "Pictures?"

Diego nodded. "Seems to be a trend with kids these days."

Jaylen reappeared at the door to the conference room. "Tracy was on shift according to the scheduling nurse, but I think we should go down there and talk with others who were on that night. See if there are any irregularities."

"I'll go with you," Abel said. "Throw around some weight."

"And let's dig into Beth Martin," Charlie added. "Seems a more likely connection than any political one."

"I'll get started on that," Diego said.

Her team activated, she thought how best to use Sean and his resources. "Can you get your hacker on Martin's phone records?"

"Did someone say hacker?"

Charlie spun toward the Texas accent that boomed from the doorway... and rocked back on her heels. The voice wasn't wholly unfamiliar—she'd spoken to Agent Marshall on the phone twice—but it was louder and deeper in person, not crackling over a patchy line. And Agent Marshall himself looked nothing like what she'd expected. He was spindly Jefferson Marshall's son and a cyber legat for the FBI. She'd pictured a likewise spindly agent, rumpled and overworked, who lived on Red Bull and nothing else. At no time had she pictured a man as big and broad as Abel, in his midforties with bronze skin, a sprinkling of silver in his dark hair, and flecks of amber in his dark eyes. Add to that the wide-brimmed white hat and pointed-toe boots, the worn Levi's and rust-colored Long-horns T-shirt, and Emmitt Marshall shouted *cowboy*.

Nothing about him shouted *hacker*.

More surprising than the agent's appearance, though, was Sean's reception to his arrival. Barreling past Charlie, he practically launched himself at Agent Marshall.

Marshall stood firm and returned the fierce hug, slap-ping Sean's back. "It's good to see you, Hale."

Sean drew back, one corner of his mouth lifted. "Missed you too, though I gotta say"—he patted the other man's T-shirt covered chest—"not exactly funeral attire."

Agent Marshall straightened Sean's coat and tie like he'd done it countless times before. "You're fancy enough for the both of us."

His voice was rumbly and affectionate, and Charlie suddenly felt like an intruder. Like the roller coaster her life had been on lately had taken another unexpected turn.

Thank fuck for Maggie, who had absolutely no problem butting into the agents' reunion. "Umm, Sean, care to introduce us to your friend?"

"Pardon, ma'am," Agent Marshall said, beating Sean to the introductions. He removed his hat and shot Maggie a grin. "Emmitt Marshall." And damn if Maggie didn't put a hand to the table to catch herself.

Charlie bit back a laugh that died when Agent Marshall's dark eyes landed on her. A warm smile stretched across his ruggedly handsome face. "You must be Charlie." He crossed the room, a hand outstretched. "I've heard a lot about you. All of it good."

Her gaze shot to Sean, who ducked his chin but not before she saw the streaks of red hit his cheekbones. Agent Marshall's hand closed around hers, bringing her back to the man directly in front of her. She cleared her throat. "Agent Marshall," she said. "Good to put a face to the voice."

"That's enough of that *Agent* shit," he said with a wink. "Just Marsh, please, and tell me how I can help." He jutted a thumb over his shoulder at Sean. "Should I start by getting that one in line?"

She lifted a brow. "You think you can?"

His dark eyes twinkled with mischief. "Oh, I know I can, sweetheart."

Standing next to a collared priest, a raised casket, and a freshly dug grave, the funeral director waved them over. Two more of his staff waited in coveralls a few rows back, wiping sweat from their brows, their shovels leaned against a nearby headstone.

"We're not done with this conversation," Marsh said to him, making sure Sean knew he wasn't off the hook. Payback no doubt for the earlier needling. As Marsh stepped forward, hand outstretched, Sean hung back. After a few words with the director and priest, Marsh circled to the opposite end of the casket and removed his hat. Sean joined him, offering silent support as the priest recited a generic service. When the five minutes were over, and Jeff's casket was being lowered into the ground, Marsh handed his hat to Sean and knelt at the side of the grave, tossing in a fistful of dirt. With his other hand, he withdrew a rosary from his coat pocket and began the recitations in Spanish. When he was done, he stood, crossed himself, and pocketed the rosary.

"You do that to piss him off?" Sean asked as he handed Marsh back his hat. They reversed several steps from the grave, the funeral staff coming forward to close it.

"Mostly." He swiped a hand over his brow and into his hair, slicking it back before resettling his hat. "That and the whole Catholic guilt thing. Hard to shake."

"You didn't think anyone from the town would want to be here?"

"I can't imagine he suddenly stopped being an asshole."

Marsh's reply garnered a disapproving glare from the

funeral director, and Sean decided to wait until he and his staff cleared out before continuing.

"From what I've seen of this case and heard from Trevor, he didn't."

"I asked Mom if she wanted to come."

"Oh boy." Sean couldn't wait to hear the rest of this story. Marsh's mom was a riot. So was her wife.

Marsh grinned. "She told me she had to help Irina birth a calf, then they were gonna get drunk on Dom and fuck all night long."

Sean laughed out loud. "I love your moms."

"They love you too." Marsh turned from the grave, moving in the direction of the exit. "Speaking of moms, anything further from Marie?"

"Saul's vitals are weaker, but he's still hanging on."

"Doesn't want to leave his lady. Or you."

Sean cleared his throat and ignored his stinging eyes. "Once we get this case and things sorted, I need to get up there. She said not to come until after, but—"

"But you want to be there. I get it. Maybe not for that asshole"—he jutted a thumb over his shoulder toward Jeff's grave—"but if anything were to ever happen to Mom or Irina, I'd be on the first plane out."

"You're here for me, yes, but also for your dad." Sean reached out and ran a hand over Marsh's upper back. "Don't sell yourself short."

"Thanks, Hale." He patted the hand still on his shoulder. "Now, speaking of sorted, you mentioned Trevor."

Yep, not off the hook. Sean nudged him a different

direction, physically and conversationally. "You can meet him later. Someone else I want to introduce you to first."

Marsh, however, wasn't to be deterred. "Charlie's a looker," he said. "I can see why you're hooked."

Heat hit Sean's cheeks and he looked anywhere but at his friend.

Marsh's laughter boomed around the wide-open cemetery, sending several crows scattering off headstones. "That blush, Hale. There's a reason you could never do undercover work."

"Says the giant cowboy."

"You got that right. There's a reason I work behind a computer." He added a quiet "mostly" that made Sean slow and loop an arm through his. That *mostly* had cost them a dear friend, and the loss, while a couple years old now, still stung whenever it came up for either of them. Marsh, though, as was his way, didn't let them linger on the sadness for long. "So, where do things stand with your exes?"

"I'm working on it." After the scorching kiss with Trevor earlier and the heat that seemed to flare anytime he was within ten feet of Charlie, he wouldn't deny wanting to know what would happen when all three of them were in the same room again. And with the knowledge they were going to be in DC too... Possibilities that included him in their plan to move on were hard to look away from, *if* he could make them happy again.

"Am I going to be a problem?" Marsh asked.

"You're gay and not poly, so no."

Marsh lifted a brow. "Charlie know that?" And lifted it higher. "Trevor?"

Sean blew out a breath. "No, I need to have that talk with them, but there are a few other conversations that need to come first." He drew to a stop and tilted his head toward the angel statue in front of them.

"Alice?"

Sean nodded, and Marsh removed his hat, approaching respectfully. That same night Marsh had let slip about Brax, Sean had confessed the secret he'd been carrying for years. A secret he couldn't keep from Charlie and Trevor if he wanted another shot with them. "They both deserve to know why I left and stayed away. And they deserve to know the truth about Alice's death if they don't already."

Marsh circled Cal's grave. "You think they know?"

"There've been a few times where I thought she might. And when we identified the next victim as Ophelia..."

"Guilty of conspiracy."

Sean rolled his eyes. "Everyone's a Shakespeare expert but me. I had to get the damn CliffsNotes."

Marsh smirked. "Probably because you were too busy chasing a certain pair in college."

"Oh, and you weren't chasing all the guys?"

He twirled his hat, caught it by the brim, and landed it perfectly on his head. "I can multitask." He made a go-on gesture. "Now, you were saying about Alice?"

Arms crossed, Sean rested against Mitch's gravestone. "She tried to hide it, but Charlie reacted strongly when it was suggested Trevor could be the next victim."

"It could be something else."

"What else could there be?"

"It's been ten years, Sean. A lot could have happened."

He flew off the gravestone, bearing down on Marsh as the sting of betrayal burned in his chest. "You investigated them?"

It was a bedrock of their friendship, one of the first ground rules he'd laid down when they'd become tight and when he'd discovered what Marsh could do with a computer.

Marsh met his charge, and in the blink of an eye, he had both of Sean's arms twisted behind his back and his torso forced over Cal's headstone. Fuck if Sean didn't forget about that whole military training thing sometimes. "You know me better than that," Marsh hissed in his ear, all humor gone from his voice. "I only dug when you asked me to."

"I'm sorry," Sean relented, justly scolded. He forced his body to go limp and waited for Marsh to release him.

When Marsh didn't after a few seconds, Sean twisted his head and looked back at him. "You gonna let me up sometime today?"

"I dunno," he said, humor returned like the last five seconds hadn't just happened. "Maybe I like you there."

"Barbecue in it for you."

Marsh shifted so his hold was one-handed and doffed his hat with the other. "Did you forget I'm from Texas?"

"Fine," Sean sighed, knowing what his friend was really after. "A dozen chocolate glazed."

"Now we're talking!" Marsh yanked him up, both of them laughing, and Sean made the extra few steps to fold his arms around him again. "I'm glad you're here." His parents, then Saul and Marie, had never been shy about affection, had drilled it in to him to always let the ones you love know it in case you might lose them. And he'd almost lost Marsh once. He wouldn't hold back.

And he was done holding back with Trevor and Charlie too.

CHAPTER FIFTEEN

"What happened to staying at the Sand Dollar last night?"

Charlie glanced up from the stack of files on her desk to find Trevor standing in her office doorway. Dressed in sweatpants and a T-shirt, he held his duffel in one hand, a tray of coffees in the other, and wore an unamused expression to match his unamused voice. "You were supposed to stay somewhere safe."

Charlie closed the file she was working on and laid her pen on top of it. "I was safe."

"Charlotte—"

"I slept there." She pointed at the couch to his right. "Safe and sound."

He tossed his bag onto said couch and crossed the office to her. "You pulled an all-nighter?" He rounded the corner of her desk and rested a hip beside her, unloading the coffees to a spot she cleared for him. "Did you get any sleep?"

"A few hours." She spread her hands, indicating the files on her desk. "This Shakespeare case isn't our only one. It's summer season." She gestured at one stack. "I've got half a dozen break-ins." At another. "DUIs." At a third. "Couple domestic disturbances." At the tallest teetering one. "And that hodgepodge of mostly teens behaving badly. Needed to catch up."

"You should've called." He snuck a foot under her chair and gave it a teasing push. "I would've kept you company."

She hooked her ankle around his, keeping herself from rolling too far and keeping him close. "I'm not sure how much work I would've gotten done with you here." Their eyes clashed, held, and heat tumbled in her belly, remembering again that moment yesterday in the cell downstairs, remembering all those moments from a decade ago when Trevor used to try to distract her—with tickles, touches, and tastes—during tutoring sessions. She still felt bad about that C he got in calculus. If his mouth hadn't been so damn tempting...

Then and now, turning up in a sexy grin. Charlie suspected he was remembering the same moments she was, confirmed as he reached out and traced his fingers up her thigh. "I'll try not to distract you too much today."

She tangled her hand with his but didn't move it away. "That's a lie if I ever heard one."

He shrugged, not the least bit sorry, and took a gulp from one of the coffees. "You can send me back to the motel, but fair warning, if I have to stay another hour in that room next to Craig's as he bitches and moans about *all the work he has to do*, poor Wally is gonna quit from having to play referee. I can't tell you how many times I banged on the wall the past two nights."

She leaned back in her chair and laughed, only righting herself when the scent of freshly brewed coffee wafted close to her nose. "Probably didn't help your headache."

"Not at all." Trevor handed her the coffee. "Think you can get this case done today?"

"Someone's in a hurry." She lifted the cup and took a sip of ambrosia.

"Sean told me about DC."

And nearly scorched the back of her throat. She'd expected another quip about Craig; not *that* revelation. How did he know? How long had he known? Was he pissed she hadn't told him? Once she was sure she wasn't going to choke, she set the cup down, reclaimed his free hand, and started with her last concern, the most impor-tant. "I'm sorry I didn't—"

"It's fine, honey." He squeezed her fingers. "I'm sorry I didn't say anything either. He told me Monday night, but I didn't want you to be biased going into the interview."

"And then yesterday got away from us."

"There's a lot going on, but when this case lets up, we need to talk. All of us."

Her gaze shot from their entwined fingers to his face, her heart jumping from her chest into her throat. "Trevor, what are you saying?"

Shifting, he set aside his cup and brought his warm

hand to her cheek. "I think we need to consider *all* our options."

She angled her face into the warmth, into the hope his words offered. And offered some of her own. "Then we'll solve the case today."

A knock came at her door, and Trevor lowered his hand. She rolled in the chair so she could see around him and spied Diego poking his head into the room.

"Got a lead, Deputy."

A good start. "I'll be right there."

As she stood, Trevor lifted his hand and snapped his fingers. "Abracadabra."

She rolled her eyes and grabbed their coffees, shoving Trevor's against his chest. "Shut up and drink your coffee."

Laughing, he slid off the desk without the proffered cup and grabbed his duffel off the couch. "Take mine to the conference room. I'm going to duck into the locker room and shower. Hot water at the motel is iffy."

She wrinkled her nose as she followed him out. "So *that's* why you stink."

"Shut up and drink your coffee," he said, throwing her words back at her. "No one needs your precaffeinated crazy."

He wasn't wrong. As he headed toward the stairs, she entered the conference room, Sean holding the door open for her. "Where's Trevor headed?" Sean asked, his eyes tracking Trevor across the bullpen floor.

"To shower and change downstairs."

"Good." Trevor disappeared down the stairs, and

Sean's attention refocused on her. Or rather the coffees in her hand. "Which one's Trevor's?"

She lifted the left one and he promptly slid it from her hand, claiming it for himself. "Probably better we discuss this before he gets back."

She closed the door behind them. "Discuss what?"

Marsh's deep drawl echoed from the far end of the table. "Beth Martin's phone records."

Charlie's attention swung to him, and though he might not have liked his father much, she recognized the dark jeans, black shirt, and black cowboy hat for what it was. Mourning. She'd been there herself not so long ago; still was to a degree. She walked the length of the table and took one of Marsh's hands in hers. "I'm sorry for your loss," she said. "And I'm sorry that wasn't the first thing I said to you yesterday. It should have been."

Marsh's eyes flicked over her shoulder in Sean's direction, and if she weren't mistaken, Charlie saw a glint of approval in them. And that same twinkle of mischief she'd glimpsed in them yesterday. He brought his gaze back to her, lifted her hand, and kissed the back of it. "He always said you were one of the good ones."

"I'll try better to live up to that." She squeezed his hand, then after a shot of caffeine, turned toward the papers he'd spread on the table. "Now, tell me what you found?"

"Abel said you might recognize this number." Marsh tapped a finger next to several highlighted entries on Beth's phone records, all outgoing calls to the same local number.

A number Charlie knew well. "Tracy."

"According to those," Abel said from across the table where he stood next to Diego, "Beth called Tracy multiple times during the past two weeks, including at three o'clock the morning Julian was killed and again at nine, right after the crime scene techs cleared out of the house."

"Did you confirm Tracy was at the hospital that night?"

"We did, with two nurses and the surgeon she was assisting. I spoke to one of the nurses again just now, and she said Tracy slipped out midsurgery."

"Do either Tracy or Beth have any connection to Jeff?"

"Both," Sean replied from his perch on the windowsill.

She raised a brow, prompting him to go on.

"Going on Trevor's tenure theory, Tracy was married to Trevor when the troubles with his tenure started, correct?"

"Correct."

Abel slid another piece of paper across the table while Sean continued. "Yesterday afternoon, Trevor made a list of the female tenure candidates Jeff had railroaded. Anyone's name look familiar?"

Her eyes froze halfway down the list.

Beth Martin.

"Fuck." She glanced again at Sean. "You still think it could be a frame-up?"

He shrugged. "Possibly, or they may have their own motives."

"Is Tracy at the hospital now?" she asked Abel.

He nodded.

"Go. Bring her in once her shift is over. She's less likely to be spooked if it's you she sees coming."

"On it, sugar."

She turned to Diego. "Where's Beth Martin?"

"She had class at nine this morning. I diverted Jaylen on his way in to pick her up."

Charlie glanced at her watch. "It's nine thirty. They should be here by now. Call Jaylen and see what the delay is."

Diego withdrew his cell and followed Abel into the bullpen, skirting by Trevor in the doorway.

Trevor stepped into the room as he pulled his wet hair into a knot. "Good lead?"

Charlie flipped over the phone records before he could see them. "Promising, though we're going to need to keep you here a little longer."

"Why?" he asked, though judging by his faded jeans, flip-flops, and HU gym shirt, he'd already planned for a day at the station. Or Annie had and packed his bag accordingly.

Diego appeared in the doorway, interrupting before she could answer. "Beth was a no-show at class. Jaylen got her address and went by her house."

"And?"

"No one's home. From a peek inside her windows, Jaylen said it looks like she left in a hurry. I told him to sit on it until we got there with a warrant."

"I'll call in the APB," Charlie said. "Get started on that warrant."

"Let me know when you have the warrant ready,"

Marsh interjected. "Judge Abernathy was the JAG on base where I was stationed. I'll get it expedited."

"Will do," Diego said.

"Thank you," Charlie added.

"Sure thing," he said with a wink as Sean handed his cup to Trevor and walked around the table to Marsh's other side.

"You better get going," he told him. "They're reading the will at ten."

"Keep me posted."

"Of course." Sean squeezed his shoulder. "You need anything, call me."

Curiosity tickled Charlie's senses again, but now wasn't the time to ask or interfere. Marsh—and by extension Sean—had enough on their minds. As Sean walked Marsh out, Charlie grabbed her coffee and took a seat, beckoning Trevor to do the same.

He remained standing, glaring at his coffee cup. "This is empty."

"Blame that one," she said, gesturing to Sean, who was on his way back across the bullpen.

"Thief!" He growled playfully as Sean reentered the room. "What's going on with Beth Martin?"

"You know her?" Sean asked around a smile.

"Personally, no, but I've passed her on campus from time to time. She teaches French. I do know she was on that list I made yesterday." He tossed the empty cup at Sean, then claimed the seat next to Charlie. "Is she missing now? Is she a suspect?"

Sean pitched the cup into the trash can and lowered

himself into the chair on the other side of Trevor. "Maybe let us do some more digging first."

"Just tell me."

Charlie took a deep breath and lowered the hammer. "We think Tracy might be involved."

"Clear," Jaylen called from one side of Beth Martin's cottage.

"Clear," Diego returned from the living room on the other side.

"Clear," Charlie confirmed from where she stood in the kitchen at the rear of the house.

"Bedroom drawers are tossed." Jaylen entered the compact kitchen, ducking his head to avoid the over-door transom. "Clothes are half gone, the rest falling off hangers. She packed in a hurry."

"Any hits on the APB?" she asked Diego, who'd followed Jaylen into the kitchen.

Shorter than Jaylen, he didn't have to duck, but he did have to turn his broad shoulders sideways to get through the narrow door. "Nothing yet, but Rachel's alerted the highway patrol in all surrounding counties and states."

"The alarm by her bed was set for six this morning," Jaylen said. "It was switched off, so either she never turned it on, or she turned it off this morning before she left. If she didn't leave until this morning, then she can't be more than a state or two away by now."

"Charlie!" Sean shouted from outside. "Get out here!"

She exited the back door off the kitchen, Diego and Jaylen behind her, and found Sean standing by the trash bins.

He held open the black trash can lid with a gloved hand. "Take a look."

She peered inside, seeing only white trash bags at first, but upon closer inspection, she spied a red plastic bag sticking out from beneath the top white one. There was an imprint on it, partially obscured, but she'd bet Sean's Harley it was a biohazard symbol.

She called Diego over. "Get in here and take pictures before I pull the bags out." She stood beside Jaylen as Diego snapped pictures with his phone.

"Clear," Diego said after a minute, trading places with her again.

Charlie pulled out the first white trash bag and exposed the red biohazard bag. She nodded to Diego, who took another round of pictures, before she removed the bag and set it on the trash can lid. She carefully unsealed it and held open the flaps.

Sean whistled over her shoulder. "Jackpot."

Indeed. The bag contained several used syringes and empty Diprivan vials.

"Diego, snap a few more pictures, then get this inside." She ripped off her gloves and moved out of the way. "Jaylen, call the station and get CSU down here. I want a full sweep."

Once Diego and Jaylen were finished, she asked Sean, "Did you check the other bins?"

He shook his head. "Got lucky on the first one."

"You take blue. I'll take green."

He moved to the recycle bin as she lifted the lid on the compost. Her breath caught and she released the lid as if she'd been burned.

"Nothing here," Sean called.

"Here either," she lied.

"CSU will be here in ten," Diego shouted from the window.

Sean took her elbow in his hand. "You okay?"

She nodded sharply.

"You're lying." His fingers tightened on her elbow. "Tell me what's wrong."

Her eyes cut to the compost bin, and Sean's other hand followed, lifting the lid. He peered inside, then lowered the lid slowly.

"Beth could've had those for any number of reasons."

"I know that," she said, voice flat, though the tremor in her limbs likely gave her away.

"There's little reason to think this case has anything to do with your family beyond the connection to Trevor."

Except it could if someone else knew the truth about her mother's death. A cover-up. And their killer was letting Charlie know they were in on the secret by leaving behind a bouquet of red roses, her mother's favorite flowers. The ones Charlie regularly took to the cemetery, that she'd tossed into her father's and brother's graves.

"Charlie, what aren't you telling me?"

She was saved from answering by a text alert. Shrugging out of Sean's grasp, she retrieved her phone and read the message from Abel. "Tracy finishes her shift at two. We need to get back to the station."

"Charlie," Sean said, his eyes searching, full of concern.

"I'm fine." She mustered as calm a stare as possible, which he either bought or decided not to question. Following him to the door, she glanced once more at the compost bin. They had the evidence to close the case today, but something told her it wasn't the full story.

CHAPTER SIXTEEN

On his way back from the restroom, Sean checked the conference room for Tracy. Not seeing her there yet, he continued across the bullpen to Charlie's office and watched from the open doorway as she moved the same file to three different stacks on her desk, opened and closed a different file three times, and clicked her pen at least twenty times. Only one reason he could figure for those jitters. "You're still spooked about what you found at Beth's place."

Charlie froze for a half second, then carried on arranging files on her desk. "Sorry?"

He stepped the rest of the way into her office and sank into a visitor chair. "Those roses spooked you. You let go of that compost bin lid like it bit you, and you were restless the entire drive back to the station, missing gears and compulsively checking your rearview mirror."

When she didn't respond, he leaned forward and

reached out, ceasing the futile rearranging. "It's probably just a coincidence," he lied.

"Does anything about this case feel like a coincidence to you?"

He didn't lie to her a second time. "Did you know Beth Martin?"

She shook her head. "I also checked Dad's and Cal's old files. There's nothing in there that mentions Beth."

He squeezed her arm. "We'll figure this out."

"What if this isn't just about Trevor?" She finally looked up and the fear in her eyes was unmistakable. "What if it goes further? What if it's about my family? If Annie or Trevor..." Her voice wavered and cracked. "I can't lose any more of my family, Sean."

"It's going to be fine." He stretched to wipe away a renegade tear that had escaped her eye. He hadn't stopped to think how much that tear cost her, how much she was holding in.

A soft knock on the door interrupted them, and Sean turned in his seat to find a blushing Rachel in the doorway. "I'm sorry to interrupt," she said, the blush intensifying. "Tracy's here. In the conference room."

Charlie cleared her throat. "We'll be right there," she said, voice free of its earlier trembling. She stood and circled the desk, but before she reached the door, Sean lightly took her wrist and turned her toward him. "It's going to be fine." He wiped away another tear.

"How can you know that?"

He curled his fingers around hers. "Because I'm going to do whatever it takes to make it that way."

Sean and Charlie entered the conference room, and Tracy's gaze shot to them. "Why am I here?"

She looked like hell. Elbow on the table, head in hand, her fingers drummed a quick rhythm against her unwashed hair. It wasn't the skittish eyes, wringing hands, or nervous fidgeting Sean typically saw with guilty suspects. It was the tired, on edge, has-a-million-other-things-to-do fidgeting that he'd expect from an overworked wife who found her cheating husband brutally murdered.

His first clue they had the wrong woman.

Charlie approached with measured steps. "We need to ask you some questions."

Tracy's eyes blazed with barely contained fury. "I don't have time for this. We're short-staffed at the hospital, so I'm still working fourteen-hour shifts and trying to plan my husband's funeral without the damn body because you haven't released it yet, and I haven't slept since—"

"You're having trouble sleeping?" Sean asked.

Her incensed glare shot to him. "Of course I'm having trouble sleeping. What kind of a stupid question is that? Our house is a crime scene, I'm sleeping at the hospital, and every time I close my eyes, all I see is my husband butchered in our bed."

Our.

Not *my*. Not *his*.

She hadn't fully processed Julian's death despite being the one who'd found the body. Not the language of a murderer.

His second clue they had the wrong woman.

He glanced at Charlie, and judging by the deepening divot between her brows, she'd caught the tell too. With a subtle double tap of his right toe, something they'd practiced in police academy, he indicated he wanted to take the lead. Charlie nodded, a small smile turning up one corner of her mouth. She retreated to the windowsill while he took the chair across from Tracy.

"Do you know Beth Martin?" he asked.

Tracy's eyes narrowed. "Yeah. Why? Did that nosy bitch have something to do with this?"

"Nosy?"

"She volunteers at the hospital. She's always in everyone's business. Gossips like an old bitty."

The highlighted phone record appeared over his shoulder. He took the paper from Charlie and pushed it across the table. "She called you a number of times over the past couple weeks."

"That's right. She got my number from one of the nurses."

"Why did she call you?"

Tracy leaned forward and answered matter-of-factly, "To tell me my husband was having an affair with a student. She'd confiscated the girl's phone and had pictures."

"You weren't surprised?"

"I'd already had one unfaithful husband." She fired a scathing glare over his shoulder at Charlie. "I knew the signs."

Charlie was at his side the next instant, her hands

braced against the edge of the table. "Trevor was never unfaithful to you. *You* cheated on *him*."

Tracy's ice-cold laugh sent a shiver racing up Sean's spine. Attempting to diffuse the mounting tension, he shifted forward, refocusing Tracy's attention on him. "Did you say anything to Julian about the affair?"

Her gaze drifted back to his, regarding him coolly. "We were in a nice, big, refurbished house, and Julian was good to me. I knew the kind of man he was when I married him. I knew there would be other women. He didn't promise to love only me and then force me to sit across the table from the object of his affection every week at Sunday dinner."

"You've got some nerve," Charlie said.

Sean didn't disagree—Trevor was the last person who would ever cheat—but they couldn't afford to get mad. They needed more information on Beth, and they weren't going to get it if Tracy shut down. He grasped Charlie's thigh beneath the table and turned his face to her. "*Check it*" he mouthed and held her stare until the tension eased from her arms and she retreated.

Once she'd resumed her perch on the windowsill, he turned back to Tracy. "As a volunteer at the hospital, did Beth have access to needles and meds?"

"Directly, no, but I wouldn't put it past her to swipe someone's keys to the surgical carts or storage room."

"Could she have accessed those unnoticed?"

"It's possible. Most of us actively ignored her to avoid the gossipmongering."

"Beth called you twice the night Julian was murdered. What did she say?"

"Nothing."

"Nothing?" Charlie asked from behind him.

"Nothing," Tracy repeated. "The first time, she had the desk nurse pull me out of surgery, claiming it was an emergency, but when I got to the phone the line was dead."

"What about the second call?"

"I let it go to voicemail, and when I checked it, there was no message." She straightened in her chair. "Do you think Beth had something to do with Julian's death?"

Not for Sean to disclose. He dodged her question with another. "Do you know if Beth had any connection to Jefferson Marshall?"

"She told me he convinced the tenure committee to turn her down. I guess she thought I was still harboring some resentment for him doing the same to Trevor."

"You weren't?" Sean asked.

An ugly sneer marred her face. "I would have given Professor Marshall a medal if I'd ever met him. I didn't want Trevor to get tenure. I wanted out of this town, and him not getting tenure was the surest bet to making that happen."

Charlie was back at Sean's side before he could blink, betrayal and outrage coloring her rising voice. "But then you married Julian, a dean at HU."

Tracy shrugged, keeping her icy glare on him but aiming her spiteful retort at Charlie. "Like I said, I knew what I was getting and what I wasn't."

Charlie leaned forward, her temper on full blast. "Trevor loved you."

Tracy lurched to her feet and slapped her palms on the

table, mirroring Charlie's attack posture. "Not as much as he loved you."

"Maybe if you'd supported him—"

"Like he'd notice. He was too busy supporting you and your family."

"Enough!" Trevor barked from the doorway, drawing everyone's attention. "The whole station can hear you." He looked back and forth between the two women, seemingly unsurprised, and Sean got the impression this was not the first scene of the sort he'd broken up. "Sean"—he nodded toward Charlie—"get her out of here."

"No need." Charlie backed off herself. "I'm sorry. That was uncalled for." But she didn't let Tracy have the last word. "My best friend loved you. He would have made you happy and given you a good life. We would have welcomed you into our family. I'm sorry you didn't give him or us a chance."

Maybe Charlie's words would sink in eventually, but today was not that day, not with Tracy already on the defensive. "It would have just delayed the inevitable." Sean was surprised when Tracy's gaze swung to him. "You're back." Followed by a snide remark aimed at Trevor. "You can have your happily ever after now."

"You never got it, did you?" Trevor shook his head, then looked to Sean and Charlie. "Give us the room, please."

Charlie exited in front of Sean, making a beeline for the stairs. He paused in the doorway, catching Trevor's tired hazel eyes. He wasn't looking forward to this conversation, but the determined set of his shoulders and spine indicated to Sean he was going to have it, regardless. It was long overdue. Sean waited for his nod, then followed Charlie out.

Abel was waiting for him at the top of the stairs. "Tracy's not involved," Sean told him. He glanced around the chief at Jaylen and Diego waiting in his office.

"Go," Abel said. "I'll fill them in."

Raised voices from the conference room drew his gaze back that direction. "Maybe I should help Trev."

Abel's line of sight followed his. "That blow-up's been comin' for years. Might as well let 'em have it out here where we've got the means to contain it. Go." He jutted his chin toward the stairs. "Make sure Charlie's okay. I'll send Trevor your way when he's done."

Confident Abel could manage, Sean nodded and followed his concern for Charlie down the stairs. "Charlie?" he called at the bottom, not sure if she went the direction of the gym, the locker room, the morgue, or the holding cell.

"In here," came her voice from the locker room directly across the hallway.

He pushed open the cracked door and stepped into the dimly lit room. And smiled at the trail she'd left on the floor. Red pumps on their sides just inside the door. Black blazer in the open area near the sinks. The claw clip that had held up her hair in the aisle between the lockers. He picked up the discarded items as he made his way to where she sat, midway down the second-row bench, elbows to her knees, cradling one hand in the other. A quick scan of the surrounding lockers revealed the unfortunate victim of her pent-up anger—a crumpled metal door in the back corner.

He leaned against the locker across from her. "You couldn't hit a bag instead."

She glared up at him through a thick fall of dark hair. It had been a month since he'd run his hands through the rich brown locks, a month since he'd twirled his fingers around an errant lock like he used to do in bed—and right then his fingers itched to reacquaint themselves with the sensation.

"I wanted to change first," she said, distracting him from his impulse to reach for her. "But my inner hulk couldn't wait."

"I can see that." He dropped the suit jacket and hair clip on the bench beside her and the pumps at her feet. "Why do you insist on wearing those things when you're kicking them off all the time?"

Proving his point, she kicked them aside. "Because I've lived my entire life with men over six feet. And they're pretty."

He knelt in front of her and took her right hand in his, gently prodding each scraped and swollen knuckle. "You did good to back off."

"I shouldn't have let it get that far at all, especially here at the station. It only feeds her delusions."

"Light crowd on the floor, and she did bait you. Repeatedly. I was about ready to explode myself." Knuckles checked, he curled her fingers into a fist and got a curse for the effort. He set her hand on her thigh. "Wraps in your locker?"

"Yeah, number—"

"Twelve."

She smiled. "You remembered."

"Twelve. Pizza. Raisinets. Cheerwine. Lagavulin. *The Departed. The Wire.* October..." He continued to rattle off her favorite things as he popped open her locker, dug around for her boxing gloves, and found the wraps and tape shoved inside.

"An update to that list," she said.

He opened the first aid cabinet over the sinks and gathered supplies. "And what's that?"

"Ardbeg."

Pain pierced his chest and stole his breath at the remembered taste of the peaty scotch on her and Trevor's lips that night a month ago. From there, a cascade of other memories assaulted him—the salt and cocoa butter taste of her skin, Trevor's firm muscles under his hands, her sure hands running over his chest as Trevor's wove through his hair, her legs clamped tight on either side of his hips, her muscles clenched tight around his dick, his mouth full of Trevor's.

"Sentimental favorite," she said softly.

He met her gaze in the mirror over the sink, and black diamonds glittered back at him. He was seconds away from dropping the supplies in the sink and sprinting the ten feet to her, but then she broke the heated staredown. "You still know your way around."

Letting her have that play, he carried the wraps and first aid supplies to the bench and crouched in front of her. "Your family doesn't change much when it comes to police business." She jerked her face to the side and swallowed hard, and Sean's chest clenched for a different reason. It was on the tip of his tongue to ask about Alice—why else would she react so strongly at the mention of her family's history at the station?—but then Charlie swerved again. "You and Marsh seem close."

"I've only known him a few years. Since he was assigned to our legat office. But we've been through some shit together, and he was there for me when I needed a friend." He chuckled. "I ran away from all those cowboys in Kansas City only to end up with one as my closest friend."

Charlie's hand jerked in his, and Sean's gaze shot to her face, catching the hurt expression there before she wiped it away. Only she couldn't completely hide her curiosity. "Go ahead and ask," he said, figuring he knew the question that would answer for both her reactions. He did not, however, figure the question would come from behind them.

"Were the two of you ever together?" Trevor's question —the one Charlie was too polite to ask—was punctuated by the locker room door banging closed.

Sean shifted from his crouch to the bench beside Charlie, wanting to see them both and wanting both of them to see him, to read the sincerity and truth in his account of past events and his hope for the present direction. "Once," he said. "The night our boss was killed in a terrorist attack. An attack that may have been averted if political bickering hadn't tied up our funding. We were frustrated, angry, and most of all sad we'd lost a colleague and friend. We got drunk and both needed more comfort than the bottle could provide that night. That was the one and only time."

He was surprised when Charlie pushed back her hair and asked, "Do you want there to be more? Do we need to figure out how to make that work too?"

"We will," Trevor added, "if that's what it takes to make this"—he gestured among them—"work."

"Do you mean that?" Sean could barely keep his seat, hope surging out to his fingers and toes, coloring his voice as well.

Trevor's "Yes" nearly tripped over Charlie's, and Sean nearly tripped over himself in his haste to reach out to them. Trevor saved him the broken limbs, closing the distance and kneeling in front of him and Charlie. "We've got a shot here. I think we should take it, however that looks."

"It looks like the three of us," Sean said. "I love Marsh, but only as a friend. Plus, he's gay and not poly."

"You and he can still have a relationship," Trevor said, proving yet again he got it and also how big his heart was. "Separate and apart from ours."

"If that's what you need," Charlie added. "This past week, having you here"—she glanced at him, then at Trevor—"feeling the connection between us again." She swung her gaze back to Sean, her words back to their earlier conversation. "I don't want to lose this either."

"We need you with us, Sean," Trevor said. "That's how this"—he gestured between them again—"works best."

"Marsh doesn't work that way, and he deserves to be the center of someone's world." He notched a hand in the crook of Trevor's neck and laid the other on Charlie's thigh. "Like you two are of mine."

Trevor's pulse kicked beneath his hand, Charlie's thigh slid closer, and that was all the go-ahead signal Sean needed. He floored it on the next beat of their hearts, leaning to the side and slamming his mouth onto Charlie's. All that existed, all that mattered in that moment was Charlie's lips against his—her taste, her moan, her tongue as it dueled with his—and Trevor's breathy moan beside them, his hand covering Sean's on Charlie's thigh and inching it higher. She shifted forward, her legs opening to their touch and arms opening to Trevor. Sean broke their kiss, then with his hand around Trevor's neck, drew him to Charlie. The sigh of relief that always accompanied their first kisses found its way into Sean's soul and settled right where it belonged. The sense of peace and belonging like nothing else he'd ever found with anyone.

The peace, however, was snatched away too soon by footsteps in the hallway, headed in their direction. "We've got company," Sean said, and Trevor and Charlie broke apart just in time to avoid another uncomfortable run-in with Rachel.

"Charlie, you in here?" the receptionist called from the door.

"Yeah, here." Sean hung back with Trevor as Charlie straightened her top and poked her head around the end of the row, not that Rachel couldn't see them over the top of the lockers, her gaze bouncing over them. "What's up?" Charlie said, bringing Rachel's gaze back to her.

"Beth Martin's in custody. Abel's called for a victory

lap at Pearl's." Charlie glanced over her shoulder at them, and Sean could read in her expression the same thing he was thinking. A victory lap was premature, a jinx if he were superstitious.

"Wallace wants to celebrate being off jackass duty," Rachel said with a smile. "Abel's gonna have 'em shut the place down—police only—so we can relax."

Caution, disappointment, and duty all sped across Charlie's face, all of which Sean felt too. He gave a reluctant nod. "Sure," Charlie said. "We'll meet you there."

CHAPTER SEVENTEEN

Charlie was halfway down the station's front steps, on her way across the street to Pearl's, a twenty-four-hour sports bar and pool hall that was a favorite of cops and college kids alike, when her sister's car swung into one of the visitor spots in front of the station.

"Hey, A," Charlie greeted with a smile. "What're you doing here?"

"I brought another bag for Trevor." Annie returned her hug, then drew back with a wry grin. "Don't take this the wrong way, sis, but you look beat."

Chuckling, Charlie ran her fingers through her sister's waterfall of white-gold hair. "No offense taken. I'll sleep better once this case is over."

Annie stepped away and reached into the back for another of Trevor's duffels. "Any developments?"

That familiar wave of guilt rose up, for worrying Annie and for not keeping her updated. "Federal marshals picked up our prime suspect in Georgia an hour ago. They're going to drive her here in the morning."

"Her?"

"Beth Martin. She teaches French at HU. Do you know her?"

Annie shook her head. "Not personally, but I saw her around the hospital and the library from time to time. She gossiped a lot, and then a couple weeks ago, she started harassing Trace."

"About Julian's affair?"

Her sister nodded.

A thought occurred to Charlie, a way to silence the doubt still lingering in her mind. "Hey, can you do me a favor?"

"What's that?"

"Pull her library record. Electronic and hard copies. I want to see if she's checked out any Shakespeare lately."

"I can do that," she said. "Just get me a warrant."

"Will do." Charlie grasped her sister's free hand. "Thanks, A."

Annie smiled, squeezing back, but her smile disappeared, and she lifted the bag. "So Trevor doesn't need this? Is he even here?"

"He's at Pearl's with Sean."

Annie lifted a brow.

"We're talking things out," Charlie said with a laugh. She slipped the bag from Annie's hand. "I'll take this. Make sure he gets it."

"Is he okay?" Annie asked.

"He's had a rough few days, but I promised him this

case would be solved today, and it looks like we're on our way."

"Good, I'm glad." Annie leaned against the side of her car. "Did Sean say yet why he left? What kept him away?"

Charlie's smile dipped. She had hope, but she was still missing answers. She sensed Trevor had maybe a few more than her, but in the chaos of the case, some of the details between her, Sean, and Trevor had gotten lost. Details that needed to be sorted before they went any further. "We're going to talk about that tonight," she told Annie. "Good thing you brought this. Might turn into an all-nighter." Red slashed across Annie's cheekbones, and Charlie reconsidered her words. Then blushed herself. "Shit, I didn't mean it that way."

Annie giggled. "You go get 'em, sis."

Charlie laughed out loud and threw an arm around her sister's shoulders, kissing her temple. "You want to come to Pearl's with us? Jaylen will be there."

Annie blushed harder as she pulled away. "We've got a date tomorrow. I think I'll take tonight for myself."

"If you change your mind," Charlie said as she tossed Trevor's bag into the Mustang, "you know where we'll be."

"Sounds good." Annie stopped in the open doorway of her car and turned half-around, her smile gone. "We're all we've got. Be good to him."

Before she could reply, Annie disappeared into the car, Charlie's "Love you" lost beneath the crunch of gravel and the heavy feeling that something wasn't quite right with her sister.

An hour later, Charlie's doubts had grown from a mole hill to a mountain, fretting over Annie, over risking her friendship with Trevor, over the truth about Alice's death they needed to tell Sean, and most of all, the case and what she was increasingly sure was a premature victory lap.

"I don't know." She refilled her water glass from the pitcher on the table. "It seems too easy."

"Easy?" Maggie scoffed from across the booth next to Rachel. "You call the past five days easy?"

"Not at all, so why should the solution be?"

"Sometimes the simplest solutions are the right ones," Rachel said with a shrug.

Charlie didn't think so. "I just have this feeling the case is connected to my family, but before this week, I had no idea who Beth Martin was. Trevor and Annie only knew her in passing from HU, and there's no mention of her in Dad's or Cal's old files." She'd run a check through the digitized records a third time before leaving the station.

"Your gut thinks it's connected to your family," Maggie corrected. "Your head just gave us all the reasons it's likely not."

"The roses—"

"Are sold at every supermarket, convenience store, and florist in town."

Her friend wasn't getting it, and she desperately needed someone else to get it. She aimed her next question at Rachel. Maybe she'd be easier to sway. "What about the connections to Trevor?"

"Trevor's lived his whole life in Hanover," she said. "He's gorgeous, everyone loves him—especially after what Tracy did to him—and he's one of HU's most popular professors. He's bound to have a lot of connections to people in town. It's probably just a coincidence." She mimicked her earlier shrug. "Simple."

Not getting it either. Nothing about this case was a coincidence. She was sure of that, but the only person who would believe her was playing pool with Trevor and Marsh across the bar. Resisting the urge to growl in frustration, Charlie asked another pertinent question of her less-than-cooperative audience. "What's her motive?"

Maggie threw up her hands, nearly hitting a passing waitress. "I don't know. You're the detective. I'm just the lady who hangs out in the dungeon with dead bodies."

"Rules," Rachel reprimanded, even though there was no food in sight. "No more case talk, and definitely no more dead-body talk. Your suspect will be here tomorrow. You can ask her why then. For the time being, there's nothing more you can do."

"Except drink." Maggie held up her glass of whisky for a toast.

"Hear, hear," Rachel seconded with her own.

Clinking her glass against theirs, Charlie nursed her water while mentally repeating her litany of issues with Beth Martin as their prime suspect, hoping something would click. Midway through her fourth repetition, Maggie asked the inevitable. "So about that Trevor and Tracy blowup at the station. I've heard differing accounts of what went down."

Setting aside her glass, Charlie propped her elbows on the table and covered her face with her hands, mumbling behind them. "I overreacted to her accusing Trevor of cheating."

"He never cheated." The volume of Maggie's voice caused Charlie to cringe.

She lowered her hands and dropped her forearms back to the table. "I'm not sure he convinced her of that today either, but it's the truth. We made our case."

"We?" Rachel said. "Did I interrupt something in the locker room?"

Maggie lifted a brow. "What was going on in the locker room, Henby?"

"Sean, Trevor, and I talked about giving it another try."

Maggie's "Woot!" had the whole bar looking their way.

And Charlie tossing back the untouched shot of whisky Maggie had bought for her too.

"So Trevor's officially off the market?" Rachel asked, subdued compared to Maggie.

"TBD." Charlie lowered her voice to match, aiming to bring their conversation back into their booth instead of broadcasting to all of Pearl's. "We need to talk. Put all our cards on the table. And I'd be lying if I said I wasn't sure about taking a chance on Sean again, especially with Trevor's friendship on the line too."

"But you're moving to DC with Trevor?" Rachel said, the sharp edge of impatience in her voice catching Charlie's attention. "Sean's overseas."

Charlie shook her head. "Not anymore. He's going to be in DC too."

Rachel gasped and reached for her hand. "For real?"

"Okay, look," Maggie said, and Charlie prepared herself for the assault. Only it wasn't the attack she'd expected. "I've kept my mouth shut for years. I don't know what happened. I don't know why Sean left and stayed away or why you and Trevor never went after him. I've respected your wishes to keep that to yourself, and I still mean to, but from what I've seen the past few days, that man is still in love with you." Her eyes cut to Sean by the row of pool tables, his hand grazing the small of Trevor's back. "And with your best friend."

"I thought you wanted me to go for it with Trevor?"

"I did. I do. But you're afraid that won't work without Sean. Well, Sean's back, and it looks like he means to stick with you two this time, and more than anything, I want you to be happy."

Rachel squeezed her hand. "Me too."

Charlie smiled, thankful for the support of her friends, but then her face fell as she thought about the hard truths she, Trevor, and Sean still needed to talk about. Including the ones connected to the case.

"Charlie?" Rachel called, reading the rapid decline in her mood.

"Sorry, I had another thought about the case."

"Stop that," Maggie chided. "Time to switch that brain of yours off for the night."

Charlie went through the motions again, clinking her water glass against theirs, as she snuck a glance across the bar to where Sean and Trevor were focused on their game of pool, their fingers loosely entwined beneath the table's rail. She hoped like hell the truth wouldn't break all their hearts.

Same as she'd done Sunday morning, Charlie parked her car between Sean's bike and Trevor's truck. Only this time she was in front of the Sand Dollar, not the station, and she was staring at room twelve with both eager anticipation and dread. The future was within their grasp, but they had to tackle the past first. Not a small feat, and rehashing painful past events would not be easy.

The room door opened, and Trevor stood over the threshold, backlit by the lamplight. Hair down, barefoot, in jeans and a tee, he looked like home, like comfort. Those life-altering events of the past would be easier to recount with her best friend by her side. Her best friend who was on the verge of becoming something more again. Eagerness twisted with dread. She ached to love him again romantically, but she was terrified of losing anyone else she loved.

He tilted his head, beckoning her inside. When she didn't move to get out of the car, he pushed off the door and crossed the walkway to where she was parked. He propped an elbow on the corner of her windshield. "You want me to get in the car?" He eyed the passenger seat on the other side of her. "We can leave right now if you're not ready for this or if you don't want it."

Her gaze flicked in the direction of his feet. "You're barefoot." Then back to his face, all the beautiful angles thrown into sharp relief by the moonlight overhead and the shadows cast from behind. "And you want this."

"I do, but you will always come first, Charlotte." His serious-as-a-heart-attack expression gave way to a smirk. "Shoes or not."

She leaned her head back and laughed at the moon and stars above, a little of the tension leaving her. "I want this too," she admitted. "So much it scares me."

He pried one of her hands off the wheel—not all the tension was gone—and linked their fingers together, setting them on the open window. "Talk to me."

"We have to tell him about Mom. I think it's relevant to the case." She skated her thumb along the side of his as she recalled Sean's words from the cemetery the other night, recalled where she'd found him. "I think he might already know." No surprised jerk, no wide eyes, no inhaled breath. "You're not surprised," she said.

"I think it might have to do with why he stayed away," Trevor said, surprising her. He stroked a thumb across her palm, calming the flare of nerves. "Either way, we have to talk about it, case or not. No more secrets."

"What if it pushes him away again?" she said, putting words to her fear.

"I don't think it will, but if it does, we move on."

"How with all of us in DC?"

Trevor chuckled and slid along the outside of the door, closer to where she was leaned back against the headrest. "It's DC, Charlie. Not Hanover. It's a big fucking town. What other excuse you got?"

She closed her hand around his and drew him down,

his forearms resting on the window ledge, his face only a few scant inches from her own. The kiss in the locker room today wasn't enough, neither were the kisses earlier that month or all the kisses of ten years ago. "I want this, Trevor. I don't want to lose what this might be."

He leaned forward and their mouths met, glided together as if it were the most natural thing in the world. More of that comfort, more of that sense of home. Her lips parted, and Trevor's tongue dipped inside, taking his time and kissing her so thoroughly, so perfectly, she had to close her eyes and catch her breath when they finally parted.

His fingers twisted in her hair, and his lips rained soft kisses across her face. "I want this too, Charlie, and I will fight for us this time."

With that knowledge, Charlie's eagerness overcame the fear, and she climbed out of the car. Hand still clasped in Trevor's, she tugged him toward room twelve. Toward the other person who would make that sense of home complete. "Let's go fight for him too."

CHAPTER EIGHTEEN

Trevor followed Charlie back inside the motel room, and Sean's gaze went immediately to their joined hands. One corner of his mouth hitched up, and he did such a piss-poor job of trying to hide it, ducking his chin and pretending the scotch he was pouring was the most interesting thing in the world, that Trevor laughed. "You're not fooling anyone."

"Who said I was trying to?" Smiling, Sean capped the bottle and set it aside. "Outside on the patio? I can pull out another chair."

"Inside." Charlie untangled their hands, claimed a glass, and led the way to the seating area. She gestured at the room around them. "What I have to say needs to stay inside these four walls. Just between the three of us."

"All right," Sean said as he lowered himself onto the near end of the couch.

When Charlie claimed the chair, Trevor joined Sean on the sofa, sitting on his other side. As soon as his ass hit the cushions, Charlie tossed back her scotch and bolted up. Sean moved to stand too, but Trevor put a hand on his thigh. "Let her get this out."

"But I know."

Charlie froze midstride between the dining table and them, her dark eyes connecting with Trevor's, then skipping to Sean's. "You know?"

"I know how your mother really died that night. Do you?"

He knew.

Trevor was caught between relief and pissed-off anger. What exactly did Sean know? How long had he known? Why hadn't he said anything? Apparently, pissed-off anger was winning, his white-knuckled grip on Sean's thigh eliciting a hissed, "Trev."

He eased his hold as Charlie stepped closer, gripping the back of the chair. "It wasn't a stranger who ran Mom's car off the bridge. It was my brother."

Sean nodded, encouraging her to go on.

"It was raining, and he was speeding, racing to come get me from a date gone horribly wrong."

"Craig Rowan?"

She nodded. "I called Trevor and Cal, I..." Her words drifted off, eaten by the lump in her throat she visibly strained against. "Another something that was my—"

Nope, they weren't going there again. "Don't say it," Trevor interrupted. "We went through this after we got the letter. It was not your fault. If anyone's to blame, it's Craig."

"The letter?" Sean asked.

"From Cal," Trevor told him. "We got it the day after the funeral."

If Charlie's guilt over Mitch's and Cal's deaths had been crushing, it had been twice as bad when she learned the truth about Alice's. They'd hashed it all out that night over homemade pasta, a bottle of Chianti, and several boxes of tissues, discussing and dispelling the guilt and anger they both felt, and ultimately concluding Craig was the party truly responsible for that awful night their senior year of high school. He'd been the one who'd set in motion the tragic chain of events. That said, Trevor had had to remind Charlie of that on the regular the past month, her tendency toward self-blame compounded by the losses that just kept coming.

"The same day I left again?" Sean asked, and when Trevor nodded, he lowered his chin and ran a hand over his nape. "Fuck, I'm sorry."

Charlie circled the chair and sank back into it. "Is that when you found out?"

Sean lowered his arm. "No, I found out the first time I tried to come back to you."

Trevor almost bolted up himself at that revelation, but Sean clasped his leg, keeping him seated. "Let me get this out, please."

Trevor simmered down and Sean removed his hand, reaching out to snag his glass for a long swallow. "We need to go back a little further first," he said. "To the day we graduated police academy." Trevor sensed this was the part of the story he'd gotten some of the other night. "I got a call from Marie in the parking lot right after the ceremony. You two had already left for the house to get things ready for the party. Cal was there with me and overheard the call. Saul was in emergency surgery. They weren't sure he was going to make it. Cal told me to go, and he'd let you two know what had happened and why I'd left in such a hurry. I gave him my new badge, my necklace, and the wedding band I'd proposed to you with for safe keeping."

Trevor touched the base of his throat where his necklace used to rest. "You had yours on you?"

"In my pocket, since I couldn't wear the necklace with the uniform and since we hadn't announced the engagement yet."

Trevor's heart and stomach sank, betrayal a heavy boulder dragging them down. And if he felt that way...

Charlie trembled where she sat, her face a ghostly pale. Thank goodness she'd sat back down because Trever didn't think she'd have the legs to stand. He sure as shit didn't. "He told us you left and weren't coming back. He gave me the badge, and Trevor the ring and necklace."

"I figured maybe that's what happened when you wouldn't answer my calls." Sean tossed back the rest of his scotch and slid his glass onto the coffee table next to Trevor's. "I tried to come back anyway, once Saul recovered, but then Cal used *his* badge to hold me up at the airport."

Charlie's trembling took on a different tenor, morphing into anger. "He did what?"

"That's when he told you about Alice?" Trevor asked. He shared Charlie's mounting anger, but Sean needed to get this out and they needed to hear the full story, once and for all.

"He said I shouldn't come back and cause another scene," Sean continued. "That you both were furious I'd left, that if I came back it would be worse, that our unconventional relationship would draw more unwanted attention, and that others would use our drama to their advantage against the Henbys and against you with HU. They'd dig and find out the truth."

"Others like the Rowans." Trevor propped his elbows on his knees and scrubbed his hands over his face. "Craig was just back in town. He came at me at Pearl's about a week before your police academy graduation, saying the reign of the Henbys was over, and I wouldn't be *protected* anymore. That he'd use his pull with HU to get me kicked out of the doctoral program. Cal was with me."

"Dad, Cal, and Abel would all have been kicked out of the department too," Charlie said. "For covering up the accident." Her gaze shot to his. "And Craig was still pissed at you for breaking his nose at that party the night of the accident."

"And *you*"—Sean reached for her hand with one of his —"would blame yourself, for all of it. Cal feared that more than anything, and so did I." He took Trevor's hand in the other. "I didn't want to risk your futures. I didn't want to do anything that might bring harm to you or your family. And I was likely going to have to take over Paxton sooner than expected. I couldn't ask you to leave your family and your futures here in Hanover. Not when they were just beginning."

Trevor closed his eyes, mentally rewinding to that day that had begun so beautifully and ended so tragically. A proposal, a graduation, an abandonment. Except that last one wasn't true. Cal had intervened, again prompted by fucking Craig Rowan. The course of their lives had been irrevocably altered a second time. But even if it was about protecting them, how could Cal do that, to Charlie, to him, to Sean? How could he live—Trevor's mental film reel fast forwarded to the answer. Cal hadn't been able to live with himself. "The overdose," he mumbled.

Sean's gaze darted between them. "What overdose?"

"About a year after you left, Cal almost OD'ed. A friend called me from a bar over in Southport. Cal was strung out on pills and halfway through his second bottle of vodka. I found him at a nearby motel, unconscious."

"He barely made it," Charlie said, voice a mere whisper, some of the anger leeching out as realization dawned for her too. Pieces coming together.

Trevor stood, circled the coffee table, and sat on the arm of Charlie's chair. Needing to be near her as he finished telling Sean this part of the story. One of the other worst times of their lives. "I sat by his hospital bed for the next forty-eight hours, convincing him to live."

Charlie laid a hand on his thigh and leaned against his side. "We never knew what set him off. Took him a lot of therapy and a new partner to train to recover and refocus, but he never completely shook the sadness."

The guilt. On multiple levels.

"We talked to Abel," Trevor said. "After Mitch and Cal died and after we got Cal's letter. Cal didn't remember anything after the accident that night." Charlie shivered and Trevor wrapped an arm around her shoulders, offering and taking comfort as the memories crept even closer. "He woke up at home the next morning, barely a scratch on him, the previous twelve hours a blank. Abel told him he'd hydroplaned and run off the road several miles short of the bridge. Mitch made sure the police reports said Alice's accident was a hit-and-run."

"We were eighteen." Charlie sniffled and wiped at her eyes, stopping the tears before they fell. "Abel told us he and Dad thought the guilt would crush him, that it would crush me."

Trevor hugged her tighter. "Not an unfounded concern."

"When did Cal learn the truth?" Sean asked. "He never let on while we were at HU."

"It didn't come back to him until police academy," Charlie said. "In bits and pieces."

None of them had seen it, but Cal's life had been spinning out of control, and Sean had unwittingly been caught in the storm. Trevor reached out, drawing him to them, wrapping an arm around his waist and holding him close too. "I'm sorry, baby."

Sean wove his fingers into his hair. "I'm sorry I wasn't here for you both."

Charlie cut off his lament, reaching three fingers up to his lips. "You felt a duty to Marie and Saul. You love them, Sean. We're not going to hold rushing to their side against you."

"I know what it's like." Trevor rested his head on

Sean's chest and nuzzled into the heat. "When good people take you into their family and ask nothing in return. You want to give them everything back."

Sean kissed his head. "But you were my family too."

"And you were still trying to protect us," Charlie said. "Even though Cal told you we didn't want you here anymore."

"We should have come looking for you," Trevor said. "Fuck, I debated it half a dozen times. I was so fucking angry and hurt, but Cal talked me down every time."

"Me too," Charlie whispered. "I can't believe he..." Her words drifted off again in the same sea of anger and regret that Trevor was wading through.

"We were twenty-three-year-old kids, *including* Cal." Sean curled his fingers around Charlie's, holding them to his chest, and Trevor kissed her knuckles. "He was just trying to keep his family safe and close. Hanover too, I imagine, from the Rowans. I can't hold that against him, especially now that I've met Craig. And after what Cal told you, together with the badge, ring, and necklace, and with me joining the FBI, you tried to move on because you thought that's what I was doing too. I can't hold that against you either."

They stayed curled together for several long minutes, wrapped in each other's arms, grieving the time they'd lost, mourning good intentions that had resulted in pain and anguish, and yet acclimating to a fresh sort of peace that was settling now that the truth was out there. Reality, however, eventually intruded, Charlie's phone ringing insistently. Trevor told her to ignore it, but after it rang a third time, she rose, kissed each of them firmly but briefly, and retrieved the device off the dining table.

"What've you got?" she answered. A quick conversation later, she hung up, left the phone on the table, and returned to them. "Marshals will be en route with Martin tomorrow morning. She should be here by two. I still don't know—"

Sean's and Trevor's fingers collided on the way to putting them on *her* lips. They laughed, the earlier melancholy beginning to fade. "We'll question her tomorrow," Sean said. "We'll get to the bottom of the case, just like we got to the bottom of things between us." He curled a hand around each of their necks. "I missed you both *so much*. I want to move forward with you, but I don't want to compromise your futures or your family now. I won't hold—"

Without a second thought, Trevor sealed their lips and let Sean know just how much he'd missed him too. And what he thought about their futures. "I want to move forward with you too."

Charlie stepped close, arms circling their waists, making her thoughts on the matter clear as well. "I'm in this too. I want to make it work this time." Her eyes locked with his. "We fight for each other and our family." She rose, her lips colliding with his, and it wasn't like the kiss in the locker room earlier. Or like when his lips had reconnected with Sean's then or in the batting cage. Or hell, even like their kisses a month ago. None of them were trying to prove anything. They'd all but confessed they were it for each other. Their kisses were a continuation of their catharsis that had started that night and finally been fully realized, years of longing finally getting its proper due. Trevor was going to savor this victory and commit every second of it to memory.

Touching his tongue to Charlie's lips again, she opened for him immediately. Diving in, he tangled his tongue with hers and she responded—hot, hard, and demanding—eliciting a moan from deep within his throat. He hauled her into his embrace, one arm circling her waist, his other hand curving over her ass and under her thigh, hitching her up against him. The heat of Sean's body lined up behind him, hands on his hips, and he directed them toward the bedroom. Good thing, as Trevor's lips were making a survey of Charlie's neck, his mouth trailing kisses down her throat.

She wove her hands into his hair, holding him to her. "Yes," she moaned, grinding her hips against his abs, not hiding her need for him either.

His dick strained behind the fly of his pants, and when Sean reached a hand around, palming his erection, he damn near dropped Charlie in his rush to thrust into the touch. "Dammit, Sean," he cursed. "Let me get her to the bed first."

Charlie threw back her head and laughed, and he nipped her collarbone for making fun of him. Rotating, he sat on the edge of the bed, Charlie in his lap, and he reached up to hold her face in his hands. Looked higher at

Sean standing behind her, shirt gone, blue eyes bright. "I love you both. As much as I did ten years ago. We will make this work. *I* will make this work."

Sean leaned over Charlie's shoulder to press his smiling lips to Trevor's. "Fucking romantic."

Charlie laid her hands over Trevor's. "*Our* fucking romantic." The sweet words and gesture were belied by the demanding roll of her hips.

Trevor thrust up to meet her and they gasped against each other's lips. "Fuck, Charlie."

Grinning, she trailed her mouth over his jaw and neck while Sean climbed onto the bed beside them, helping Charlie to undress him. They wrestled Trevor out of his shirt, then Sean flicked open the button of his jeans and reached a hand inside his boxers to stroke his cock. Trevor closed his eyes and braced a hand behind him on the mattress, needing the support as his lust kicked into overdrive. His love and need for these two people fueling the train.

Sean's hot breath floated across the side of his face. "What do you want, Trev?"

He rolled his hips and thrust his dick into Sean's fist. "This to never end."

Charlie skated her nails up his chest. "It won't, baby." She rose again, and before she brought her body back down, Sean freed Trevor's cock, and the resulting friction of fabric against his bare shaft about did Trevor in.

He needed to get Sean and Charlie as undressed as he was if he had any chance of the three of them coming together. He righted himself, and on Charlie's next downward grind, he yanked her shirt free and slipped his hands under the hem. He spread his fingers over her warm skin, climbing her torso and pushing the fabric off over her head. Beside him, Sean rocked an impressive erection against his side. Trevor tilted his face for a kiss, and when Sean was done devouring his mouth, Trevor growled against his lips. "Get your cock out and get it in me."

As Sean raced to strip and grab the lube out of his bag, Trevor focused on getting Charlie out of the rest of her clothes. He popped the front clasp of her bra, slid the straps down her arms, then palmed her breasts, pinching and twisting her stiff nipples, causing her to throw back her head and moan. The next time she rose, he stopped her descent with a hand between her legs, cupping her center. With his other hand, he lifted a breast to his mouth and sucked a nipple between his lips, flicking it with his tongue. She wobbled on her knees, but Sean steadied her while working free the zipper of her pants. As she writhed in their arms, teased to the extreme, whispering pleas for more, Trevor reached a hand inside her panties and plunged two fingers inside her.

"Yes," she gasped, and that throaty sound, the warm wet heat clenching around his fingers, had him barreling close to the edge again. Eyes closed, he pumped his fingers in and out, his thumb circling her clit, building her higher and building his own need faster.

"Trev." Sean's voice cut through the lust. "I'm gonna come all over Charlie's backside if you two keep it up."

Blinking open his eyes, Trevor feasted on the sight of

Sean naked beside them, hard and flushed, with a fist around his balls. "Not a bad proposition."

Sean's gaze darkened. "I thought you wanted me in you."

A better proposition. Made even sweeter as Charlie lightly touched his cheek, bringing his attention back to her. Her dark eyes were hooded, her lips deliciously plump, and her hair a wild halo of dark brown. "And I want you in me. All together. Always."

If he'd thought his lovers were sexy a decade ago, it was nothing compared to now. Nothing compared to how fiercely he needed what Charlie and Sean were promising.

They shed the rest of their clothes and crawled toward the middle of the bed, Charlie lying on her back and letting her thighs fall open. Trevor sank between them as Sean blanketed his back, cock notching against his ass.

"Protection?" Sean panted as they rolled in a simulation of what they were seconds from making a reality.

"IUD," Charlie said. "Last test was negative."

"There's been no one else for me since the two of you earlier this month," Trevor said, looking down at Charlie, then over his shoulder at Sean. "Negative."

"Same," Sean said. "But if you want—"

"I want to feel all of you," Trevor said. "Both of you."

"I'm good with that," Charlie said, echoed by Sean's "Me too."

Trevor hung his head, overwhelmed at their trust, at their love, and at the miraculous fact they'd somehow gotten this back. A second—hell, a third—chance.

Charlie nudged his chin up with a kiss. "Make love to me, Trevor. I want to feel all of my best friend."

Powerless to hold back, he surged over her. With his forearms on the mattress on either side of her head, his hands framing her face, their eyes locked, he drove inside her, hard and deep. Charlie gasped, nuzzling her face into one of his hands and nipping his palm.

"Home," Sean whispered behind him, and Trevor's heart stuttered. Leaning over him, Sean ravaged his mouth again with a deep, plundering kiss, contradicting the simplicity of that single word.

Sean pulled away, kissing down Trevor's spine. Overload threatened again as Charlie kissed across his chest and hitched her legs higher, taking him deeper. And when Sean's tongue glided down his crack and circled his rim, there was no stopping his forward thrust. Into Charlie while Sean held tight to his hips and pushed his tongue into him. Asked to make a choice which was better, Charlie's center clenching around his cock or Sean's tongue breaching his hole, he'd refuse to answer. He didn't have to choose. He was lucky enough to have both.

Mind-blowing, intimate, extraordinary.

Charlie bowed beneath him, her heels pressing urgently into his ass, and Trevor sharpened his focus on her. He wanted to make this wonderful for his best friend too. Needed to. His strokes were deep, claiming, and Charlie met him thrust for thrust. Sean kept up with them as well, taking hold of Charlie's ankles and driving Trevor in deeper. Together, they pushed her harder and faster until she careened over the edge with a shout. Three strokes later, Sean shoved two spit-slicked fingers into Trevor's hole, aimed directly at his prostate, and Trevor planted to the hilt inside Charlie and groaned his release into her neck, joining her in oblivion.

And then he was ripped out of it in the best way possible. Sean hauled him up and back, across his spread thighs, and trickled cool lube down his crack, spreading it around and in his hole. "I'm not gonna last long." His voice sounded as wrecked as Trevor felt. "Watching you two, tasting you on my tongue again. Fuck, I want in here."

"Then get in there," Charlie said from in front of them, her legs still spread, and Trevor stretched forward with his upper body. He licked a long, slow swipe through her folds, lapping up their combined release and humming in pleasure. He lingered there for a blissful moment, in the taste and smell of them, before continuing to her clit and sucking hard on the bundle of nerves, causing Charlie to buck.

"Fucking hell," Sean cursed behind him, then tunneled into Trevor's ass, burying his dick inside him.

Trevor groaned. His senses, his soul, were full. Of the taste of him and Charlie that he couldn't get enough of, continuing to lick and suck and building her up again. Of Sean thrusting inside him, pegging his already sensitive prostate. Just this side of pain but fucking incredible. Of the scent of sex and the sounds of Charlie's keening and Sean's grunts, music to his fucking ears.

A perfect three-part harmony that played a hell of an encore, Charlie's thighs trembling on either side of his head as she bucked off the bed, coming hard a second time against his mouth. Sean burying himself with one last thrust and coming inside Trevor, the warm gush of his come—the "I love you" and "Come, baby" from his partners—the final sparks that lit Trevor from the inside and had him coming again in the arms of the two people he'd never stopped loving.

Never would.

CHAPTER NINETEEN

———————

Bound and gagged, Craig Rowan sat shaking on a starting block in HU's natatorium. Moonlight streamed through the ceiling windows of the huge building, reflecting off the water in the pool and giving the shadows a life of their own. It had been close to nine when he'd left the gym, needing to get in a good work out after being cooped up in protective custody. Given the position of the moon overhead now, he guessed it was past midnight. He'd been out for several hours.

Sweat soaked his gray gym shirt, staining his collar and running down his back, a by-product of his agitation and the humidity of the room, but his limbs weren't slick enough to slip out of the ropes binding his wrists and ankles. All he'd managed to do since waking an hour ago was scrape his skin raw and add the stench of his blood to the heavy chlorine-scented air.

Even if he managed to loosen the bindings, they weren't the only things holding him in place. Thicker, heavier-duty ropes circled his waist and neck, and tied to their ends, sitting on his knees, were two giant cinder blocks. Struggle or shake too much and one or both cinder blocks would fall. And so would he. Into the deep end of the pool below him.

He couldn't believe this. The officer who'd been his shadow for the past two days, ever since that bitch Charlotte Henby had dressed him down in front of the entire HPD and an FBI agent, had told him the threat had passed. They'd caught their prime suspect. So either they had the wrong person in custody, or this was something else. Someone jerking his chain, out for a good laugh, he hoped. Or someone trying to force his hand or seeking retribution, he feared.

In either event, he couldn't say with certainty what for. The potential list was a long one. He was no saint, and he hadn't hesitated to use his family name or city hall to get what he wanted. That's the way his father had done it and his father before him. One of the perks of being a Rowan. He was pretty sure, though, that neither his dad nor his granddad had ever found themselves in this kind of situation.

A shadow moved, drawing his gaze from the blocks on his knees to the corner of the room. When the shadow took form and stalked the end of the building closest to him, Craig reared back, almost knocking off a block.

"Careful, Craig," the figure spoke, voice disguised by a modulator. "I need you to send a message for me before you die."

Die?

Fear shot through him, causing his heart to pound and his vision to blur. This was not some prank.

"I'm going to ungag you now, and you're not going to scream. If you scream, I'll knock those blocks off your knees. Nod if you understand."

He nodded carefully as beads of sweat ran down his forehead and into his eyes. He blinked furiously to clear his vision. Maybe if he recognized his kidnapper, if it was someone he knew, he could use his connections to plead his case. His hopes died, though, when his kidnapper approached from behind, untying the gag and removing it from his mouth. The cloth made a small splash in the water.

Hearing a click to his right, he scanned the shadows again and found the unmistakable red dot of a camera. He was being recorded. Before he had time to contemplate further, his attacker spoke again.

"Do you know why you're here?"

He licked his lips and stretched his jaw, forcing his mouth to function again after being gagged. "No," he croaked. He cleared his throat and started again. "No, I have no idea."

"You're guilty, Craig."

"Guilty?"

"You were a star back then, weren't you? Captain and starting tailback for the Raiders. I bet you thought you could have any girl you wanted."

"What the fuck are you talking about?" he asked, distracted. He'd begun working again at the bindings behind his back.

"And if a girl didn't want you, you'd just slip a little something into her drink."

His fingers froze. "I never did that."

"No?" It wasn't so much a question as thinly veiled outrage. The pacing behind him stopped. "You never took Charlotte Henby to a party her senior year of high school, plied her with a roofied wine cooler, and pressured her to have sex with you?"

It took everything in him not to move, to suppress the bile that rocketed up his throat and stung his nostrils. The struggle only intensified as the kidnapper carried on with the litany of his sins.

"And Trevor Caldwell never broke your nose when he came to rescue her. You never returned the favor. Your best friend, Thomas Teller, never pulled Trevor off you and threatened to tell his father, the HU Pirate's baseball coach, what Trevor had done so he'd lose his scholarship. You never threatened to press assault charges if he or Charlie reported what you'd done. You never did any of those things, did you, Craig?"

"H-h-how did you know all that?"

Footsteps grew louder, charging up behind him, and he closed his eyes, forcing himself not to rock forward at the force of the person's words or the spittle flying onto the side of his face. "You ruined a good family that night. Then you grew up to cover the same crimes you committed. Anyone who's lived in Hanover a minute can see what a despicable man you are."

The warm breath retreated, and the names began

again, names he'd never forget. "Hannah Meyers, Patricia Gilbert, Meghan Abbott."

As the assailant's angry voice filled the cavernous building, Craig had to fight harder to control his shaking, the cinder blocks wobbling precariously on his knees, threatening death at any second.

"Three HU cheerleaders, drugged and raped at an alumni party in Atlanta after the Pirates won their bowl game last New Year's Eve."

Shaking only his head, he spouted his practiced response. "HU and Atlanta PD conducted an investigation. They found no evidence connecting any HU players to the events of that night."

"Because you, our esteemed mayor, covered it up. You and Thomas Teller up to your old tricks again."

His attacker was still in the shadows, not close enough to glimpse, to confirm who they might be. Either way, he had to try to negotiate for his life. He knew the camera was rolling, that he was admitting his guilt, but between certain death and a jail cell, he'd take the cell.

"What do you want? Money? Restitution for those girls? We can handle this quietly. I'll talk to Thomas. I'm sure we can make some sort of deal. Just tell me what you want and let me go. Whatever you want, just let me live."

"Would you give up the mayor's seat?"

He'd hate it, relinquishing the power of city hall, cutting off the future career path for his son. But right now, his attacker had all the power, and he had none. "If I have to."

"Not good enough. You have to pay for your crimes,

Craig. For the wrongs you've committed and the tragedies you've caused."

"Please," he begged. "Whatever you want."

Arms snaked from around him, hands on the cinder blocks. "I only want one thing for the lives you've destroyed, for the lives lost because of your crimes."

He gulped. "What do you want?"

"For you to get what you deserve."

"Please," he whispered a final appeal. "You don't want to do—"

The cinder blocks fell and dragged Craig Rowan into the water with them.

CHAPTER TWENTY

Sean balanced the tray of Bojangles' breakfast goods in one hand and with his other withdrew the motel room card key from his pocket and swiped it in front of the door lock. The electronic lock clicked, and he pushed inside... and nearly dropped the tray.

Charlie sat on the end of the dining table in one of his dress shirts, unbuttoned, and nothing else, so far as Sean could tell from the doorway. Between her spread legs, Trevor stood in his boxer briefs, running his hands up her thighs as he rained kisses over her face, Charlie's quiet sighs making Sean hard in an instant.

Her command making him even harder. "Close the door, Sean."

He kicked it shut behind him, then looked for another place to set his wobbly tray of food because it looked like the table was well on its way to not being an option.

"Was somebody hungry?" Trevor asked as he kissed a path down Charlie's neck.

Charlie laughed, deep and throaty, and with an easiness that had been missing since Sean had been back in Hanover. "He wanted to mark another off his list."

"Chicken biscuits for you and me," Sean said as he crossed the room on the other side of the table. "Bo-berry biscuits for Mr. Sweet Tooth." He set the tray on the coffee table, then turned back to the even sweeter, hotter sight. "I hope those are still acceptable."

Trevor righted his head, face turning to Sean, and the languid heat in his hazel eyes was as intoxicating as Charlie's earlier laugh. "The only thing acceptable right now is you out of those clothes and standing here with us." One of his hands crept under the hem of Charlie's borrowed shirt, and Charlie spread her legs wider, braced both hands behind her, and dropped her head back between her shoulders. The shirt fell the rest of the way open, revealing nothing else indeed, other than her gorgeous breasts and Trevor's thumb working her clit.

As Trevor sank two fingers inside her, Sean hustled to join them, shedding his shirt and dropping his pants, never happier he'd gone commando.

A growly Trevor approved. "Get in here." He shifted enough for Sean to slide between them on his knees, adding his tongue to the pleasure Trevor was already giving Charlie while stroking Trevor's cock. He groaned at finding them both wet and eager. And they groaned above him too, two hands landing on his head, Trevor and Charlie directing him together. He loved giving up control to them, pleasuring them like this.

Without goodbye looming over them.

Charlie moaned and writhed, the roll of her hips, the pants of her breaths, and the keening *please*s and *fuck me*s escalating, until she came with a shout and a slap of her palm against the table.

Trevor dragged him up the next instant, turned his back to Charlie, and grasped their dicks in his fist. He pumped them, hard and fast, Sean's spit and their precome making his grip smooth and wet. Wetter still when Charlie recovered, wrapped herself around Sean from behind, and teased his rim with her own slick finger. "You know what would make this better?" she whispered hotly in his ear.

Oh, he knew, remembered it fondly. "You pegging one of us."

"Next time," Charlie promised as she pinched his nipples.

Sean tipped forward and came with a fantasy-fueled grunt against Trevor's lips, then nearly combusted a second time when Trevor lifted his come-covered hand and Charlie licked it clean over Sean's shoulder. Trevor thrust against his groin and covered it with his own release.

Sweaty and panting, the three of them rested against the side of the table, Charlie recovering her voice first and nipping his earlobe. "Maybe don't leave us alone if you don't want to come back to trouble."

He twisted to steal a kiss. "This is the kind of trouble I like to come back to."

Trevor nuzzled the other side of his neck. "Did you say Bo-berry biscuits?"

They were still laughing when a knock sounded

against the motel room door. Charlie righted her head, gaze snapping to him, "Who—"

The knock came again. "Sean, you in there? It's Abel. Open up."

The lightness of a moment ago evaporated on a dime. Charlie's eyes filled with the same foreboding that had haunted them all week, and Sean was walloped with a terrible sense of déjà vu. This could not be good.

Trevor sensed their tension too, going rigid behind him. "Why's Abel here?"

Charlie began the process of untangling them. "We need to clean up and get dressed."

"What's going on?"

Sean brushed the hair out of his face. "Get us some towels." As Trevor made a beeline for the bathroom, Sean called out to Abel. "Just a minute." Sean darted forward, grabbing his shirt and jeans from where he'd dropped them. "He know you're here?" he asked Charlie, who was likewise hastily gathering her and Trevor's clothes.

"Yeah, he knew I was still worried." They caught the two towels Trevor tossed their way, wiped off, then began yanking on clothes as Trevor retreated into the bathroom with the clothes Charlie had handed him. "I told him I'd be here and that I'd keep Trevor here too. Though not necessarily like this."

"Look at it this way," Sean said. "It saves him a trip." His attempt at humor was forced as was his smirk, and both fell flat, doing nothing to lighten the tension.

Once they were dressed, Sean opened the door. One look at the chief's grim face and Sean knew what was coming. So did Charlie, given the sudden stiffness of her shoulders.

Abel made no mention of the fact she was in his room, no remark about the rumpled bed behind them, and paid barely any notice to Trevor as he opened the bathroom door. All Abel's attention was focused on Charlie. "There's been another murder."

"Where?" Trevor asked, at the same time Charlie and Sean asked, "Who?"

"The HU natatorium."

"Fuck." Trevor raked a hand through his loose hair. "Ophelia."

Abel nodded.

"Who?" Charlie asked again.

He didn't answer right away. Instead, he approached Charlie and grasped her shoulders. "Charlotte, you need to brace."

Sean's stomach sank. This was bad, worse even than Julian. "Who is it, Abel?"

"Craig Rowan," he said, eyes still locked with Charlie's. "They found him in the pool along with twelve dozen red roses."

***

"Stop the video, Charlie." Sean meant it as an order, same as he had the last three times he'd given it.

Charlie, sitting to his left on the fourth row of metal bleachers, ignored him, same as she had three times before, her index finger sliding the cursor back across the tablet screen and replaying the horrific death scene.

With each viewing, Charlie's pale skin blanched whiter, her eyes grew wider, and her body shook so badly the tablet wobbled on her knees.

As wobbly as those cinder blocks had been in Craig Rowan's lap.

Yet she remained transfixed, unable to look away. Then again, Sean wasn't sure which sight was worse: Craig's nocturnal death tableau or his lifeless body lying on a stretcher in the light of day, next to the pool blanketed in red roses.

Either sight was terrifying, both confirming what Charlie had suspected. What he had feared. This case wasn't over, and the evidence pointed strongly to a connection to Charlie, Trevor, and the Henby family.

"Charlie, stop the damn video and hand me the tablet."

When she still didn't respond, he shot out a gloved hand and snatched the tablet from her grasp. He turned it off and placed it in the evidence bag Maggie had left at the end of the row. Snapping off his gloves, he turned back to Charlie and found her staring at her empty, shaking hands. He took one then the other in his own and rolled off her gloves.

"How many people know?"

"Know?" She seemed confused by his question.

He rubbed her ice-cold hands between his, trying to ward off the shock and refocus her. "About what Craig did to you at that party." Together with what he'd learned yesterday, Sean finally understood the hostility he'd witnessed between Charlie and Craig. And why Trevor hated him so much too. He was the root of so many tragedies, including those in the lives of the people Sean loved. Scooting closer, he squeezed Charlie's hands, offering as much comfort as he could in a building full of cops and crime scene techs. "How many knew, Charlie?"

Charlie curled her fingers around his, closed her eyes, and took several deep breaths. "I called Cal and Trevor that night. Trevor showed up. And the only other people I ever told were Abel, Annie, Maggie, and Rachel." She blinked her eyes open, and the haunted look was still there but so were bone-tired weariness and lingering anger. "Craig talked, though. He told people we had sex that night even though we didn't."

"Fucking bastard," Sean cursed through clenched teeth.

She swept a thumb across his palm, cooling his anger.

"And the alumni party last year?" Sean asked.

Another of Craig's sins called out in the video.

"Wasn't in our jurisdiction," Charlie answered. "With Thomas being Craig's best friend..."

"It was hushed up."

Charlie nodded. "And our killer knew about both."

Feeling her pulse quicken as her eyes drifted to the pool again, Sean tightened his grip on her hands. She needed something more to focus on, tangible police work to settle into, or else she'd spend all morning staring at those roses and imagining the worst. "Hand me your phone. Unlocked." She dug the device out of her pocket, entered the passcode, and handed it over. He opened her notes app, then handed it back. "You need to make lists. Best you can remember, everyone who knows the truth about what happened at that party, everyone involved in the HU incident last year, and everyone who knows the truth about your mother's death. Let's see if there are any matches. In the meantime, I'll follow the roses, and Marsh can hack the tablet."

"Follow the roses?"

"That's a lot of roses, even for red ones. Someone would notice a purchase that large."

"Charlie. Sean." Abel called to them from where he stood with Officer Sylvan next to the evidence table at the end of the pool closest to them.

"We'll be right there," Sean said before speaking quietly again to Charlie. "Take a minute to gather yourself." He waited for her to nod, then stood and climbed down the bleachers, taking the tablet in its evidence bag with him.

"I'll leave you to it," Officer Sylvan said. "HU Administration has been ringing me from outside every five minutes for the past hour. I better go talk to them."

"Stall for now," Abel said.

"Yes, sir."

Once he was out of earshot, Abel asked Sean, "How is she?"

"Shaken but pulling it together. Just give her a minute."

He set the bagged tablet on the table next to two other evidence bags. One held the latest note—a slip of paper that read: #3 – SWEETS TO THE SWEET. The other bag contained an unmarked bottle of pills, likely the same pills that had drugged those cheerleaders and maybe Charlie too. All three items—the tablet, the note, and the pills—had been waiting for them on the starting block where Craig had taken his last breath. Politicians and their power trips. There was a certain irony to Craig being powerless in the end. Sean wondered what his constituents would think now, especially if that video was ever leaked.

He looked back up at Abel. "What've you got?"

"Just got off the phone with the marshals. Beth Martin was in a holding cell in Athens all night, and she's been in their car since six this morning."

"Does she have any connection to Craig?"

"None that we've found so far, but Jaylen and Diego are at the station digging." And watching over Trevor. "Marsh is on it too."

He caught his friend's worried glance from the top row of the bleachers on the other side of the pool. They'd exchanged only a few words on the car ride over. Marsh had read Sean's anxiety the moment he'd opened his motel room door and wisely hadn't pressed beyond questions about the case. The whole time, though, Marsh's thumbs had beat a steady rhythm against the steering wheel, no doubt wondering why Trevor and Charlie had also exited his motel room. They'd get into that later. Right now, Sean's immediate concern was keeping his family safe.

"Once CSU logs that"—he nodded toward the bagged tablet—"Marsh gets it. If there's something to be found, we need it before Beth arrives."

"I'll go tell the techs to double time it," Abel said.

The clack of heels alerted him to Charlie's approach. "Do you still think Beth's involved?" she asked. "There's no mention of her in any of Dad's or Cal's files, and other than being a colleague, Trevor didn't know her either."

"It's looking unlikely since she was in custody last night, but we can't discount that she could be working with an accomplice." It was a stretch, but it was all they had to go on. "We need to talk to Trevor again. As much as I hate to admit it, it's clear this latest murder has something to do with your family. But we can't deny our killer may also be doing this for Trevor. Jeff tried to railroad his tenure. Julian stole his wife. Craig almost cost him his baseball scholarship. You need to make your lists, have him look over them, and see if he can make any connections we're missing."

Charlie's phone vibrated in her hand, an alert lighting up the screen. "Shit, I'm supposed to be staking out Julian's funeral in an hour. I told Annie—"

"Go," he said. "But not alone."

"I thought you wanted to talk to Trevor."

"I do." He flagged down Marsh, who snapped his laptop shut and unfolded from his spot on the bleachers, slowly making his way down, his cowboy boots clattering. "Marsh will go with you." Charlie started to object, but Sean gave her reasons not to. "One, he's good backup. Two, he'll be right there. Give him your list. He'll start the cross-checks immediately. Three, he's big enough to break up a brawl if things escalate again with you and Trace."

She chuckled weakly, but he'd take it.

"We'll get through this. I promise." He lowered his head and kissed her, hard and fast. A firm press of his lips, enough to make his point but not enough to be indecent in front of others, including Marsh who cleared his throat behind them. "Sorry to interrupt you kids."

Sean glanced over his shoulder. "Oh, so I can start calling you old man now?"

"You do and there will be consequences."

Charlie laughed, more strength to it than before.

Sean was happy to keep needling Marsh if it kept her laughing. "Well, if you're not too old to break up a catfight today—"

"Hey!" Charlie shoved his chest and continued her mock offense by pointedly turning her back on him and addressing Marsh. "If you wouldn't mind a return trip to the cemetery, I could use some backup."

"Happy to help." Marsh grinned as he flicked his eyes at Sean. "Especially if it gets me away from that asshole."

Charlie snickered and Sean reached around her to slap his friend's shoulder. "You're a fucking riot. And just for that, one more thing on your to do list." He snagged the evidence bag with the tablet, gestured to Abel, and when Abel gave him the thumbs up, handed it to Marsh. "I need you to dig into this. Anything you can find."

He glanced at the tablet, then back up, dark eyes dancing with mirth. "Too much to hope for porn?"

Charlie's laugh was music to his ears.

CHAPTER TWENTY-ONE

Trevor paced the length of the conference room for the—he'd lost count an hour ago—time. It had been multiple hours since Abel had dropped him off at the station, and while he appreciated Diego's and Jaylen's efforts to make him comfortable and keep him distracted, no amount of pastries or coffee, no amount of lifting weights in the gym, no amount of answering work emails and sending lesson plans to substitute lecturers was going to make him forget Abel's words at the motel.

"Craig Rowan... They found him in the pool along with twelve dozen red roses."

Christ, Charlie was right. This did have something to do with their family, and while she and Sean were out there being useful, he was stuck at the fucking station. The fact that he couldn't be there for her, couldn't tackle this with her like they had Cal's letter, was maddening. Granted, Sean was with her, which was some comfort, but he wanted to be there too. The woman he loved, his best friend, was hurting, and he couldn't be there for her.

"So it's your day to pace?"

Trevor whipped around, surprised and dismayed to find Sean in the conference room doorway. Without Charlie. "What are you doing here? Why aren't you with Charlie?"

Sean closed the door behind him. "Marsh is with her. She's safe. They're on their way to keep an eye on Julian's funeral."

"Fuck." He raked his hands through his hair, fisting it behind his neck. "That's today? I didn't send—"

"Trev, no one expected you to send flowers." Sean rounded the table, coming to his side and gently taking his hand. His thumbs smoothed a pattern over the back of his palm. "You need to take a breather."

"That's what I've been doing all morning."

Sean shot him a judging glare. "No, you've been stewing."

"Because I don't know what's going on." His gaze drifted over Sean's shoulder in the direction of Charlie's office, and he wished like hell she was in there, working too damn hard like always, running herself ragged trying to do all the things. Like going to Tracy's funeral, even if it was in an official capacity. He should be the one doing that. He should be with her. "I need to be helping somehow." He returned his gaze to Sean and gestured at the room around them. "More than this."

Sean spun out the closest chair and nudged Trevor into

it. "I'll catch you up." He lowered himself into the adjacent chair. "Then I'll tell you how you can help."

"Is she okay?"

"No." Sean talked over his curse. "But she's distracted, at least for an hour or so, and Marsh is the best backup she could have besides me."

He jammed an index finger against the table in front of Sean. "Then why the fuck are you *here?*" He hated how accusing he sounded, how rough his voice was toward Sean, especially after last night, but his frustration needed an outlet, and Sean was there.

He was strong enough to take it and knew Trevor well enough not to take offense. He scooted closer, a knee braced against Trevor's under the table, an arm stretched across the back of his chair. "One, to check on you. How are you?"

"A fucking mess," Trevor admitted. No use mincing words. Sean had read him right from the second—

Sean's mouth pressed against his, lips rough and demanding, parting Trevor's and coaxing his tongue to play. The gentle, playful, confident kiss silenced the rambling in Trevor's head for a few blissful moments. "What was that for?" he asked as Sean drew back.

"Because I wanted to. And because what I'm about to tell you isn't going to make things any less messy."

Trevor eyed the hand Sean placed on his thigh. "You know I'm on to you and Charlie and this containment thing. How you box me in and minimize the damage when I'm upset. I've always been on to it."

"We do what we can for each other." Sean smiled, tired but true. "That's why it works, why *we* work."

The last of the frustration gusts went out of Trevor's sails and he slumped in his chair. He braced an elbow on the armrest and rested his head in his hand. "Get on with the messy part."

Sean ripped the Band-Aid off. "Craig was pushed off a starting block into the pool at HU. His hands and feet were bound, and cinder blocks were used to weigh him down."

Trevor closed his eyes. "Ophelia."

"The killer left a video. They made Craig confess his crimes before they pushed him off the block and into the water."

"And they knew about the party that night? That's the basis for conspiracy?"

"The video also describes a cover-up by Mayor Rowan and Coach Teller of several alleged date rapes at a New Year's Eve party."

"Cheerleaders who were at an alumni party after the bowl game." Trevor righted himself in the chair. "Nothing alleged about it."

"That's what Charlie said."

"But it's not just about Craig and Teller, is it? Abel mentioned the roses."

Sean withdrew his phone from his pocket, tapped the screen a few times, and set it on the table in front of Trevor.

One look at the picture—Craig's body on a stretcher next to the pool of roses—and Trevor shot out a hand to flip the phone over. "Fuck, if I never have to see that again, it'd be too soon." He propped both elbows on the table and buried his face in his hands, then plowed them through his hair when all he could see behind his closed eyelids was that same horrific sight.

Sean's hands on his thigh and back were the only things grounding him in the here and now, keeping him from falling into the abyss of nightmares. "How do we stop this?" He angled his face toward Sean and bit back his gasp at seeing the haunted look in Sean's eyes. He'd been hiding it before, but it was clear now he was as terrified as Trevor, as Charlie also had to be. Trevor lowered an arm and wrapped a hand around the one still resting on his thigh. "Get to the how I can help part now, please."

"We need you to review Charlie's lists and make similar lists of your own."

"Lists of what?"

Sean lifted one finger. "People who knew Craig Rowan tried to rape her at that party your senior year of high school." Another. "People involved in the alumni party incident last year." And a third. "Anyone who knows the truth about Alice's death."

"Then do what? Cross-check them?"

Sean nodded.

"I can, yeah, but don't you want Diego or Jaylen or Abel to do that? I play at being police, but they're real police."

Sean chuckled. "You finally watched *The Wire* with her?"

"She wore me down." Trevor couldn't help but smile, remembering that epic marathon-watching session. It was a three-day holiday weekend, a rare one that Charlie got off, and neither of them had left the beach house for days. Trevor's pleasant memory was wiped away, though, by Sean's next words.

"I don't think this case is just about the Henbys." He flipped his hand over under Trevor's and laced their fingers. "It's about you too. You might even be at the center of it."

Trevor flinched, hard. "How do you figure?"

"Jefferson Marshall tried to railroad your tenure. Julian Hirsch stole your wife. Craig Rowan almost cost you your baseball scholarship."

Trevor hung his head. "Christ, I never asked for this."

"Then help me stop it." Sean squeezed his hand, then released it and retrieved his phone. "Who did you talk to about that party senior year?" he asked as he opened the notepad app.

"Cal, obviously. Annie, Rachel, who I was dating at the time, and later on, Tracy. But there were a lot of people at that party, Sean."

"Beth Martin, maybe?"

He shook his head. "She didn't grow up here. Besides, Beth was in custody."

"Evidence indicates she's still involved somehow." He tapped at his phone again and brought up another picture. A sharps bag in a trash can. "Those were at Beth's place." He swiped across the screen to a picture of empty vials. "It's an anesthetic only available locally at HU Med."

Trevor put together where Sean was going. "Tracy."

"Did she know about Alice's death?"

"Not that I'm aware of. Charlie and I didn't know Cal was responsible or about the cover up until after his and Mitch's funeral, and by then, Tracy was remarried to Julian. We hadn't spoken in months." Trevor closed his eyes and that nightmare image flashed again, along with a horrifying realization. "But she knew about the roses. Every Sunday, I used to bring Charlie red roses to take to the cemetery after dinner. But why, Sean? Why would Tracy kill for me when she hates me?"

"Revenge, to frame you, to get your attention," Sean rattled off. "It's a thin line between love and hate, even thinner when you throw in an unhealthy dose of obsession. She said it herself. She was tired of playing second best to Charlie. She's demanding your attention."

Sean's phone vibrated on the table, an incoming text from Charlie flashing onscreen. "What's it say?" Trevor asked.

"They're at the cemetery. And she attached her lists."

His face fell, and Trevor could guess at what he read. "Tracy on there?"

He nodded, brow furrowing. "When we questioned her, I didn't think she had anything to do with it."

"Maybe she's a better actress than we thought."

He didn't miss the shudder Sean tried to hide as he stood, opened the door, and began issuing orders. "Call the hospital and see if Tracy was on shift last night," he said to Jaylen. Then to Abel, who'd stepped out of his office, "Can we get an extra squad car out to the cemetery? Charlie and Marsh may need to bring Tracy in."

"Ah, fuck," the chief cursed. "She a suspect again?"

"Maybe," Sean said. "Pending what Jaylen finds out from the hospital."

Abel started across the bullpen floor toward the dispatch officer, and Sean turned back into the conference room. Trevor waited until he closed the door to voice the fear that had been steadily crawling up his throat. "Sean, if this is because of me..." He gulped, swallowing the lump in his throat, ignoring the goose bumps that rose on his arms. "How am I supposed to live with myself? After what it's done to Charlie, to our family, to the victims..." He tracked Sean as he rounded the table and came to stand beside him. "We have to stop this," he pleaded. "I don't want anyone else to die because of me."

Sean tugged him out of the chair and into his arms. "We'll figure this out, Trev."

He wound his arms around Sean's waist and burrowed closer, hiding from the potentially catastrophic truth. "But at what cost?"

CHAPTER TWENTY-TWO

Charlie glanced away from the crowd gathering at Julian Hirsch's gravesite to the man beside her in the squad car's driver's seat who was rooting around in a yellow Taqueria Perez bag. "I'm sorry to drag you back to the cemetery. I'm sure this wasn't how you planned to spend your afternoon."

Marsh produced two burritos from the bag, handed one to Charlie, then slid back in his seat with the other, tearing away the foil. "Worth it for good Mexican food."

"I also realize this is you distracting me from the events of this morning."

"Is it working?"

Smiling, Charlie peeled back the wrapper around her own burrito and took a bite. She hummed in approval.

Marsh chuckled. "I can't remember the last time I staked out something other than browser histories or network servers." He paused to take a bite of his burrito. "And this food is damn good."

"Burritos and college towns seem to go hand in hand."

"Good cheap eats," Marsh said. "Taqueria Perez is run by Diego's family?"

Charlie drank from her bottle of Cheerwine, then set it back in the cup holder. "Yep. His parents and aunt relocated from Corpus Christi when he and Maggie had their first kid."

"They have more?"

"Restaurants?" she replied, looking back out the windshield. The groundskeeper had let them take the maintenance road into the cemetery, and from their shadowed spot next to one of the utility sheds, they had a bird's-eye view of the funeral. And of a mournful Tracy approaching the gravesite. She looked worse than when they'd last seen her. Her somber black suit hung loosely on her frame, and her face appeared pinched and drawn. Seeing her so frail, Charlie seriously doubted Tracy was the one who'd dragged Craig into the HU natatorium last night and questioned him with the force and morbid glee their killer had exhibited on that video.

"Kids," Marsh said, snapping Charlie back inside the cruiser.

"Three in all."

"And they manage okay with their schedules?"

"They do. It helps having family around. You thinking about kids?"

Dark eyes lifted to hers, a little winsome, a little wary. "I hadn't really thought about it until recently. A friend in San Francisco has an almost three-year-old, and she's so stinkin' cute it makes me wonder, though I'm pretty sure she threw her daddy's chess game the other day."

She jutted her chin at his phone on the dash. "Is that what you're always doing on there?"

"A lot of the time," he said as he tore away more foil. "When things went sideways at work a while back, I went radio silent on him. Promised not to do that again."

Charlie took another bite before getting back to Marsh's earlier question. "I think kids and a career in law enforcement is doable if you want both. Plenty of folks do it, my father and grandfather included."

"You?"

She smiled, remembering similar conversations from a decade ago. "Sean, Trevor, and I used to talk about adopting. If they still want to, I'd be down." She took another bite, then shot a smile the cyber agent's direction. "I'm sure they'd appreciate some cousins."

"Gotta stop falling for unavailable guys first."

Charlie nearly dropped her burrito. She caught it at the last second but not her gasp. "Sean said—"

"I'm over it now," he said with a dismissive wave. "Same way I'm over my friend in San Francisco. I see how happy he is with his husband, how happy Sean is with you and Trevor, and that's all I want for them." He took another huge bite of burrito. "But I do seem to be cursed."

Charlie set her burrito on the dash and took a swig of soda. "I thought the same for a while. When Sean left and it didn't work out with Trevor, I never connected with anyone else. It felt like a curse."

"You broke it somehow."

She smiled. "I hope so."

He bumped her shoulder. "Me too."

They finished their burritos in comfortable silence while keeping an eye on each new arrival at the funeral. No unexpected visitors so far. No sign of her sister yet either. She'd just picked up her phone to text Annie when a call from the station lit up the screen. "Talk to me."

"Tracy alibied out," Abel said by way of greeting.

Sean had texted her that Tracy was on Trevor's lists too, and they were running down her whereabouts at the time of Craig's murder. "She was on shift last night?"

"Accounted for all night. Got off at six this morning and went straight to the funeral home. Wasn't her in the video."

She leaned back in her seat, staring at the roof and silently cursing another dead end. "So either she had an accomplice, or she's not involved."

"If Beth was also an accomplice, that'd be three people involved," Abel said. "That's stretching it, sugar."

"Charlie," Marsh said, gesturing out the windshield. "We may have a situation here."

Glancing forward, Charlie spotted her sister approaching the gravesite and Tracy cutting through the crowd toward her. "Abel, we gotta go." She ended the call and slung open her door, Marsh exiting on the other side. They hustled to where Tracy and Annie stood arguing at the edge of the crowd. Charlie picked up speed when Tracy grabbed Annie's arm and gave her a violent shake. "Tracy!" Charlie shouted. "Let her go."

"Oh, perfect." Tracy shoved Annie away as her gaze

swung to Charlie. "You're here too. You Henbys can't leave well enough alone, can you?"

Charlie curled an arm around her trembling sister's shoulders. Despite the tragedy that had befallen Tracy, Charlie had never been angrier with her than she was right then, not even after what she'd done to Trevor. "Marsh and I are here as part of the investigation, in case your husband's killer makes an appearance. My sister is here because she's your friend. And this is how you treat her? Manhandling her and embarrassing her in front of half the town?"

"Charlie, it's okay," Annie whispered at her side.

"No, it's not. All you've ever tried to be is a good friend—"

"Bullshit," Tracy spat, and Annie flinched against Charlie's side. "She was only friends with me to stay close to Trevor and then after as a spy for you."

"Annie has never said a bad word about you, not even after the divorce."

"I haven't, Trace," Annie said. "I promise. I'm your friend too."

"I don't believe either one of you." Tracy took a menacing step forward, and Charlie shuffled in front of Annie, Marsh at her side.

"Fine, don't believe us," Charlie said. "But when you wake up tomorrow or ten days from now and realize you've lost one of the best friends you'll ever have, do not come looking for my sister. I don't want someone like you around her anymore."

"Charlie." Annie squeezed her hand. "Let's go."

"Do I make myself clear?" Charlie said, her eyes still locked with Tracy's.

Tracy sneered. "Crystal."

"Good." She turned her back on Tracy and the onlookers they'd drawn, gathered Annie to her side again, and headed away from the gravesite.

"I was just trying to be a good friend." Annie leaned into her. "Tell her I'm sorry."

"I know, sweetie, but you've got nothing to be sorry for."

"Get her home," Marsh said when they reached the walkway that would take them to the cruiser or Annie's car out front. "I'll keep watch here."

"Thank you," Charlie said as she handed off the cruiser keys. "For more than just today. I'm glad Sean has a friend like you."

Charlie waved her thanks to the officers in the cruiser that had tailed her to Annie's then to the station. She'd hated having to leave her sister so quickly, Annie still shaken from the altercation with Tracy, but Sean had texted that Beth Martin was at the station, attorney in tow. As they were already pushing the limits on holding and transporting her, Charlie couldn't delay.

She strode across the bullpen toward the conference room but was intercepted halfway by Trevor's "Charlie!" Before she could blink, he was right there in front of her, arms circling her waist and drawing her into his embrace. "Thank fuck you're okay."

She returned the hug. "I'm fine, babe."

He drew back enough to frame her face with his hands. "Annie?"

"Tracy caused a scene." She smoothed her fingers over his forehead before it got too wrinkled with anger. "Annie's shaken but home safe." His heartbeat slowed a little beneath her other hand on his chest. "How are *you*?"

"Scared for everyone I love, but a little less so now that you're here." He leaned his forehead against hers and heaved a weary sigh. As much as this was wearing on her, she could at least focus on the police work. Trevor, on the other hand, was at the center of a storm that just kept intensifying around him. "What the hell is going on?"

"We're going to figure it out. I promise."

"Charlie," came Sean's voice from the conference room.

She leaned back and patted Trevor's chest. "Let me go talk to Beth. See what else we can find out. We'll check in with you after."

Trevor reluctantly released her, and she half suspected it was only because it was to go to Sean. He held the conference room door open for her and the short, balding man across the table, Beth's attorney Charlie assumed, stood. The bedraggled-looking woman, however, remained seated. Her mousy-brown hair was limp and greasy, and her brown eyes were dull and ringed with dark circles. She looked tired, scared, and confused. What she didn't look was guilty.

"Ms. Martin," Sean said, "this is Deputy Charlotte Henby. Charlie, this is Beth Martin and her attorney, Aaron Goldstein."

Charlie held out her hand, shaking both of theirs before lowering herself into the chair next to Sean. "We'd like to ask you some questions."

"I'm being set up," Beth blurted.

Aaron admonished his client.

"No." She laid a hand on his forearm in a way that spoke to more than just an attorney–client relationship. "They have to understand I didn't do this." Her wide eyes swung back to her and Sean. "I was in Georgia last night. I wasn't even here when the mayor got killed."

Sean leaned forward, bracing his forearms on the table. "Did you know Mayor Rowan?"

"Other than seeing him on TV or around town in passing, no. I stay out of politics. I've got way more interesting things to do with my time."

The remarks were dismissive in the way someone would speak of any politician, not of a murder victim targeted for his past misdeeds. If his furrowed brow and narrowed eyes were any indication, Sean thought the same. She tapped his foot twice beneath the table, and with a slight head tilt, he gave her the go-ahead to lead.

"Ms. Martin, why did you take off for Georgia yesterday morning?"

"I've been following the case in the news. I mean, like, how could you not? It's been the lead story all week. It's like a novel come to life—gruesome killings, the FBI investigating, police and press crawling all over campus. I've never been somewhere where the news happens right under my nose. I've been telling all my online friends about it. So exciting. But never in a million years did I think I'd wind up in the middle of it. Leave me out of that part of the novel. Those marshals were hot and all but so not worth it."

"Beth," Aaron warned, attempting to curtail his client's ramble.

"Sorry, got carried away there." She folded her hands on the table. "I'm here because you found that sharps bag in my trash, right?"

"Yes," Charlie said. "Would you care to explain that?"

"I took out my trash yesterday morning and found that bag in there. I volunteer at the hospital, so I know what goes in those. I already had on a pair of cleaning gloves, so I opened the bag. I'd heard enough about the case to figure those guys had been drugged, and when I saw the syringes and Diprivan bottles, I freaked. I have no idea where they came from. I know I should have called 911 or something, but I panicked. My fiancé lives in Georgia. Both he and his brother"—she patted Aaron's arm—"are criminal defense attorneys. So I ran to them for help."

"You couldn't have just called?"

"Like I said, I was freaked. Like way the heck out."

"My future sister-in-law acts before she thinks sometimes," Aaron added.

Consistent with a busybody who talked and acted before she thought. Inconsistent with a murderer who carried out brutal, calculated killings.

"You said you didn't personally know Mayor Rowan," Charlie said. "Did you know Julian Hirsch?"

"Unfortunately." Beth shifted forward in her chair and affected a conspiratorial whisper. "He asked me out last year, but I was engaged already. Even if I wasn't, I wouldn't have touched that man with a ten-foot pole, no matter how hot he was. Might as well have had love 'em and leave 'em stamped on his forehead. Then I found out he was sleeping with one of my students, Sarah Barnett. I know his wife, Tracy, from the hospital. She's kind of a bitch, but I didn't want that man taking advantage of Sarah. So I told Tracy. They hadn't been married long. I thought she'd pitch a fit, maybe get him to back off Sarah. She's a good girl, real smart, and I knew her father was running for office. I didn't want her to get in trouble. That's why I asked her about your officers coming to talk to her. I feared the worst."

Charlie inched back, distancing herself from Beth's gossipy tone. Why someone would willingly insert themselves into such a sordid mess when they had no personal stake in it was beyond her.

Sean, who'd pushed his chair back even farther, redirected. "We also understand Jefferson Marshall vetoed your tenure."

"See?" She threw up her hands, right back to panicked. "This is why I ran. I knew this would all come back to bite me in the ass. I was just trying to help them out."

"Them?" Sean queried.

"Sarah and Tracy. Girl power and all that. I couldn't care less about Professor Marshall. Being denied tenure at

HU was the best thing that ever happened to me. I guest lectured at UGA last year, met my fiancé, and UGA offered me a tenure-track position. I'm out of here at the end of this summer, assuming my offer isn't yanked after all this." She placed her hand on Aaron's arm again as she pulled out her phone with the other. "I need you and Daniel to call your contacts at UGA while I reschedule the appointment with my real estate agent."

"Beth," Charlie said, zeroing in on her phone. "Tracy Hirsch's phone records indicate you called her the morning Julian was killed, once at three and again at nine."

"No, I didn't."

"Then how do you explain the calls?" Sean asked.

"My phone went missing last week. I searched everywhere for it, then found it in my desk drawer Monday morning. I thought I'd lost it in a pile of papers, but maybe..." She looked at her phone as if it might bite her and tossed it on the table. "Maybe someone took it or cloned it or something. That always happens in the movies."

"Beth," Charlie said, "can anyone verify your whereabouts between the hours of two and five on Monday morning?"

She nodded. "I was home alone, but I was online, chatting with friends."

"In the middle of the night?"

"I was in a video chat room, live-streaming a K-Pop concert."

"I'm sorry, what?" Sean asked, bewilderment tingeing his voice.

"I'll explain—"

Aaron thankfully silenced her. "Give them the names, Beth."

"They're all on there," she said, chin jutting toward the phone. "Under the group name K-Pop Fangirls."

Beside her, Sean spun his chair to the credenza, withdrew gloves and an evidence bag, then gloves on, picked up the phone and dropped it into the bag.

"And where were you Friday night?" Charlie asked.

"In Georgia with my fiancé."

"His info on the phone as well?"

"Yes, Daniel Goldstein. He had a hearing this morning, but he's on his way here now."

"If you have no further questions..." Aaron moved to stand, but Charlie halted him with a raised hand.

She was ninety-five percent certain Beth wasn't involved, but she needed to lock down the final five percent. She withdrew her own phone and opened a picture of Trevor. "Do you know this man?"

A quick glance down, then Beth fluttered her lashes coyly. "Everyone at HU knows Trevor Caldwell, though we've never formally met. He's the hottest professor on campus, but I'm taken." She wiggled her ring finger with its massive rock. "And well taken care of, thank you very much."

Her future brother-in-law half chuckled, half groaned. "Any further questions?"

"That's all we have at this time," Charlie replied.

Beth's eyes lit with relief. "I don't have to stay in police custody any longer?"

"Just stay local for the next few days," Charlie said as they all rose. "In case anything comes up."

As Sean ushered them out, she signaled Jaylen over with a tilt of her head. She grabbed the bagged phone off the table and handed it to him. "Take this down to CSU. Ask them to run it for prints, pull the contacts off, and email me the numbers."

"On it, Deputy."

She waited in the conference room for Sean, who closed the door behind himself when he returned. "Beth Martin's a busybody," he said, "but she's no murderer." The same conclusions Charlie had reached. "Ten to one her alibis check out."

"And Tracy was on shift at the hospital the night of all three murders," Charlie said, addressing their other prime suspect. "Any luck with the roses?"

Sean shook his head. "Florist took in a delivery last night for a wedding. They were gone this morning. Lock picked on the backdoor. No surveillance on the shop or entrances."

"Fuck, we're back to square one." Twenty-four hours ago they'd had this case solved, and now their two prime suspects were in the clear. "We've got nothing."

"Not nothing. We've got a pattern with one victim left."

"Lady Macbeth." She kicked off her heels and began to pace. "The actually guilty one."

Sean rested against the table's edge, out of her way. "She's ambitious, manipulative, and goads Macbeth, among others, into murder."

"Given our killer's MO, I don't think they'd flip their script and kill someone innocent. That doesn't make their point, doesn't satisfy some wrong."

"Agreed, but given Lady Macbeth's actual guilt, I don't think the victim is necessarily a man this time."

"Makes sense." She continued to pace as she put together the pieces of their last victim's profile. "So if the pattern holds, we're looking for a person the killer perceives as power hungry, as an accessory to murder, is connected to my family and maybe the night of my mother's death, and somehow did Trevor wrong."

Sean's lack of a rejoinder brought her to a halt in front of him. She startled at the haunted look in his eyes.

"Sean?"

"Charlie, sit down." His voice was quiet, tight, laced with dread.

Slowly, she lowered herself into the chair beside him. When he didn't sit or explain, she laid a hand on his thigh. "Sean, you're scaring me. Tell me what you're thinking."

He covered her hand with his. "I see two possible victims, and you will too if you stop and think for a minute."

It didn't take her a minute. It took her less than ten seconds to connect the dots, and when she did, her stomach hit the floor and her breath caught in her throat. Leaning forward, she rested her forehead on their clasped hands and whispered the horrible realization.

"You... and me."

CHAPTER TWENTY-THREE

From his perch on Charlie's office windowsill, Trevor futilely scanned Main Street below. "I don't like this. Why couldn't I go with her?"

"She wanted you safe," Abel said. "Here at the station."

Trevor turned to the man he considered an uncle too. "That's not all of it. She and Sean were wired when they came out of the conference room. And then for some reason it's good for the three of us to go off in separate directions? Her to Annie's and Sean to the natatorium. How does that make sense?"

"There's a patrol car on Charlie. Wally's already at Annie's. Marsh is with Sean. It's safer this way."

Trevor exploded off the windowsill, all the pent-up fear and anger going nuclear. "What the fuck is that supposed to mean?"

Abel held his ground, one of the few people who was bigger than Trevor and also someone who had known

Trevor at his scrawny middle school worst. Had saved him a time or twenty from his parents' brawls. "You and she seem to be at the center of this thing," he said. "Maybe Sean too. Each of you is guarded, safe but separate. Better than having you all in one place like sitting ducks."

Or put another way... "We're all sitting ducks in separate places instead. Waiting to see which of us the killer comes for."

Abel sank into Charlie's desk chair, head in his hands. "That too. Their plan, not mine. And I'm as worried as you are." He pointedly eyed the visitor chair across from him and Trevor begrudgingly took a seat. "She's the deputy chief of police. She's armed and well trained, not to mention known to everyone in town. All the prior murders happened at night. It's four o'clock in the afternoon in broad daylight. She'll be fine." He picked up the stack of papers on Charlie's desk—the ones Trevor was supposed to be reviewing—and held them out to him. "Now, let's get back to these and see if we can help identify a suspect."

Fuming, Trevor snatched the papers and a highlighter. He was on the second page when a sharp rap sounded against the door behind him. He twisted in his seat and was on his feet the next second. So was Abel. One look at Rachel, trembling and white as a ghost, and they both knew something was seriously wrong.

"Rachel," Abel said as he lightly grasped her elbow.

Trevor moved in to steady her from the other side. "What's wrong?"

"I went downstairs to get something out of my locker, and they were there."

"What were there?" Trevor asked.

Her frightened eyes bounced between them. "Roses. A vase of red roses."

Trevor was halfway to the stairs before she finished her sentence. Taking them three at a time, ignoring the pounding of Abel's feet behind him, he cleared the bottom step in seconds. He darted across the hall to the locker room, slammed open the swinging door, and skidded to a halt in front of the bench where he, Charlie, and Sean had talked yesterday.

In the exact spot where Charlie had been, now sat an elegant crystal vase, a blood-red ribbon tied around its middle, and a dozen red roses spilling out the top. Their ploy had worked, but not in the way they'd anticipated.

Trevor moved to step closer, but Abel's hand around his upper arm stopped him. "Trevor, wait! We don't want to contaminate any evidence." He hollered down the hall. "Mags, gloves."

Every wasted second ticked in Trevor's head like a time bomb. Charlie was the target; he was certain of that now. And if Sean was right and the killer was doing this in some part for him... Trevor turned and covered his mouth, choking back the threatening sickness.

"What's with all the—" Maggie stepped past him, next to Abel. "Whoa."

Trevor listened as they went through the motions behind him—snapping on gloves, taking pictures, opening an envelope. A card tucked in among the roses.

"Trevor, you need to see this," Abel said. "There's a note."

He took a deep breath, steeling himself, then rotated back to Maggie and Abel. Approaching, he clasped his hands behind his back to avoid touching anything, and Abel held the note out in front of him. Same paper, same red ink, same block-style letters.

#4 – OUT DAMNED SPOT. OUT.

"It's *Macbeth*."

Abel dropped the envelope and note into the plastic evidence bag Maggie held open. "Did you see anyone go in or out of here in the last hour?"

"No." Maggie sealed the bag. "But I just got back from another crime scene over in Supply. Their coroner is out this week, so I'm pulling double duty."

"The rear entrance door," Trevor thought aloud. He'd come in and out of it numerous times that week, always after someone opened it for him. "It's always locked, right?"

"That's right," Abel said. "Only those who work for the department have keys."

"That should narrow things down." He thought further about the hallway. "Security cameras?"

Abel shook his head. "Only after hours."

"Fuck!" He left the others in the locker room and stepped into the hall, making a three-sixty rotation, his eyes searching for anything they might have missed. Nothing. Fucking nothing. The killer had been right under their noses, and they'd missed them completely.

What if Charlie had been in that locker room? Would Rachel have found her body instead of a vase of roses? His breathing grew ragged, and he spun for the wall, bracing his forearms and leaning his forehead against the cool plaster.

A small, warm hand smoothed across his back. "Breathe, Trevor." Maggie spoke softly at his side. "Nothing's going to happen to Charlie. We'll find her."

He opened his eyes and held her steady gaze, letting Maggie's calm confidence settle his panicked mind. Letting Abel's issuing of orders calm him more.

To Maggie: "Have CSU run the vase and note for prints."

To Diego, who had followed the commotion downstairs: "Coordinate with Jaylen to cross-check the lists Charlie made against anyone who's worked here, past or present, who had keys."

"Someone needs to check on Rachel," Trevor said. "She was pretty unsteady."

"Unsteady?" Diego said. "She seemed fine upstairs just now. She said she had an early dinner with her sister at the hospital."

"Fuck, she's a surgical nurse, isn't she?" Trevor asked Maggie, who nodded.

"Trevor, you can't think—" Abel started, but Trevor didn't hear the rest of what he said, his mind already connecting the dots.

Rachel knew what Craig did to Charlie in high school. She'd dated Trevor. She had the means to get her hands on Diprivan and she had keys to the station. And by virtue of her job, she knew everything going on in Hanover.

The person who'd told them about the roses downstairs.

Because she'd put them there.

Abel must have reached the same conclusion. "Put out an APB on Rachel Hawkins," he told Diego.

The detective hesitated, no doubt reluctant to consider his colleague a murderer or to incur his wife's ire for putting out an APB on her best friend.

"Do it," Maggie seconded.

As Diego hustled up the stairs and Maggie hustled to the lab to grab a tech, Trevor turned to Abel. "It all fits, except Rachel doesn't know about Alice." Abel lowered his chin, noticeably deflating, and goose bumps rose on Trevor's skin. "Abel, she doesn't know, does she?"

The chief glanced up, guilt swirling in his dark eyes. "I told her."

CHAPTER TWENTY-FOUR

They'd been scouring the natatorium for twenty minutes when Sean's phone vibrated with an incoming call. He backed out from under the bleachers, yanked off his gloves, and withdrew the device from his pocket, Trevor's name lighting up the screen.

"Hey, Trev—"

"You need to get to Charlie!"

Sean's pulse kicked at the sheer panic in Trevor's voice. And at the sirens he heard blaring in the background. "What's going on?"

"It's Rachel! Rachel's the killer!"

Sean flailed a hand for the nearest solid surface, not believing his ears.

Marsh was by his side the next instant, a wall of steady. "What's happened?"

Sean clicked the phone over to speaker. "Run that by us again."

Abel's voice was a touch steadier, but only just. "A vase of red roses was found in the locker room."

Trevor cut back in. "Right where we were sitting yesterday, Sean."

"And Rachel put them there?" he asked.

"We were in Charlie's office when she told us about them," Abel clarified. "Looked mighty frightened. But Maggie doesn't think she heard anyone else come or go, and now she's in the wind. Said she had dinner with her sister, but she was a no-show."

"I ran a background search on her," Marsh said. "Clean, nothing pinged. Owns her house and her car. She's active in the community, organizes all the department events, and babysits her sister's kids a lot if the frequency of Chuck E. Cheese charges on her debit card are any indication."

"Her sister is a nurse at HU," Trevor said. "We also dated in high school, she knew about Craig's misdeeds— both times—and she apparently knows about Alice because she and Abel are a thing and he told her."

"*What?*" he and Marsh squawked together.

"We've been keeping it real quiet," Abel said. "Didn't want to upset anyone with all that was going on. She found me drunk at Pearl's the night after Mitch and Cal were killed. I told her then. I needed to tell someone."

Sean roughly ran a hand over the back of his neck and cursed. "Fucking hell."

"We're headed to Annie's now," Abel said.

"Did you call Charlie?"

"She's not picking up," Trevor said, voice trembling.

"Neither is Wally, who was also supposed to be at Annie's."

"Fuck, we're on our way." He hung up the phone and shoved it in his pocket. When he dug into the other for the keys to the borrowed cruiser, he came up empty. He patted himself down frantically. "Fuck, where are my keys?"

Marsh clasped his shoulders. "Easy, Hale."

He caught Marsh's dark eyes, similar to Charlie's, and the case began spinning through his brain again. He shook his head. "A lot of the pieces line up, but I'm not buying it."

"Maybe you don't want to believe your friend is capable of murder."

"Would you?"

Marsh shot him a sympathetic look, then lowered his hands. "She's in the wind, Sean. It doesn't look good."

"I know," he said. "But so was Beth Martin, and she turned out to be innocent."

"All we can do is get out of here and find out. Now where might your keys be?"

Calmer now, he retraced his steps. "Maybe under the bleachers." He turned back in that direction, and sure enough, a glimmer of metal caught the shifting reflection off the water.

And so did something else.

"You find them?" Marsh asked behind him.

"Yeah, but there's something else under here." He snagged the keys, then pulled his phone back out and hit the flashlight. And gasped. "I need a new pair of gloves," he called to Marsh as he inched closer to snap a photo of the lone red rose at the edge of the shadows.

Knuckles tapped his leg and Sean traded Marsh the phone for the gloves. He tugged them on, carefully picked up the rose, then backed out from under the bleachers. He sat on the bleacher beside Marsh and examined the rose. Something shiny reflected in the center of the bloom. Probably what had caught his eye. "You see that?" He tilted the rose toward Marsh.

"Sure do." He held Sean's phone close to the bloom, spread his fingers on the screen to zoom, and snapped another picture. "Got it."

Very carefully, Sean pushed the petals aside and pulled a single hair out of the center.

"So our killer has blond hair," Marsh said. "Rachel still fits the bill."

A resigned curse was on the tip of Sean's tongue when another terrible possibility tore through him. A knife twisted in his chest as a horrifying picture came together, one he should have seen before but had been willfully blind to, the truth too awful to imagine. "Rachel's hair is dark blond and curly." He held up the long, straight, white-blond strand.

Marsh's eyes grew wide, realization dawning. "Sean, you can't think..."

"It all fits. All of it fucking fits. She must know about Alice." He doubled over in agony, clutching his knees and gasping for breath. Gripped so tight in fear's jaws he couldn't think, couldn't move, could barely breathe. "Call them back," he wheezed.

Marsh didn't need to be told twice, using Sean's phone in his hand to call Trevor.

"Sean!" Trevor answered. "Are you on your way? You're closer."

"I don't think it's Rachel," Sean managed to choke out.

"But the evidence—"

"Also points to Annabelle Henby."

CHAPTER TWENTY-FIVE

Juggling a box of Annie's favorite red velvet cupcakes and a tray of coffees, Charlie waved off the patrol car that had followed her over, then strode into Annie's house, the soft hum of the dishwasher the only sound that greeted her.

"Annie?" she called to no response. "Wally?"

A half-full laundry basket sat on the floor by the open back door. She was probably outside fighting with the dryer again. Probably recruited Wally to help her too.

Charlie paused in the kitchen to unload the cupcakes and coffees and dropped her bag on the end of the counter by a set of keys. They weren't Annie's usual keys. Those were on a gilded stack-of-books key chain she and Trevor had given Annie when she'd graduated her MLS program. These were on a plastic Cape Hatteras Lighthouse key chain like the ones you'd get at the gift shop there. The key chain was familiar, but Charlie couldn't immediately place it.

She unclipped her weapon and set it on the counter next to the other items before making her way outside. Hearing the dryer buzz, she rounded the back of the house in the direction of the utility room, then froze midstep, her instincts and mind processing the scene in front of her.

Rachel, bound and gagged, unconscious on the utility room floor. A person, dressed in all black, looming over her, a loaded syringe in one hand, one of Cal's old bats in the other.

Cal's station keys, Charlie's mind clicked. He'd been carrying them on that lighthouse key chain when he'd been killed. A split second after making that connection, Charlie understood the rest, comprehending exactly the scene before her.

Their killer was someone with ties to HU and HPD, who had been a student at the former, was an employee of the latter, and liaised between the two. Someone who had likely heard about Jefferson Marshall's tenure-voting tendencies, who must have known about Julian Hirsch's extramarital affairs, who was on the case last year involving Teller's players, who, with the help of a badge, could likely access the drugs and syringes that had incapacitated their victims, could access Beth Martin's office, could access the equestrian center and natatorium. Who had been at those crime scenes. Someone who had been tight with Cal and who, Charlie had always suspected, had had a crush on Annie.

Someone who had recently lost a friend and work partner and a potential love interest.

Sean was right. This case was about vengeance and

unhealthy obsession, but they'd gotten the who of it wrong. It wasn't Trevor at the center of this storm; it was Cal and Annie.

And Officer Wallace Sylvan.

He stared at Charlie from over Rachel's body, his light blue eyes full of anger and resentment.

Charlie's gaze flicked down to Rachel. "Did you kill her?" She reached for her sidearm and cursed herself for removing it. But fuck, she hadn't anticipated needing her gun in her sister's backyard. Where was Annie? She took a step forward, then halted abruptly when Wallace drew his gun and pointed it at Rachel's head.

"She's not my target, but one more step and she'll be collateral damage. There's a lot of that in Shakespeare's tragedies."

"Where's Annie?" she asked, worrying about other collateral damage.

Stepping over Rachel and out of the utility room, Wallace stalked toward her with the gun and the loaded syringe. "Annie took a walk like she always does when she gets home. A little earlier today than usual, but after that scene at the cemetery..."

Charlie's gut churned. She'd asked for Wally on backup. She began back tracking toward the house, toward her gun on the kitchen counter. "Let's talk about this, Wallace."

His eyes flashed dangerously, and in that instant, Charlie knew there'd be no reasoning with him. Spinning on her heel, she bolted for the house and ran smack into Annie coming out the back door.

"Get out!" she shouted at her sister, as she kicked the laundry basket over and shoved Annie toward the living room on the other side of the raised dining bar. "Go, go, go!"

Annie teetered, confused and off-balance, into the living room, knocking over lamps and tables. Continuing to track her movements as she raced parallel through the kitchen, Charlie reached for her gun and curled her fingers around its grip, only to have it knocked loose when the baseball bat came hurtling down on her outstretched forearm. Bones cracked, and Charlie's legs gave out from under her, pain making her dizzy. The gun skidded down the counter out of reach, knocking the box of cupcakes and coffees to the floor.

"Annie, get out of here!" She screamed from her knees, clutching her arm.

To her horror and dismay, Annie stopped dead in her tracks less than a foot from the front door. Her wide, terrified eyes were locked on a point over Charlie's shoulder. "Wally, what are you doing?"

A telltale click echoed in Charlie's ear, followed by the press of steel against her temple.

Wallace's voice was as cold and hard as the gun pointed at her head. "Making sure *you* get everything you deserve by taking it all from her."

Annie's wrecked gaze fell to her, searching for an explanation, beseeching her older sister to make it all better, but all Charlie managed was a whispered "I love you" before a needle pricked her neck and her world faded to black.

CHAPTER TWENTY-SIX

Sean careened into the circular driveway of Mitch's old house—Annie's now—and brought the borrowed police cruiser to a screeching halt behind two other cruisers. Charlie's Mustang was parked in front of the garage, a spark of hope. Snuffed out as he looked past the car to the front patio, its screen door hanging off its hinges.

He shoved open the car door and barely missed colliding with Marsh in front of the car as they ran toward the house. "Are they here?" Sean shouted at the uniformed officer—not Wallace—who stepped outside. "Are Charlie and Annie here?" he repeated. "Where's Officer Sylvan?"

"They're gone," the officer said. "We followed Charlie here earlier. She waved us off. Wally's car was here." She pointed toward the cruisers, then removed her cap and ran a shaking hand over her hair. "We turned around as soon as we got the call from dispatch."

"Where's your partner?" Marsh asked.

"Utility room." She gestured the opposite direction,

toward the backyard. "We found Rachel tied up and unconscious. She was just starting to come to when we got here."

Sean moved toward the door, but Marsh stepped in front of him. "Careful, Hale, this is a crime scene," he reminded before leading Sean through the patio and into the house.

Sean froze the instant Marsh stepped aside, his insides clenching at the destruction.

Cupcakes and coffee spilled on the kitchen floor. Charlie's holstered gun teetering on the edge of the cracked kitchen counter, a baseball bat and used syringe beside it.

Sheer terror overwhelmed him. Charlie was injured. He'd just gotten her back. He couldn't lose her, not again. He couldn't let Trevor lose her either.

Fuck. Trevor. How was he going to react to this? Was there enough power in the universe to contain him?

"Lock it down." Marsh's stern order— Sean called it the army voice—cut through his panicked haze. "Lock it down and focus. What do you see?"

Taking a deep breath, he beat back the terror and forced himself to detach and examine the rest of the scene. Beyond the mess in the kitchen, at the opposite end of the galley, by the open back door, a laundry basket was tipped over, clothes scattered on the floor. To his left, the living room was in disarray. End tables toppled, two broken lamps, muddy shoe prints on the floor. There'd been a chase, an attempted escape, a struggle. Charlie had gone for her weapon, but Annie had gotten the upper hand, wielding the bat and syringe. She'd knocked Charlie out and dragged her out of the house. Had Wally helped her? Was he unconscious somewhere too?

"Where's Abel?"

"Right here," came the older man's voice, followed by a "Holy fuck" in a second voice Sean hadn't expected.

Trevor stood over the threshold, his face white as a ghost, his hazel eyes wide with fear.

Behind him, Jaylen and Diego didn't look much better.

"Annie's got her," Sean said as they stared past him, gazes jumping from one horrific sight to the next.

Marsh clasped Trevor's shoulder while Sean addressed the others. "Wally's missing too."

Abel shook his head, dazedly looking around the rooms. "How'd we miss this?"

"Abel," Sean spoke sharply, mimicking Marsh from earlier. "We don't have time for that right now. We have to get to Charlie and Annie and find Wallace."

"Wally has them."

The three of them spun toward the scratchy voice. Rachel stood just outside the patio door, leaning against another uniformed officer. Abel moved first, lunging for Rachel and wrapping her in his arms. "Baby, you okay?"

"I'll be fine." She accepted his embrace, but her attention remained locked on Sean.

As did his on what she'd said. "Wally has them?"

Rachel nodded. "Wallace Sylvan is the killer, not Annie." She sniffled and cuddled closer to Abel. "I thought it might be Annie too after the roses at the station, so I came here to talk to her, but Annie was on a walk and

Wally attacked me." Her voice cracked, tears winning out, and she turned into Abel's embrace.

And Sean turned back to the scene, considering it anew. Considering past events in a new light too. The nosy young officer with light blue eyes, a too-thin nose, and peeling sunburnt skin at Mitch and Cal's funeral. An officer who had been at the other crime scenes this week, including at the natatorium. The officer who had told Craig Rowan they had a suspect in custody.

"He's municipal affairs, right?" Sean asked. "Dealing with HU and city hall?"

"That's right," Jaylen said, a terseness in his voice Sean had never heard there.

"Voluntarily?" Marsh asked.

"Said he needed a break," Abel supplied. "After everything with Cal and the Salazar case."

Threads began to come together in Sean's head. "And he was tight with Cal?"

"Cal was his partner. He and Annie were close too."

"Always thought he wanted more with her," Jaylen said, his voice gone brittle.

"Was he involved in the Teller case last year?" Sean asked.

"Yeah," said Diego from the doorway. "He was HPD's liaison with Atlanta PD."

"Fuck me," Trevor said beside him, clearly coming to the same conclusion.

It was never Rachel. Nor Annie. It was Wallace Sylvan. And he was targeting Charlie as Lady Macbeth. For calling Cal to come get her the night of the accident, which he'd somehow learned about. For taking Alice, Mitch, and Cal from Annie. For climbing the HPD ranks.

The rose with Annie's hair in it beneath the bleachers.

A gift. A clue the killer couldn't help leaving.

Sean shivered. "We need to get an APB out on Wallace Sylvan."

"On it," Diego said, turning back for the driveway.

Marsh grasped Sean's arm. "My tablet's in the car. I'm going to go grab it and start running searches."

"Let me get Rachel checked out," Abel said, "and I'll get on the horn too."

Sean figured Jaylen would follow them out, but he stepped closer instead, lowering his voice. "I need to get Annie back." He wiped a hand down his face, and the professional mask fell away, the full weight of his distress becoming obvious. "I love her, and she's the mother of my unborn child."

Trevor's unsteadiness intensified, and he rocked into Sean's side. "Annie's pregnant?"

Jaylen nodded. "Annie wanted Charlie to accept the FBI job first. She didn't want either of you to pass up your futures to stay here with her." He returned his gaze to Sean. "Please, man, we gotta get them back."

"We will." Sean squeezed his shoulder. "Give me two minutes here, then we'll sort a game plan."

Jaylen said his thanks, then joined the others in the driveway. Beside Sean, Trevor was a different deteriorating story. His breathing had become erratic, his head frantically shaking back and forth. The fear in his eyes was an emotion Sean understood all too well.

Sean angled to fully face him and framed Trevor's face with his hands. "Trevor, focus." He waited the couple of seconds it took for the other man's breaths to settle. "Wallace needed to get away quick. A car would be too obvious. We could intercept. How else could he get out of here fast?"

Trevor stared wide-eyed at him for a moment, then hung his head. "The boat."

"What boat?"

"The family boat we keep at the marina at the end of the street."

Sean grabbed Trevor's hand and dragged him out of the house to the driveway where Diego and Jaylen were waiting. "Get down to the marina," he told the officers. "See if the Henby boat's missing. Slip number?" he asked Trevor.

"Twelve. *Wild Pitch.*"

"Got it." Diego took off running to his police cruiser, Jaylen on his heels.

Sean headed for the borrowed cruiser, Trevor still in tow. "That boat have GPS on it?"

"Yeah, of course."

"Ping the GPS on the boat," he said to Marsh, who was leaning on the front fender. "I think I know where Wallace is going, but we need to be sure."

Trevor gave him the registration number.

"Call when you've got a lock on it," Sean said, ducking into the driver's seat and shouting out the passenger window to Trevor. "Get in. You're with me."

CHAPTER TWENTY-SEVEN

Heavy.

Everything was so heavy. Her limbs, her eyelids, the ache in her head, the knot in her stomach.

Charlie peeked open an eye and swiftly slammed it shut against the blinding sun. Groaning, she tried to move her arms from where they were bent uncomfortably behind her, rope binding her wrists, but then a searing pain shot through her right one, clearing the remaining brain fog. Recent events came crashing back.

Wallace Sylvan was their killer, and he'd attacked her and Annie.

Annie.

She croaked out her sister's name, her voice like sandpaper over her dry throat and cracked lips, a side effect of the Diprivan.

"She's fine," Wallace's too-calm voice said from behind her. "Just taking a nap."

Charlie slowly blinked open her eyes, letting them adjust to the bright sunlight. She was lying on her side, facing the bow of the family boat, the tall reeds of the Intracoastal Waterway passing on either side of the prow. Angling her head, she looked past her bound feet to where Annie lay prone against one side of the deck. Her wrists were bound in front of her, and blood dripped from a wound on the side of her head. Wallace must have cold-cocked her with the gun, knocking her out, but judging from the steady rise and fall of her chest, she was breathing normally. But she needed to get that head wound seen too ASAP, which meant Charlie had to get them out of this situation ASAP.

She curled upright, and pain throbbed in her head and arm. She leaned against the steering column, taking deep breaths and trying to focus despite the nausea. After Wallace had incapacitated her, the world had gone mostly black, only bits and pieces cutting through the fog. Annie crying, begging Wallace to let them go, even as he forced her to tie Charlie's hands and feet. Annie mentioning a baby. Wallace carrying Charlie across the rocking marina docks to the boat. Then nothing until the rhythmic bump and swish of the boat and the vibrating phone in her pocket had pulled her toward wakefulness.

It couldn't have been long between the house and now. A quick survey of their surroundings confirmed Wallace had navigated out of the marina, into the sound, then up the waterway. He slowed the boat's speed and steered into one of the many inland streams that fed the marshy waterway between the mainland and coast.

Five minutes later, the dilapidated bridge where her mother had died appeared before them. Charlie's fear skyrocketed. What sort of vengeance was Wallace planning? Why did Annie need to be there? How did Wallace even know the truth about Alice's death?

Her phone vibrated again, silencing the spiral and focusing her. She counted back the calls since she'd begun to wake. That was the fourth one. Sean would know by now that something was wrong, and the boat had GPS. Trevor would know that. So would Abel. She just needed to buy more time for Sean and HPD to reach them.

The boat rammed ashore near one of the crumbling bridge foundations, sending Charlie skidding across the deck toward Annie. Charlie scooted in front of her, hands fumbling behind her back for Annie's wrists to check her pulse. Strong, delicate fingers curled around her own. With Wallace bearing down on them, a gun in one hand, a Bowie knife in the other, Charlie didn't dare look back and give away that Annie was awake. Instead, she squeezed her fingers and whispered "Stay down" under her breath.

"Get up," Wallace said.

"You don't want to do this, Wally," she tried coaxing.

His face contorted in anger. "Don't call me that." He leaned forward, brandishing the knife. "Only Annie gets to call me that."

Charlie shifted and swept out her legs, bound as they were, toward Wallace's shins. He stumbled, and for a second, Charlie thought she might get the upper hand, but Wallace regained his balance and brought his gun down in a pistol-whip to her broken arm. Charlie cried out and lost her balance, falling to her other side, away from Annie.

By the time the blinding pain and blackness receded and Charlie managed to right herself again, Wallace was standing over Annie's prone body with a gun. She hadn't heard a gunshot and saw no more blood than was previously on Annie's head. She was still pretending to be passed out, thankfully not inserting herself into the scuffle.

"Please don't hurt her." Charlie would have pled with her hands up if her right arm wasn't broken and tied to the other behind her back.

"I don't want to hurt Annie," Wallace said. "I'm doing this *for* Annie. But if you don't cooperate, I'll have to."

"Okay, I'll go with you, but let me say goodbye first. Please."

He hesitated but then retreated a few steps, keeping the gun trained on them. "No funny business. I'm a trained officer too. I can hit either of you from here."

Inching over to her sister, Charlie bent forward and kissed her forehead. "Please stay here," she whispered. "By now, HPD is tracking the boat. They'll be here soon. Whatever happens, I love you, Annie, and I'm so sorry for any pain I ever caused you. I never meant to. You are the best sister I could have ever had. I'm the lucky one. Take care of Abel, and Trevor, and Sean."

A single tear escaped the corner of Annie's eye, and Charlie wiped it away with her cheek, hiding it with a kiss. Turning, she discreetly pulled the phone out of her back pocket and dropped it next to Annie's hip before Wallace cut the bindings on Charlie's feet and hauled her up and over the side of the boat.

On the sandy shore, he yanked her up by her injured arm and pushed her toward the incline, gun at her back.

"Wally—"

"I told you not to call me that. Now go."

Charlie dragged her feet as they climbed the embankment, stumbling a few times as waves of pain crashed through her. "Why are you doing this?" she asked between pants, in agony and out of breath once they crested the ridge.

"Because you're guilty."

"Of what?"

Wallace shoved her out onto the buckled wooden slats of the bridge. "You're power hungry, ambitious, and worst of all, you ruin the lives of good men."

"Lady Macbeth."

"One after another." Wallace kicked Charlie's legs out from under her, sending her crashing to her knees. "You call Cal to rescue you from that party, and he races to you in the middle of a storm because he'd do anything for you, and he kills your mother. Leaves Annie without a mom."

Charlie gulped. "How did you find out?"

"Cal told me. I was his friend, his partner, he needed someone to talk to, and he didn't want to hurt you. He never forgave himself for what happened to Alice or for sending Sean away. He sent his best friend away because he was protecting you. Always *you*," he spat as he paced back and forth on the bridge, armed and looking increasingly agitated. "And let's not forget your case—your determination to prove yourself to the FBI—got my partner and my chief killed."

"Wallace, please." Her voice cracked, that particular wound tearing open. "You have to know I didn't want that to happen. I never wanted them to get hurt."

Wallace charged, pointing the gun directly at Charlie's forehead. "But they wouldn't have been there if not for you. They wouldn't have died."

Charlie hung her head, unable to stare down the barrel of the gun or the truth. "I'm so sorry."

The gun safety clicked back on, and Charlie looked up as Wallace tucked the weapon into his waistband at the small of his back and resumed pacing. "You know, I ran into Sean at the funeral. I saw how he looked at you and Trevor. The way Trevor looked at you. They still love you. I thought maybe Cal's letter would do the trick, would expose the truth and tarnish the Charlie shine, but nope, they still fucking do your bidding."

"You knew about the letter?"

Wallace sneered. "Who did you think convinced him to write it? And who did you think was there helping Annie clean out your dad's attic when she found the real case file from the night your mother died." He jabbed himself in the chest. "*Me!*"

Fuck, so Annie knew already too. And Charlie hadn't been the one to tell her. Another sin to atone for if she got them out of this alive.

"You know what's the kicker? She was mad at Cal, not you. Never Charlie. She didn't want to compromise your life, your career, or your love." Wallace ranted on, his voice sounding forlorn and broken. "Why do you get all the love —friends, family, colleagues, your exes—but I get none? I just want to love her."

The pieces began to click. "Annie?"

"I've loved her since I set foot in the library as a freshman at HU, and she helped me find the copy of Shakespeare's *Four Tragedies* I needed. She introduced me to Cal, and I knew what it was like to have a real friend. I joined the department and got to work with Mitch too, someone I liked and respected. And then you took them all from me."

Turning her face away, Charlie cursed herself for having missed this. She suspected Wallace had had a crush on Annie, but she thought he'd moved on, especially after Annie had gone public with... Jaylen. Is that what had triggered Wallace? Together with Cal's death? The two people he was closest to. Gone. Charlie knew something about that sort of loss.

"You don't get to leave town and get your happily ever after," he seethed. "You're guilty. You have to pay for your crimes."

As Wallace's misery swung back to anger, he swung her direction with the knife again, and Charlie flailed for anything to stall him. "Why Professor Marshall?"

"To help Annie's friend. To clear the way so Trevor could stay here. That's what she would want."

"And Julian and Craig?"

"Julian because he hurt another of Annie's friends. And to throw you off the trail." He grinned, full of malice. "Craig because he was evil and because he gave you the opening to take everything from Annie. You just keep hurting her. The only way I can help her, maybe get away from that man *you* set her up with, is to get you out of her life for good."

"Wallace, this isn't love. This is obsession."

He closed the distance between them, yanking Charlie up by her hair and holding the knife to her throat. "You do not get to tell me what love is. You, who takes and takes and takes and never gives anything. *You* don't know what love is."

"Yes, she does," came the last voice Charlie wanted to hear right then.

Wallace released her hair and spun them around to face Annie, who stood at the edge of the bridge.

"Annie, go back to the boat," Charlie urged, fear straining her voice. "Please."

Annie ignored her and locked eyes with Wallace as she slowly approached. "Charlie left me in that boat just now because she loves me, because she wanted to protect me. She made sure after Mom's death, after Dad's and Cal's, that I had people to support and love me. She's stayed here in Hanover and is considering passing up a career-making job and a second chance at love and her own happiness to keep our family together and the truth about our mom from being exposed. To make sure I'm happy. That's how much she loves me."

Wallace's lip trembled, and Annie took a step closer, almost beside them, drawing his attention away from the direction she'd come. On purpose it would seem, as

Charlie glimpsed Sean and Trevor cresting the embankment at the end of the bridge.

"I appreciate everything you've done for me." Wallace's attention focused on her while Sean ducked behind one of the trestle pillars and Trevor inched toward them. "But do you think I'd want you to hurt Charlie? She's all the family I have left. Please don't take her away from me. That's not what I want."

"How do you know you wouldn't be happier without her?"

"You don't have to kill her to make that happen," Trevor spoke up from a few feet away. "We'll leave."

Wallace whipped around, lowering his knife arm. "And you'll stay away?"

"If that's what Annie wants." He took the same path as Annie, keeping Wallace distracted while Sean snuck from one pillar to the next, inching closer. "She's my family too. I'm on your team. I just want her to be happy."

Annie extended a hand toward Wallace. "Hand me the weapons and let's work this out."

His hand shook around the knife, and he started to reach to Annie, to hand it over, but then the wail of police sirens pierced the air and chaos erupted. Annie surged forward, Trevor pushed her out of the way, and Wallace gripped Charlie by the hair once more, spinning them to face off against Trevor and Annie. Standing behind her, Wallace pressed the knife's blade against Charlie's throat.

The sirens instantly died. Sean, who was now behind her and Wallace, must have radioed them to hold.

Annie stepped in front of Trevor. "Wally, please, don't do this."

"Do you love me?"

"Of course I do."

"More than you love her?" He jerked Charlie's neck farther back, the sharpened edge of the knife skating over her skin.

Annie hesitated, and Charlie winced. It was the honest but wrong response.

"I didn't think so," Wallace said. "But you will when she's not here to confuse you, to put others in your path. Don't you see? She's Lady Macbeth. And I won't let her ruin your life anymore."

"Wally, please," Annie begged, straining against Trevor's arm around her waist.

"You'll see, Annabelle. You'll be better off without her too. Me, you, and Trevor. Our family will be better off without her. It's what Cal would've wanted." His words took on a hysterical edge. The end was near. "I'm sorry, but I can't let her ruin your life anymore."

Wallace pressed the knife harder against her throat. The fear of imminent death chilled Charlie to the bone. But then Trevor's eyes shot over her shoulder. When they came back to Charlie, they were hard and focused. He blinked twice in quick succession. Reading his message, she leaned forward and took the sting of the knife's blade for a split second before ramming her head back into Wallace's face.

Wallace stumbled, his hold loosening as the knife clattered to the ground. Charlie ripped free, falling forward into Trevor's arms at the same time Sean captured Wallace from behind. He kicked the knife out of Wallace's reach and took him down, knees to the ground. Disarming him, he tossed the gun aside with the knife and cuffed Wallace's wrists behind his back.

"I did it for you," he cried woefully to Annie. "Shakespeare was your favorite. I just wanted you to see me."

Annie ripped out of Charlie's and Trevor's arms. "Not like this, you didn't." Her voice was powerful, confident, and spitting nails. "I love my sister. All my family. And as for Shakespeare, you do not get to use the silent voices of wronged women, fictional or not, to make your fucking point." She started to turn, then paused and loomed over Wallace again, unleashing all the temper they'd inherited from their mother. "And I owe my sister for my happiness. She introduced me to the man of my dreams, and this baby in my belly will be named Charlie if it's the last fucking thing I do."

Charlie didn't think it was possible to be more in awe of a person than she was of her sister right then, and she held on tight, telling her so, when Annie charged into her and Trevor's arms. "You are the bravest woman I know."

"Right back atcha, sis."

"You okay?" Sean asked as he jerked Wallace up by his cuffed wrists.

"It's over now," Charlie said as Trevor used a fishing knife to cut through the ropes around her wrists. She swiped at her neck, coming away with a faint smear of blood. "Just a nick."

Sean nodded, then led Wallace over to one of the pillars where two officers waited.

Bindings gone, she cradled her broken arm against her chest and relaxed into Trevor's and Annie's hold. The lingering knot in Charlie's gut finally let up when Sean joined them, his arms wrapped around them.

Her family safe.

CHAPTER TWENTY-EIGHT

Trevor was half dozing on one of the waiting room sofas near Charlie's recovery room, Sean passed out against his side, when a gentle shake of his shoulder roused him back toward awake.

"Charlie's coming to," Annie said quietly. "She's asking for you two."

Trevor wiped a hand over his face and rubbed his eyes as Sean continued to snore. "What time is it?"

"About eight."

"It's only been a couple hours. That was quick."

"In the morning." Trevor's surprised jolt drew a grumble from the man tucked under his arm. "You two were so cute I didn't have the heart to wake you. And I knew if I did, you wouldn't leave anyway."

She laid a hand on her belly, and the concern that shot through Trevor woke him all the way up. "Were you here all night? With the baby, you need—"

"I was in the maternity ward. They wanted to keep me for observation." Annie ruffled her hair, flashing the bandage at her temple. "All good."

"That's good, A," Sean said from Trevor's other side, a little groggy but on his way to awareness. "Charlie awake?"

"Yeah, baby," Trevor dropped a kiss on his temple. "Let's go see our girl."

Hand in hand, they followed Annie into Charlie's room, and Trevor couldn't help but laugh at the pouty, "Everything hurts," she leveled at Jaylen.

"They had to reset your arm," Sean said, and her gaze darted to them.

Trevor tapped his nose as they moved to one side of the bed. "Now you've got breaks like the rest of us."

On the other side of the bed, Annie drummed her fingers on her collarbone. "No more perfect record."

Charlie, though, only had eyes for Annie's belly. She lifted her good hand, laying it there. "Did I imagine this part?"

"Nope." Annie covered Charlie's hand with both of hers as Jaylen threw an arm over her shoulders. "That's Charlie 2.0 in there."

"Everything's okay?"

"All good. If it stays that way, you'll be an aunt in seven months." Annie glanced up, smiling at them across the bed. "And you two fools will be uncles. I'll be sure to tell Charlie 2.0 all about how you thought *I* tried to kill their namesake."

"Annie," Sean started, but she waved him off.

"We went through this last night. You're forgiven, but I'm still gonna make you feel guilty about it from time to time."

Trevor was working up another apology to pick up where Sean's was cut off, but Charlie beat him to it. "I'm sorry I didn't tell you about Mom. I'd just gotten you back. I didn't want to lose you again."

"Same reason I didn't tell you when I found those files in the attic."

"I'm still sorry," Charlie said. "And for not getting out of your way sooner. You're amazing, sis."

"You're forgiven too." Annie beamed and gazed up at Jaylen. "You put him in my path."

He tightened his arm around Annie. "You need to get home and rest. Properly." Jaylen looked at Annie with such affection, such admiration, that Trevor had no doubt he'd give Annie anything she wanted. He'd do anything for her and their children. It settled any lingering concern he had about leaving Hanover. Annie would be just fine. Better than.

Annie knew the same; they were all just slow to catch up. She leaned over Charlie and kissed her forehead. "I meant what I said on the bridge yesterday. You go to DC. You worked hard, and you deserve this opportunity." She straightened and glanced again at Trevor. "Same goes for you. Show HU what a mistake they made letting that windbag Marshall hold up your tenure. And you"—she swung her gaze to Sean—"just make them happy this time. For good."

Sean blushed handsomely, his chin dipped in deference. "With your blessing."

She reached across the bed, covering one of each of their hands on the rail with hers. "You have it."

Charlie caught her hand as it trailed back, squeezing it. "Love you, sis."

"Love you too."

Annie and Jaylen slipped out, and Trevor claimed the closest chair. He reached through the rail, fingers brushing her hip, needing the contact but avoiding the stabilized arm that had been reset. "So, DC or bust?"

Sean smirked as he rounded the end of the bed to the chair on the other side. "Your place or mine?"

When Charlie didn't reply, both their gazes swung to her. "Charlie?" Trevor said, not liking the stormy mix of doubt and fear creeping into her eyes. Eyes that just a couple nights ago burned with hope and lust. "What's going on in that head of yours?"

"I could have been killed. If I become an FBI agent, it probably won't be the last time."

Sean rose on the other side of the bed, hands curling around the rail. "Charlie, don't say—"

"No, Sean, you've lost someone to the job. We all lost Dad and Cal. You could both lose me." She looked back and forth between them. "What happens then? Are you willing to risk that?"

Trevor inched closer, placing his hand on her hip more firmly. "Honey, any one of us could be gone tomorrow, but we've been given another chance. I don't want to pass it up." He cut a glance to Sean. "With either of you."

Sean rested an elbow on the rail and took her hand with the other. "He's the romantic. I'm the realist. It could happen."

What was he doing? "Sean!"

He lifted a hand, and Trevor bit his tongue. "Which is why," Sean continued, "at another time when you're not just out of surgery and Trevor and I have slept more than a restless night on a horribly uncomfortable sofa, we'll discuss how this works legally, what documentation we all need, how to make sure we're all taken care of and all supported. But right here"—he tapped his knuckles against his chest—"I'm with the fucking romantic on this one. Are you with us too, Charlie?"

She bit her bottom lip and tears collected in the corners of her eyes, one escaping, and for a moment, Trevor feared he was about to lose it all, but then the corners of her mouth tipped up and she nodded. "I'm with the fucking romantic too."

There was no stopping the grin that stretched across Trevor's face. He reached into his pocket and withdrew the tiny satchel he'd asked Abel and Rachel to swing by his house and raid the sock drawer for. "Good thing I brought these, then." He opened the satchel and tipped out the rings Sean had proposed to him and Charlie with a decade ago.

Sean's smile was blinding as he reached across the bed, one hand grasping Charlie's, the other Trevor's. "Last time I'm gonna ask because this time it's forever. Trevor Caldwell and Charlotte Henby, will you marry me?"

Trevor caught Charlie's dark eyes, full of glittering

hope and happiness. "Yes," they answered the man they loved, together always.

____

CHAPTER TWENTY-NINE

Six months later...

"Let's go, let's go, let's go!" Charlie clapped her hands as she stood in the doorway of their bedroom at the beach house. It was technically their second home now—their condo in DC their primary legal residence—but this house would always be home. And Charlie would be spending every spare weekend and holiday she could get off work here once her niece was born next month.

And the two naked men tangled in the bed together would be with her. Always.

Trevor rolled onto his back and threw an arm over his face, groaning dramatically. "Why is she screaming at us at seven in the morning?"

"That whole leader of the pack thing went to her head." Sean rolled with him, draped across his side and chest. "Think we could sneak out? Head back to DC?"

"We should've kept the apartment," Trevor said, referring to the apartment she and Trevor had rented for all of two months before moving into Sean's penthouse condo in the Paxton Building. "Used it as a hideaway."

"She's FBI. She would've found us."

"And if I couldn't, Marsh would." She stepped to the end of the bed, hands on her hips under the hem of Trevor's T-shirt she'd grabbed on the way to the kitchen to start the coffee. "My little sister is getting married tonight." She pointed to the beach outside the window. "Right out there. We're hosting. There's a mile long list of things to do, which involves you two cooking and me going to the airport to pick up Marie and Marsh. And Rachel will be here in an hour to coordinate the rest of the deliveries. And there's something else we have to do before all of that."

"Sex?" Sean offered as he cupped Trevor's balls.

She clapped louder. "Let's go, let's go, let's go!"

Trevor laughed out loud even has he arched his back. "You second-guessing that whole married and moved-in-together thing?"

Sean shrugged and smirked over his shoulder at her. "Little late now."

Charlie blew him a kiss, amused as always by their antics. Sean kept them from ever being too serious, and they needed that, more than ever now. Her job was far from easy, but it was good work. Trevor was dealing with departmental politics as usual, but he loved his students and loved DC. And Sean was working long hours as the head of Paxton. But each night they found their way home to each other, laughing and loving.

Using the distraction, Trevor tumbled Sean onto his back, pinned his hands to the mattress, and demanded a kiss. As Charlie watched them grapple, heat licked at the heels of humor, the match already lit by Sean's earlier fondling.

"Oh, is that how it is?" Trevor rumbled.

If he kept rolling his hips and talking in that sexy voice, they were definitely not getting out of bed. "Trevor Caldwell Henby!" she snapped. "Get your ass out of the bed."

"Hey!" He jerked half-around, now the one looking over his shoulder. "Why am I the bad guy? He's the one with his hand around our dicks." He pointed down, and Charlie was sure it wasn't a lie. "Come see."

"Is that so Henby-Paxton? Is it your fault our husband won't get out of bed on the day of his sister-in-law's wedding?"

Sean shifted his torso enough to grin at her from under Trevor. "We're trying to get you back into bed too, Agent Henby."

When Trevor's sexy smile joined the battle, she surrendered, rolling her eyes as she stripped off the shirt. "Fine, I'm just going to have to come up there and fuck both of you."

Sean snickered. "That's the kind of leader we want."

She kicked off her underwear, opened the drawer at the end of the bed, and retrieved her favorite toy and lube. She tossed them onto the bed, climbed on, and knee-walked herself up the mattress. Knees on either side of Sean's thighs, she notched herself against Trevor's back.

Trevor relaxed against her with a sigh. "Morning, honey."

"Morning, babe." She stole a quick kiss, then peered

over his shoulder, and sure enough, their husband had his hand around both his and Trevor's dicks. She winked at Sean. "Good morning to you too."

He winked back. "We're getting there."

Chuckling, she opened the bottle of lube and squirted a generous amount into Sean's open hand. He fisted Trevor again and both her men groaned as their cocks slid more easily together, rocking hard enough to move her too. Heat and wetness arrowed south, pooling hot and heavy between her legs. "Getting there faster now," she teased.

Trevor licked and kissed the underside of her jaw, thrusting harder. "Fuck, baby, you both feel so good."

She tossed the bottle aside, then reached an arm around Trevor's chest, holding him to her, teasing the nipple she could reach. She lowered her other hand between her legs, two fingers skirting either side of her clit, teasing herself, before diving deep into her own heat, opening herself up. She nipped at Trevor's ear. "For your sass this morning, I'm getting your ass."

Sean growled beneath them. "And I get his dick."

"You good with that?" Charlie asked Trevor, and given his frantic blissed-out nod, the sooner the better. Charlie withdrew her wet fingers and glided them down the cleft of his ass cheeks, reaching his puckered hole and circling the rim. He thrust into Sean's fist with each swipe of Charlie's fingers, each knuckle that breached his hole deeper.

"Christ," Sean cursed. "I'm the luckiest man alive." Charlie's eyes shot to his over Trevor's shoulder. "I love you both so much." She held his gaze, not a trace of sadness or melancholy in his bright blue eyes. No tears. Instead, they were brimming over with desire and love, a decade's worth burning hot as an inferno. "Always have, always will."

Keeping their gazes locked, she circled her tongue behind Trevor's ear, relishing the goose bumps that prickled his skin. "Let's show our husband how much we love him too." She drew him up and back, both of them on their knees, so Sean could bend back his legs and ready himself. He swiped the bottle of lube, squirted more on his fingers, and began to stretch himself for Trevor, bared for them to see as he worked one, then two, then three fingers into his ass. "This is what we get for making her the boss lady."

"Fuck," Trevor cursed as he rocked against Charlie and her fingers that were inside him again.

He wanted inside Sean, and she wanted him there too, but not quite yet. She slid free her fingers and pressed herself flush against his back. "A boss lady—a wife—who loves you and can't get enough of our kisses." She grasped Trevor's chin and angled him around so she could claim his mouth in a deep, plundering kiss. "Of your bodies and our bed." She reached around his side and fisted his dick. "Of your hearts and our love." She held up his hair and pressed a gentle kiss to his nape, right over the leather strip of his necklace.

"Fuck, baby, I need to come," he keened.

Sean removed his fingers and yanked both legs back by the knees. "Then get inside me."

This time, when Trevor lurched forward, Charlie let him go. Watched in eager anticipation as he planted his hands in the mattress on either side of Sean's head and thrust his dick to the hilt inside him. Their combined grunts were almost enough to make her come. She was close too.

She grabbed the toy, soaked both ends with lube, then inserted the thicker bulb end inside her, flipping on the vibrations that would tease her inside and out. She wanted her hands free to roam. Free to grasp one of Trevor's hips and one of Sean's legs to better position them. To spread Trevor's ass cheeks and thrust the longer end of the double dildo inside her husband. To hold on tight and close as she pegged Trevor and Trevor fucked Sean.

"Holy fuck," Trevor cursed and wobbled over Sean. "This never gets old."

She smirked against his spine as she drew back then drove in in time with the pulsing vibrations. "I promised it wouldn't."

Sean's hands glided up Trevor's torso to meet hers where they came around and splayed across Trevor's chest. "Nothing about loving the two of you will ever get old." Charlie pushed Trevor forward for the kiss she knew Sean wanted and so she could plant a foot in the mattress and work Trevor harder with the dildo, knowing that's what he wanted.

Letting her men set the pace, she closed her eyes and rode the roll of their hips, savoring their frantic movements and their escalating grunts and smacking kisses. Savoring the heat that built inside her and the vibrations from below and inside.

At Sean's shouted, "I'm coming," she opened her eyes

and watched from over Trevor's shoulder as Sean came apart beautifully, his back arching, his hands fisted in the sheets, his come streaking his chest, and the charms of his necklace in the hollow of his throat bobbing as he shouted their names. Trevor followed him over, buried inside Sean's ass and groaning so deep Charlie felt it against her chest. Her nipples ached from the tremors, and with the vibrating dildo between her legs, it was all too much, a pleasure circuit that flipped and had her inner muscles clamped down on the toy as she planted inside Trevor and came apart while holding on to the two men she loved.

When she came back to earth, her breaths calming in time with Trevor's and Sean's, she removed the dildo then carefully eased it out of Trevor, chuckling at his mumbled protest. She tossed the toy aside and collapsed into a sweaty pile with her husbands. "I rule," she huffed victoriously.

Sean, after a quick clean-up swipe for himself and Trevor with the discarded bedsheet, rolled half across Trevor to claim a kiss from her. "No one's disputing that." He pecked the interlocking hearts necklace at her throat, a wedding gift from him and Trevor, then claimed a kiss from Trevor too on his way back to the mattress. As Trevor caught Sean's hand and held it against his chest, Charlie snuggled close and enjoyed the quiet moment, the waves outside, the sea breeze, and the simple pleasures of a place that would always be home to them.

Trevor dropped a kiss on the crown of her head. "What was it you were trying to get us out of bed for?"

"Well, there's that matter of the wedding." They all

laughed, easy, free, full of love. A date to remember. She laid her hand atop her husbands', their wedding bands catching the morning light. "And there are some dates we need to mark."

Memories to be etched into the railing of their home—and hearts—forever.

Thank you for reading!

Want to be the first to know when Marsh's series kicks off? For all the latest updates on new projects, sneak peeks, and more, sign up for Layla's Newsletter and join the Layla's Lushes Reader Group on Facebook.

Reviews are an invaluable tool when it comes to spreading the word about great reads. Please consider leaving an honest review for *What We May Be* on Amazon, BookBub, or your favorite review site.

ACKNOWLEDGMENTS

This story has evolved over a span of many many years. So have Charlie, Sean, and Trevor. So have I as an author. All the pieces finally fell into place to tell this story as it was always meant to be, and I am so thrilled to share it with you.

I couldn't do it alone. Special thanks to Wander Aguiar and models Alex, Dina, and Pat for the gorgeous, moody cover photography that I've been looking for for years (no lie, half the reason this book finally got done was because Wander got the perfect shot), Cate Ashwood for the equally gorgeous, moody cover design, Kim, Anna, and Michelle for the beta reads, Kristi Yanta for shaping the Play-Doh of my first novel many moons ago (I will be forever grateful you took a flyer on me), Susie Selva for her editorial expertise, and Lori Parks for the careful proofreading. Thanks as well to the PR professionals who help get the word out: Nina and the entire Valentine PR Team and Leslie and the GRR Team!

Finally, all my love to the awesome readers and cheer-leaders in my Layla's Lushes Facebook Group. You continue to hang with me as I throw curveball after curveball, and I can't say enough how much the support and open-mindedness have helped my growth and happiness as an author. I'm writing and publishing the stories I love. I wouldn't be able to do that without you.

Final Gravity

Variable Onset:

Variable Onset

Sweater Weather

Changing Lanes:

Relay

Medley

Freestyle

Table for Two:

The Last Drop

Dine With Me

ABOUT THE AUTHOR

Layla Reyne is the author of *Variable Onset* and the *Fog City*, *Agents Irish and Whiskey*, and *Trouble Brewing* series. A Carolina Tar Heel who now calls the San Francisco Bay Area home, Layla enjoys weaving her bicoastal experiences into her stories, along with adrenaline-fueled suspense and heart pounding romance.

You can find Layla at laylareyne.com, in her reader group on Facebook—Layla's Lushes, and at the following sites:

facebook.com/laylareyne

twitter.com/laylareyne

instagram.com/laylareyne

amazon.com/author/laylareyne

bookbub.com/authors/layla-reyne

www.ingramcontent.com/pod-product-compliance
Lightning Source LLC
Chambersburg PA
CBHW060229100726